Printed by Amazon

Available from Amazon.com and other book stores

ISBN-13: 978-1514832240
ISBN-10: 1514832240

The Lost Soul

Book 1 of Enchena

K. S. Marsden

To Paula

Happy Reading

K.S. M

One

The annoying drone of the alarm clock blared, breaking through the peaceful illusion of sleep. Samantha groaned and blindly reached out to hit the snooze button. Her aim was misjudged and she winced to hear the thud of her alarm clock hitting the floor. But the good news was that the jolt had magically switched on the radio.

Samantha lay cocooned in her warm duvet, listening to the latest release of last year's X Factor rejects. The song was another blur of pop that Samantha wouldn't remember in five minutes.

Her older sister Terri had auditioned last year; she had considered it a rite of passage, to try for quick fame and fortune. She hadn't even made it onto TV, being neither amazing nor entertaining in that reality TV, cringe-worthy way.

Samantha honestly didn't see the appeal; she would never do that, or anything else that would put her centre stage. No, it was much better drifting through life as something unnoticed. Especially at school. That was Samantha's first rule for survival – be a nobody.

Speaking of school, she stretched languidly, building herself up to the momentous achievement of *moving* and getting up. God, she hated Tuesdays. And not just because of a double Maths and Chemistry whammy – honestly, what was the point of Tuesdays. Monday got to be the start of the week, and by Wednesday it was downhill to the weekend. In Samantha's opinion, Tuesday and all its associated torture could take a-

"Sam!"

Her mother's voice broke through, somehow managing to sound stressed in that one easy syllable.

"Yeah." Samantha shouted back, before dear mum felt the need to burst in.

She pulled on her only-slightly-rumpled school uniform and headed downstairs.

Samantha helped herself to some instant coffee, pulling a face at her baby brother as she did so. Malcolm had turned two, but as far as Samantha was concerned, there was nothing terrible about it. He saved his temper tantrums for the daytime when Samantha was at school, and was always ready to laugh and play when she got home. After making Malcolm giggle, she grabbed her hairbrush and took the time to tackle her dull brown hair while the kettle boiled.

"You need a proper breakfast inside of you." Her mother chided, looking at her daughter with that familiar worry.

Samantha tsked. "I told you, eating early makes me feel sick." She sighed as she caught her mother's expression in the mirror. "We've been over this, I'm not trying to lose weight."

It wasn't her fault that she was naturally skinny. Ever since her growth spurt at thirteen, her friends had been

6

envious of her 'slender' frame. At sixteen, Samantha still hated it. No matter what she ate, she couldn't lose the jutted hipbones, the noticeable ribs and the frankly repulsive knobbly spine. Most days she hid under baggy clothing.

Even now, she cringed when she saw her bony wrists in the mirror as she tied her hair back. Samantha hurried to pull her sleeves back over her hands and shuffled back to the kitchen.

"I've got to take Malcolm to the doctors this afternoon, so I might not be home when you get back from school." Her mum said, swiftly getting to business. "Your dad won't be back until six, so don't forget your key this time."

Samantha rolled her eyes, she still internally corrected it to 'step-dad', but wouldn't dare say it out loud. It was more of an acknowledgement of fact than any real angst. Steve had been part of their family for years now. He was alright as far as father-figures went. He didn't pretend to be Samantha's bestest friend, or any other embarrassing traits. The worst that she could accuse him of was hogging the TV and watched golf and snooker for hours on end.

"Sam, did you hear me?"

"Yeah. Doctors, key, dad at six." Samantha reeled off, to prove that actually, for once, she was paying attention.

*****

Samantha managed to get her stuff together and leave on time. Until she realised that her house key was still on the coffee table. Swearing beneath her breath, she ran back to the house to get it, before having to run the whole way to the bus stop. So much for being on time.

7

Samantha took up her place at the end of the queue, knowing that she would have drawn the short straw for being last.

And sure enough, when the crowded bus pulled up and they all filed on, Samantha was left with the last empty seat. Next to the slightly pudgy boy that didn't know the meaning of deodorant.

As the rest of the bus was filled with chatter and laughter, Samantha pulled her coat collar higher in defence and stared resolutely ahead.

The bus ride was only twenty minutes, crawling through the Leeds city traffic, before finally delivering its students to the school. It was more like a high-security facility than a school, Samantha mused as they passed through the high metal gate, complete with guards. Well, not exactly guards – the school groundsmen had been given a few extra responsibilities, to ensure safety. Hm, some people really didn't suit authority.

When Samantha shuffled off the bus, she made her way to 'the spot'. The spot her friends hovered at every morning, waiting for the school bell to ring.

The girls hardly acknowledged Samantha as she approached, Nissa had them all captivated by a wild (and probably exaggerated) story. Her hands flapped along, trying to pass her experience on to her friends.

Samantha half-listened, and smiled when she thought she was expected to. The only person in the group that looked how she felt was Lucy, who tried to stifle a yawn as she patted down her pockets.

The redhead glanced at Samantha hopefully. "Got a light, Sammy?"

Samantha gave a bitter smile. "You're on your last warning. If they catch you smoking again, you'll get kicked out." Samantha dutifully dug through her rucksack and found a couple of lighters. She handed the one with some fluid still in to Lucy.

Her friend gave a short bark of laughter. "This pathetic excuse of a school can't kick me out, I'm keeping up their grade averages."

Lucy paused to spark up, it was true that as one of the few straight-A students their school had managed to knock together, Lucy got a little more leniency than most. As a lacklustre C-average student, Samantha didn't want to think what her punishment would be.

Lucy offered Samantha the cigarette, which she promptly refused. The redhead shrugged and took another hit of nicotine. "Besides, I need to take the edge off before double Chemistry with Clarke – I swear, one of these days I'm gonna tell that arrogant, patronising git exactly what I think. I mean, you'd think that even *this* school would have standards – the man can't even do basic maths, and they've got the nerve to have him teach us in our GCSE year."

Samantha grimaced, and nodded along in support of her friend's rant, knowing that she was only getting started. Hanging out with Lucy was always the perfect antidote for a nobody like Samantha. She wasn't expected to contribute, Lucy could keep the one-sided conversation going as long as she had a listener.

The electronic bell was followed by a groan and the unhurried filing into the school buildings. Once inside, the corridors became clogged with contradicting traffic as students made their way to class.

Samantha dug through her rucksack as she walked, double-checking she had remembered her books this time.

There was a shout above the din of the students, and several Year 11 boys ran through the masses, laughing. Samantha felt her shoulder jolted and her books spilled onto the floor. She muttered away to herself about the immaturity of boys as she knelt down to pick them back up.

One of the lads stopped in his tracks, turning back to Samantha. He bobbed down and grabbed one of her books.

Samantha hovered, half-terrified that he was going to lob the book down the corridor to further embarrass her; and half-hypnotised by his perfect features. David Jones, the school's star rugby player and all-round ladies-choice, with his golden-blond hair and dimples, was actually in the same personal space as her.

Samantha nervously glanced away when his rich brown eyes met hers, but she still caught the apologetic smile on his lips as he handed her the book.

Samantha's fingers stiffly took it from him. She opened her mouth, before she realised that she had completely forgotten how to say 'thanks'. One simple syllable, but she couldn't for the life of her, make it come out.

Samantha blushed bright red, but at least David didn't seem to notice, he was already jogging away after his friends.

Speaking of friends, Lucy sniggered at the interaction, reminding Samantha that people had been watching.

"Sammy and David, sitting in a tree…" Lucy sang softly, before laughing again.

"Oh yes, today a smile; tomorrow exchanging actual words." Samantha replied, trying to go along with the

10

humour. With only a little bitterness, she accepted that tomorrow would go straight back to being invisible.

For now, she pulled her coat collar up to hide the annoying red flushed skin that would take an age to disappear. She followed Lucy into the classroom and slid into the seat next to her, taking care to pull at the sleeves of her already baggy jumper.

Lucy let out a weary sigh. "Y'know, I don't know why you're so obsessed with covering up all the time. You're bloody stick thin and – who knows, you might even be pretty under all that. Stop hiding and you might even have a chance at a boyfriend." Lucy paused and looked at Samantha critically. "Maybe not David Jones standard, but definitely a boyfriend."

Samantha gave her a withering look. "Gee, thanks."

"You're welcome." Lucy returned with a winning smile.

Samantha twisted the cuff of her sleeve, watching as their least favourite teacher made his entrance. Mr Clarke started to prattle on about something Chemistry-related, but Samantha's attention drifted and she glossed over the details.

Samantha didn't want a boyfriend. They seemed like hard work and far too much effort. Besides, she might as well wait until college, the boys at school were far too immature.

Samantha grimaced as she flashed back to her run-in with David. OK, she was physically attracted to him, her reaction had pretty much proven that; but there was no way she was going to entertain any fantasy where he was concerned. Definitely not.

Chemistry ticked by ridiculously slow, but the two hour torture was finally over. It was pretty easy after that with English and History. Soon enough, the bell rang for dinner and Samantha joined the rest of her friends on the stone benches outside the art block. Being early March, it was cold, but at least it was dry. Even though they sat hunched in their coats, it took more than a chilly wind to drive them away from the prime seats that were the perk of Year 11s, in that unspoken rule of high school evolution.

Samantha picked at her sandwich, drifting in and out of paying attention to the others. She tossed a chunk of bread to the ravens that always came down at this time of day. She watched them hop about awkwardly, as they hustled over the crumbs.

"Sammy?"

Samantha glanced up to see Lucy looking expectantly in her direction.

Realising that her friend hadn't been listening, Lucy rolled her eyes. "Have you decided what you're doing next year?"

"Dunno." Samantha replied, with a shrug. "Sixth form?"

Samantha always felt uncomfortable when the others spoke of the future. They all seemed to know exactly what they wanted to do, and were all pretty excited about it.

Lucy had been planning to go to vet school since they were five years old and had her A Levels firmly set; Nissa wanted to travel and volunteer in third-world countries; and the inseparable Rachel and Sally were both already signed up to a hairdressing course at the local college.

Samantha envied them all. She just hoped that in two years, she'd have her A Levels and half a clue of what to do with the rest of her life.

Apparently satisfied with her minimal response, the rest of the group wittered on, leaving Samantha to her own thoughts.

Two

"So what are you up to tonight?" Lucy asked, as they packed their things away at the end of Maths.

"Nuthin'." Samantha replied, her eyes fixed on her scuffed workbook. "I've got the house to myself for a few hours... I'll probably catch up on TV."

"Well, Danny asked me to go ice-skating with him." Lucy grinned, excited to share her news. "He just texted me. Now I've just got to try not to embarrass myself and look cute."

"That sounds awesome, you'll have to fill me in tomorrow."

Lucy's expression dropped. "Oh, I mean, we could make it a group thing if you wanted to come. We could ask the girls, he could bring a few of his mates..."

"No!" Samantha replied before Lucy could get into party-planner mode; the last thing she wanted was to get dragged to some social gathering where she'd feel awkward all evening. "No. Enjoy yourselves, I know you've been wanting to date him for ages. Honestly, I'm looking forward to a few hours at home; no baby brother, no stepdad hogging the TV..."

Samantha shivered as she stepped into the cold March air. It was rare that her mad house was quiet. A burgeoning thought occurred to her – that with her stepdad working and her mum dragging Malcolm to the doctors, it was the perfect opportunity to secure a pizza dinner. A break from that health-kick diet her mum was torturing them all with.

"I'm gonna nip to Tesco. See you tomorrow, Lucy." Samantha waved and made a quick exit through the school gates.

Samantha held her rucksack tightly against her shoulder as she navigated the busy pavement. It was so frustrating getting stuck behind the dawdling students that seemed in no rush now that they had been released from the daily torment of school. Samantha glanced up as she caught movement above, there was the black shadow against the sky, the lone raven looking much more graceful in the air than on the ground. She was envious of the bird, able to glide above all this nonsense; they didn't get stuck behind stupid slow walkers.

Samantha ducked into the equally busy shop, with so many students crowding around the sweet section. She sighed and pushed through to the chilled section, at least there was room to breathe in front of the tall fridges. Her eyes scanned over the limited selection of pizzas.

"Hey."

Samantha heard the male voice, clearly not speaking to her, and proceeded to ignore it.

The guy coughed. "Sorry about earlier."

Samantha stiffly turned to the side, to see David Jones standing there. As she was the only person in the aisle, he had to be speaking to her. Samantha told herself that

15

at this point it would be polite to say something. To say *anything*.

David's smile wavered at her distinct lack of response. He took his time to pull out a pepperoni pizza and tried again. "You're Lucy's friend, aren't you?"

"Yeah." Samantha answered. Well, that was a start. Unfortunately nothing followed.

David seemed to sense that social interaction was a lost cause and gave her an awkward wave. "Well, see you around."

Samantha watched him retreat, then felt a blush flare across her skin. Well there was a bonus, at least she didn't turn bright red in front of him. Muttering curses to herself, Samantha pulled a couple of pizzas out of the fridge, hardly noting which she had picked.

By the time she had queued and paid, Samantha had already decided that this day, and her life, were swiftly going back to normal. Talking to a cute boy wasn't going to change that. Of course, she wasn't going to mention this little interaction to Lucy or the others. Lucy would take this tiny insignificant blip in Samantha's comatose social life and turn it into something huge. No, that definitely wasn't worth the drama.

Samantha pulled her coat collar tighter about her neck as she stepped out into the grey, British spring world. Because of her diversion, she had missed the school bus home. But it would only take twenty minutes to walk it, which was no problem as long as the rain held off.

Laden with her Tesco bag and rucksack, Samantha took the most direct route, cutting away from the main road and going through the estates. Her mum never liked her taking the shortcut home, she worried about the safety of the area. But as far as Samantha was concerned, it was fine. They were just streets after all, just houses, just alleyways that receded into shadow...

The sound of scuffling made Samantha turn before she could tell herself not to look.

"I said get off. What the hell do you want?" A familiar voice echoed up the ginnel.

Samantha moved closer, fear catching in her throat. She saw David, but didn't recognise the man that stood with him. Her first thought was a street thug, picking on students for sport. But he didn't look like a thug. His black hair was longer than most guys, and his dark clothes made it hard to notice anything about him.

The strange man was only as tall as David, but suddenly threw the boy back against the wall with a sickening crunch.

A flash of black feathers made Samantha jump. She pressed back against the wall, watching a bird flap and fly drunkenly up to perch on the opposite roof.

Samantha glanced back down the ginnel to see the strange man staring her way. 'Run!' She tried to tell herself, but nothing happened. Her feet no longer belonged to her. Her heart pounded and she had to remind herself to breathe.

It must have only lasted a few moments, before the stranger looked away from the terrified girl and back to the boy that was slumped on the ground.

Samantha watched as the man picked David up and, as though he weighed nothing, slung him over his shoulder.

This was bad; very, very bad. Samantha rummaged through her bag, then swore when she realised she'd left her mobile at home.

She felt a spot of rain and gazed up at the dark, threatening clouds. She should tell someone, find a phone and alert the police. If they could get here in time.

Samantha swore again and set off down the ginnel, she had to follow them and try and help David.

The heavens opened and the cold rain pelted down as Samantha started to jog along the narrow way. It opened up again on St Jude's Way, one of the more dilapidated parts of town. Samantha was pretty sure all but one of the houses were closed up and condemned. The one exception housed the local crazy lady. An old woman that refused to move out. Everyone around here knew of her. The kids all ran past her door, half-convinced she was the wicked witch about to curse them.

Samantha caught the lumpy movement of the stranger still carrying David, barging through the door of that very house. Of course.

She swore out loud, before running across the deserted street. She felt fear well up, but somehow it seemed disconnected from her. By the time she reached the old woman's door, the rain had soaked through her heavy coat and her cold and clammy clothes clung to her. Samantha hesitated in the small porch, hardly shielded from the torrents. The door was ajar, almost inviting her to enter. Her nerves were on fire as she inched into the dark hallway. To her left a staircase led up to a shadowy first floor; and to her right, a closed door. What was she doing? This was madness! This was definitely trespassing.

She heard an almighty crash from deep within the house, which threw all logic aside. Samantha opened the door and rushed through a cramped living room. Past that was the dining room and kitchen. In the kitchen, the

18

old woman had collapsed, saucepans and broken dishes lying about her, but Samantha paid no heed to this, for beyond her, where the back door should have been, there was a whirling, smoky complex of a purple and black abyss.

"Excuse me!" Came the sharp, wiry voice, and suddenly Samantha was aware of the old woman sprawled on the floor.

Samantha helped her up and towards a nearby stool. "What- what's…?" Stuttered Samantha, unable to take her eyes off the… the thing.

"That is a portal and I am its keeper." The old woman snapped, looking at Samantha with stern grey eyes. The old woman beckoned for a walking stick that had fallen nearby, which Samantha dutifully retrieved.

"Come away, child. That thing makes my very bones ache." The old woman said, standing up stiffly and walking slowly back to the living room, leaning heavily on her stick.

Samantha hesitated, unable to draw her eyes away from the dense, coloured smoke. For some reason she felt almost at ease, comforted by the natural swirling patterns. Samantha snapped herself out of its hypnotic grip, reminding herself that this was the real world, portals did not exist.

She was suddenly filled with questions, and there was one, rather daunting, person that might be able to give answers. Samantha turned and moved towards the living room, with many a backward glance at the portal.

"Now, sit yourself down." The old woman invited as Samantha entered the room, her tones softer than before. The old woman had lowered herself onto an overstuffed armchair, propping her walking stick beside it.

Samantha shuffled past a low coffee table and perched nervously on a tea-stained settee.

"Tea?" The old woman asked, but didn't show any effort to get back up.

"Um, no. Thank you." Samantha stumbled over her words. Sitting and chatting with strangers wasn't one of her fortes, especially when that stranger had been the root of scary stories for years. Looking at her, Samantha could see why the old woman could scare children; her grey eyes still wickedly sharp, her face held no kindly edge and her voice was cutting. The old woman coughed slightly and Samantha realised she was staring and looked quickly away.

"It's strange to have company of one so young. What's your name, girl?"

"Samantha. Samantha Garrett." She shifted uncomfortably, before adding politely. "Miss."

"Well Samantha, you just call me Gran for now." Replied the old woman.

There was an uncomfortable silence in which the only sound was the beating of rain on the grimy window.

"I suppose you want to know all about the portal now you've seen it." Stated Gran, her voice sharp once more.

"A portal? Portals are fantastical doors to other places." Samantha spurted out, already guessing what story the old woman would try to fool her with.

Gran just bobbed her head, keeping her grey eyes fixed on the young girl, harshly aware of how the young were only interested in what was, and whether they had it, and never what could be anymore.

Samantha let out a nervous laugh. "But that aint real, is it? It has to be a trick."

"Be quiet you ignorant child." Gran snapped, suddenly fierce. "It is as real as you or I. Do you think all those fantasy stories you read are completely made up? They all stem from one truth or another."

"I… I'm sorry…" Samantha stuttered, shocked by how quickly the old woman's temper rose.

Gran sat thin-lipped for a moment before speaking again with more composure. "Other lands, magical journeys and such, exist. You have always known it, though perhaps never accepted it. Now, if you wish to hear what I have to say, you will not question this reality."

Samantha nodded silently. As wary and sceptical as she was, her curiosity was aroused now and she wanted to hear the truth. At least, whatever version of the truth the old woman may give.

When she was happy her message had gotten through, Gran continued. "Well, I have no idea how *you* fit into this, but if they have a purpose for that boy in Enchena-"

"Enchena?"

"It is the land connected by the portal. But as I was saying, if they have some intent, leave them be. It is a cruel place. I have lived here all my life, and before I became keeper, my mother was before me, as was her mother and so on. Of course, after me the line is broken and there shall be no ancient guard." Gran frowned as she spoke, her expression betraying an inner pain. "Yet we have camped at this very spot as grounded gypsies to guard the portal from discovery when it opens, and to protect the people from it. I'll tell you now that I have never heard any positive tale from Enchena."

21

"But… I should go after David, to bring him back…" Samantha stopped herself, still not believing this was happening. Surely David had not been dragged to another world.

"Haven't you been listening, Samantha? Enchena is a dangerous place. It would take grown men trained in war, to go and make it back with the boy." Gran insisted. "Your heart's in the right place, but be honest, you're not the right person for the task."

"So you're saying… it's hopeless?"

Gran sighed. "You youngsters are always so dramatic. Is he your friend? Boyfriend?"

"No, he-" Samantha broke off and blushed at the term boyfriend. "I hardly know him, we go to the same school."

"Then he means nothing to you. Leave the boy in Enchena, it is best to sacrifice one life, than lose two."

Samantha looked away from Gran's fierce gaze. Surely he was worth it, any life was worth it. Samantha looked up, and was surprised to see a hint of sympathy soften Gran's features.

Samantha stood up and walked over to the doorway to the dining room, she could see through to the kitchen where the portal still existed.

"So this is for real?" Samantha muttered.

"Yes, I'm afraid so." Gran replied, with surprising softness. "And I'm very sorry that you'll have to live with such knowledge. I'll let you stay until the rain calms down, then you should go home and try to forget about this."

There was a sharp knock at the front door. Samantha turned round as Gran stood up, grasping her stick.

22

"If it's that bleedin' Avon rep again, I will beat that silly little…" Gran started muttering to herself.

*****

Gran returned from the door a few minutes later to find the living room empty. As she had predicted, Samantha had gone.

"Good luck child, you shall need it."

Three

David groggily became aware of voices, every sound threatening to split his pounding head in two. He took a few careful breaths, the smell of mud and grass lingering in his nostrils. Damn, had he been knocked out on the rugby pitch again? There was something he felt he should remember, but every time he tried for a coherent thought, it skittered away, out of reach.

David cracked his eyes open and winced at the bright light. He rolled onto his back and allowed his eyes to get used to the sunlight that pierced the thick green canopy overhead.

He heard a familiar man's voice bark an order, and suddenly two hands grabbed his arms and dragged him to his feet. David winced, the back of his head felt like someone had tried to bash it in; but from what he could tell, the rest of his body was without injury. That had to be good news.

David tried to focus on what he was seeing, but it didn't make any sense. There wasn't a forest anywhere near, yet tree trunks and overgrown bushes stretched as far as the eye could see. They were in what appeared to be a clearing, although a few clear metres was a closer fit.

David lingered on the fact that 'they' were there. Aside from the two men that held him upright, there must have been a dozen others. They all wore matching black uniforms with a wide red stripe from the left shoulder to the right hip. David had never seen such a uniform before, and he was pretty sure they weren't legitimate peacekeepers. He grit his teeth, wondering what dangerous nonsense he'd gotten himself into.

David caught movement out of the corner of his eye, and saw the same man that had cornered him on the way home. He remembered now, the alley he'd gone down, a shortcut home before the rain; then the stranger approaching him… Had the man even said anything?

David's memory felt patchy, but he could see the man blocking his path, his movements agile and hunter-like. Ignoring David's questions, his impossibly dark eyes had moved over the young man with a detached assessment. He'd only looked away as something further up the ginnel had caught his attention. David hadn't dared look what it was, only used the moment of distraction to duck away from the stranger.

Everything else was blank.

As David looked at the man now, he had a feeling that he was in charge of this motley crew.

"Where am I? And who the hell are you?" David demanded.

The man's dark eyes moved over him with disinterest, before looking to one of his men.

Before David could react, a fist swung into his jaw, making his head snap back.

"You do not address his majesty without permission." His punisher stood inches away from him, his hard brown eyes daring David to step out of line again.

David slowly rolled his head forwards, his tongue tenderly running across the right side of his mouth. He was sure his teeth had cut his gum; he just wished one of the goons on his arms would give him his hand back.

After a brief struggle to test their grip, David relaxed and looked between the boss man and the mouthpiece.

"I think I earned permission when his majesty knocked me out and dragged me to this... this... shit, this has gotta be a long way from home."

A flicker of a smile crossed the man's lips, and he followed it with a swift punch to the gut that made David double over in pain.

"Lieutenant Revill." The man in charge raised a hand to pause any further punishment. He spoke quietly, but his words were articulate. "You might think yourself brave back home, but here, your insolence will get you killed. What is your name, boy?"

David bit his lip, instinctively disobeying the man, when he felt one of the guards twist the flesh of his arm painfully. "David." He gasped, shooting a dirty look to the guard. "David Jones."

Why were these guys all so keen on beating a sixteen year old? And why had the boss man, kidnapped him, when he didn't even know David's name?

While the boss looked over his prisoner assessingly, David did the same. The man looked to be in his forties, even though there was no grey in his rich black hair that hung to his shoulders. His eyes were impossibly dark, but they looked tired and bloodshot.

Whereas the man had been so strong when they met, David thought he saw his balance waver now.

There was the sound of hooves as a horse was brought forward. A horse? David's eyes widened. He'd only ever seen the animals around Elland Road on match day, and thought now what he had back then, that they were bloody huge.

"Your majesty." One man bobbed down to help the boss to mount the brown beast.

Steadier, now that he was off his own feet and sitting astride a horse, he gathered his reins and looked down at his prisoner. "David, while you are in Enchena, I recommend that you follow orders and obey me. Cooperation will be rewarded with riches, land, titles… whatever you desire. Cross me, and you will wonder how many times you can die before-"

He broke off, looking away into the clearing. David heard a thump on the forest floor behind him, and followed everybody's gaze. His heartbeat faltered as he saw a vaguely familiar figure fall to her knees. She was wearing a rather wet school uniform, with their school insignia on the jumper. He wracked his rather shook brain for a name, before realising it was the girl he'd bumped into at Tesco.

David cringed as the girl started to retch, throwing up on the grass.

"Pick her up." The boss ordered, his lip curling with disgust.

Two guards stepped carefully around the mess and grabbed the girl's arms.

David stared at her dishevelled appearance and pale face. Where the hell had she come from? David was sure she'd not been in the clearing a moment ago.

27

The girl's unfocused green eyes bugged at the sight of the guards and the forest. She twisted in the hold of her captors, desperate to see behind her.

"No." She groaned, obviously unhappy with the view of more trees.

"Do not worry, child. The gateway is still there. It is simply more obscure on this side."

David looked up at the man as he spoke, his words not making any sense.

"What do they call you, girl?"

"S-Samantha Garrett." She answered, so quietly that David hardly heard her. "Who are you?"

Remembering their earlier intolerance for questions, David strained against his captors' hold; he couldn't let them hit this innocent girl too.

"I am Hrafn, King of Enchena."

David looked up at the man, feeling suddenly cold. He had already guessed that he was royalty, but it was another thing entirely to have it confirmed.

"Why did you take David?" Samantha demanded, her voice growing stronger.

The King raised a questioning brow. "I am sure you will both have your uses."

David's heart thudded in his chest; he wasn't sure what uses the King had in mind, but he doubted that it would be anything good.

"Take them back to the palace." The King ordered, briefly focusing on his men. "I will ride ahead."

More riders came forward to join the King; the ground trembling as their horses milled around him, ready to be off.

The King turned his weary eyes to David and Samantha one last time, then spurred his horse into action.

As the dust settled from the dozen or so mounted guards, David wondered how they were expected to get to 'the palace'. He got his answer when their captors gave them both a hearty shove.

"Get moving." Lieutenant Revill barked.

Hating the man more by the minute, David staggered forwards, his head still pounding, and his joints feeling oddly loose. It was all he could do to walk straight.

Samantha walked next to him, and the guards moved to flank them. David quickly counted ten uniforms, and noted their spacing – he imagined that any attempt to break away now would lead to another beating. So walking it was. He only hoped he would stay sharp enough to spot an opportunity to escape later.

He looked over to Samantha, who seemed as rattled as he was. Her bright green eyes locked onto his face.

"Did they do that?" She asked breathlessly.

David grimaced, he had no idea how he looked, but from Samantha's expression, he guessed it was pretty dramatic.

"Yeah." He grunted, darting a look at the guards about them. They didn't seem bothered by the two kids chatting, their gaze was stony and locked straight ahead, as they followed the King's orders to the letter. Lieutenant Revill, with the arrogant air of someone left in charge, was looking busy and important fifty yards ahead; out of earshot for now.

"Look, this might be a weird question…" David started, wondering how to phrase it without sounding insane. "But you didn't happen to note *how* we got here? Wherever here is."

Samantha bit her lip, looking worried before sharing. "There was a portal, it led from Gran's kitchen to this forest. When she told me about Enchena... I didn't believe her, until I came falling out this side."

David frowned. The girl definitely had a right to be worried – she sounded crazy. "OK, let's pretend that I believe that. How do you fit into all of this?"

Samantha shrugged, an embarrassed blush darkening her cheeks with unattractive red blotches. "I don't. I was walking home when I saw that guy, King Hrafn, knock you out and carry you away. I followed him to St Jude's Way – y'know, that condemned road – and then into that house. Before I knew it, there was this portal, and that old woman rambling on about other worlds..."

"And you didn't think of – oh, I don't know, telling the police?" David asked, suddenly pissed off that his rescue party consisted solely of this half-wit. "Or anyone that has an ounce of use?"

Hearing the insult, Samantha's expression hardened, and the girl withdrew. The silence deepened, only broken by their footsteps on the uneven forest track.

David grimaced, feeling that he could kick himself. "I'm sorry, I didn't mean that. It's just been a really weird day."

"Enough chatter!"

David looked up to see his least favourite guard return. He'd never thought he could dislike a guy so bloody quickly. David bit his tongue, glancing to Samantha. For some reason, he had a feeling that his apology had not been accepted.

They marched for hours following the forest track. Even with the thick canopy overhead, the sun filtered through. David could feel the sweat trickling down his back, making his white polo shirt stick to his skin. His arm was starting to ache from carrying his coat and jumper.

But he was doing better than Samantha; the girl was starting to lose her footing more and more often. His arm shot out to support her as she staggered again. Her green eyes flashed up with a silent thank you.

Her hand touched his arm, as she stopped and looked in front of them.

The trees stopped abruptly as they came to land that was cultivated, the first sign of civilisation they had seen in this world.

With the sun at their backs, the shadows reached out like dark fingers, clawing down the steep slope before them. The guards had also stopped, to take in the spectacular view. David and Samantha gazed down the hill and across the valley, where rough roads converged and led up a gentle slope to a great wall. The wall enclosed a city that stretched far across the horizon. The only entrance seemed to be colossal golden gates that glinted fiercely in the low evening sun. From their vantage point, they could just see the rooftops of countless houses within the city wall, and rising away from them a palace, its sharp turrets protruding from the heart of the city.

"Welcome to Enchena." Lieutenant Revill said smugly. "Still think you can oppose the King, boy?"

Holding back a sudden desire to punch the man, David looked over the city with a growing dread. This adventure he'd been dragged into was suddenly becoming more real. Glancing at the gates, he had the horrible feeling that once they were inside them, there was no getting out.

"Move out!" Lieutenant Revill barked, obviously satisfied with his gloating.

The rest of the guards started to move, herding the teenagers down the rough track. The road dipped away down the valley, but the city of Enchena was always in view. As they drew nearer, the roads became firmer underfoot, and more populated. Horses, carts and pedestrians milled this way and that, in their daily business; but all moved obediently aside when they saw the guards in the King's livery.

When the party reached the main gate, the Lieutenant stepped forward and demanded entry. The huge gates swung out, revealing not the majestic palace, but the sullied streets crammed in at the borders of the city. The guards moved forward onto a walkway that led slightly to the left. The guards' uniforms stood out amongst the squalor of the ramshackle houses built on top of one another; and the people's drab attire.

The main road was crowded, and the guards closed in tighter about their prisoners, blocking them from the view of the commoners. Samantha felt a hand tightly grip her already bruised upper arm, making her wince, but she said nothing. Through a gap in the press of bodies, she saw fleeting glimpses of the countless faces of strangers, as they made their way deeper into the city. Not for the first time, she was regretting her decision to come to this place – why hadn't she listened to Gran? What help did she really think she could provide? She hated to admit it, but David was right, there was nothing she could do.

The road twisted up through the city, leading through a steadily improving area. The houses were larger, and the people they passed were neater in appearance, and didn't have the look of hunger etched into their features.

A right turn showed the palace rising up before them again, looming closer as they neared the middle of the city. David felt panic bubble up at the sight of it, knowing that they were running out of time with each step.

The way suddenly opened up in front of them and they found themselves in a large, bustling square, with market stalls lining the four walls. Without pausing, the lieutenant led them across the square. The people quietened and moved out of the way, lowering their heads as Hrafn's men passed. And any that didn't do so fast enough, felt the blunt end of the guards' swords.

A shout went up on one corner of the square, a cry that was picked up through the crowd and the noise soon surrounded them. There was movement barrelling towards them, and the guards tried to raise their swords in the press.

Not understanding the sudden mob, or frantic activity, David realised this was their one chance. He grabbed Samantha's arm and pulled her towards the first gap he could see.

"Run." He barked.

Samantha hesitated for only a moment, before following David. As one of the guards hurried to grab her again, she elbowed him with all her strength. She didn't dare turn, but she heard the man groan and his grip had gone, so clearly her aim had hit something soft.

People were fighting all around them, the commoners armed with make-shift clubs, or nothing but their fists. The guards' swords were much more effective, and it was clearly only a matter of time before the mob was subdued.

Several people tried to grab them as they barrelled past, and Samantha shrieked when one person succeeded. She twisted round to see a fierce-looking young man holding her wrist to crushing point.

"David!" She gasped, as she tried to wrench herself free.

David felt the jolt as Samantha suddenly stopped, and he turned at the sound of her panicked voice. Without pausing to think, he swung his free arm and his left fist connected with the assailant's face. There was a satisfying crunch, and the guy stumbled backwards, clutching his bleeding nose.

"Come on." David ordered, pulling Samantha down the nearest street and away from the chaos.

They didn't dare stop, until the noise of the brawl had faded completely. David led the way, purposefully taking a different route than that they'd come; opting down random streets, until he finally thought it safe to stop.

Samantha pulled her sweaty hand out of David's, and lent against the brick wall of a house, struggling to get her breath back. "What... was that... about?"

David shrugged, he knew as much about this mad world as she did. Possibly less – after all, Samantha had at least gotten an introduction from Gran; whereas David was dumped in the middle of everything. He grimaced at their predicament and decided they should focus on business first. "We need to find a way back to gate. If we head away from the palace, we'll hit the wall eventually, then we can follow it to the gate."

"Without getting caught…" Samantha muttered, hardly impressed with the plan. She looked over at David hopefully. "You don't happen to have any water on you?"

"Why would… never mind." David muttered. He hadn't really been planning to get kidnapped and dragged to a foreign land when he'd been packing for school this morning. He looked at the wall of the house – further down, it was only about six foot high. "Samantha, give us a boost."

"It's Sam." Samantha insisted, as she cupped her hands helpfully.

"Sure, sure…" David grabbed the wall and, with Samantha's support, he pulled himself up onto the wall.

Behind the house was a small flag-stoned yard and, David was relieved to see, a rain butt. He leant down to offer Samantha his hand. "Come on."

The two teenagers dropped down into the yard and took turns to drink. The water was hardly fresh, but at this point they didn't care.

At the sound of footsteps echoing down the alley, they both froze.

"They definitely came this way." A man's voice stated defensively.

"You better be sure." Came the all-too familiar sneer of Lieutenant Revill's voice. "If we don't retrieve them, you'll all taste Hrafn's punishment."

David and Samantha shifted further into the shadows of the small yard. Their eyes wide at the sound of their pursuers.

"What if the Gardyn have already got them?"

There was a pause, before the Lieutenant spoke again. "Mention the rebels again, and I will kill you myself."

The footsteps continued further down the alley, until their sound was lost in the next open street.

David held his breath and slowly pulled himself up the wall, peering over into the empty walkway. "C'mon, it's clear." David glanced down, noticing Samantha still frozen in place. "Sammy? We need to move."

Samantha blinked up at him, and snapped herself out of it. This was all getting too much for her, her heart was still thudding painfully from their last run through the city. But she got obediently to her feet, trusting that David knew what he was doing.

When they clambered back over the wall, Samantha stumbled on the landing. When David reached out to steady her again, she snatched her arm away.

"I'm fine." She snapped. "We've been going for bloody hours; I'm not used to this."

David frowned, not wanting to admit that he was also at the end of his energy. He wanted nothing more than to sit down, kick off his shoes and tuck into a big meal. But that wasn't an option; and someone had to stay strong. He should probably say something reassuring – after all, she was only a kid, in over her head. But he doubted they had the time for a pep talk, and he hadn't the energy to be sincere. "Fine, if a safe alternative presents itself, we'll stop. In the meantime, we need to keep moving and find the way out of this city."

Heading back to the streets, David kept a sharp watch for anyone that appeared overly-interested in them. "The most important thing is that we stick together, Sammy. Sammy?"

Worried by the silence, he glanced over his shoulder. David panicked as he couldn't see Samantha following him anymore. No one could disappear that quickly. "Sam?!" He hissed, torn between fear for the girl, and fear of bringing attention to himself.

Four

Behind David a door creaked open and a pair of hands reached out and grabbed him, dragging him back into a dark room. He cried out in surprise and found his mouth covered to silence him. David fought back and managed to turn around. There was a pause, then a small flicker of fire as someone lit a single candle. The light revealed a girl slightly younger than himself. Next to her stood Samantha, who looked very pale in the weak light.

Outside, the noise of life continued, footsteps and muffled conversations. The girl motioned for them to follow her. As she transferred the flame to a lamp, they were able to make out the small room in which there was a roughly hewed table with a few stools. There was also a basin and cupboards in the far corner.

The black-haired girl sat down and looked up at them with big, expectant eyes. "I cannot believe you are here." She murmured, the smile that broke out on her face making her look very pretty indeed.

"I am Jillis Deorwine, I am humbled that you should enter my house."

Samantha just stood silently. She'd had nothing in her mind except to run, and to keep running when this slight girl had stepped into her path and pushed her roughly into this house. After their less-than-pleasant introduction to Enchena, Samantha wasn't in a rush to trust anyone, least of all this young girl. "Why are you helping us? I mean, you are helping us, aren't you?"

Jillis bit her lip, and David jumped in before the bonny lass could be hurt. "We're sorry if it offends you, Jillis. But we're new here, we're tired, and we have no idea what's going on."

The girl bowed her head, in understanding. "We've been waiting for you, ever since the King left with the intention of bringing you back to Enchena. The Gardyn planned to take you by force from the King's men, which must have gone very wrong." Her brow scrunched in thought, but she soon relaxed. "Thank Minaeri you have been delivered here."

Samantha opened her mouth to say that she was still none the wiser to what was going on, when Jillis jumped up from her seat.

"I'll get you a drink." She returned shortly with three mugs of darkish liquid. "Drink, it will help calm your nerves."

David and Samantha picked up their mugs and sipped cautiously. Samantha pulled a face at the sharp tasting liquid, but it was warming and even calming. David coughed, not sure how smart they were to accept the unknown drink from strangers, but didn't say anything.

Jillis gave a small smile and broke the awkward silence. "What are you both called?"

"I'm David, and this is Sammy."

"Samantha." She cut in coldly, staring into the shadows.

Jillis nodded. "And which one of you is-"

She was interrupted as the door opened, making them all jump. The person who had entered was a tall boy who went immediately to the window, looking behind the drapes. He turned and looked confused by the presence of David and Samantha.

"Are these the ones?" He murmured to Jillis. She nodded in answer. "How…? Never mind, just thank Minaeri we have them." He stared at the newcomers. "You are most welcome within our home. You have spoken to my sister Jillis. I am Tobias Deorwine. Has she told you anything yet? Asked for your help?"

Tobias stood taller than his sister, and was clearly older, but there was a family similarity between them. But whereas Jillis was striking with her black hair and pale skin; Tobias looked tired and plain.

David and Samantha sat, clearly thinking that the Deorwines had the wrong people; what help could they offer? David looked up at the older guy. "Um, no. We just got here."

Tobias gave his sister a brief glance of annoyance, before turning his attention to David and Samantha. "We are members of the rebellion – the Gardyn." He stated quietly, leaning in so the others could hear him. "We tried to engage the King's men in the square, to free you, but you slipped past us all. In fact, someone managed to break the nose of the mission leader…"

"Rian?" Jillis gasped. "Oh no, is he awfully angry?"

David grimaced. "Yeah, that might have been me. The guy grabbed Samantha, I was doing what was right."

Tobias chuckled. "Don't worry about it. Rian needs knocking down a peg or two. The arrogant git could do with a broken nose to mess up his pretty boy image."

"But what does Hrafn actually want with us?" David asked, bringing it back to his main concern.

"So… you know nothing?" Tobias questioned in disbelief.

They both shook their heads, feeling increasingly lost.

"We're not even from this world. We came through a portal in the forest." David replied, hardly believing it himself.

"Well, we had best tell the whole story then." Jillis said, hesitating only slightly at the revelation. "From the beginning?" With a nod from her brother, she started.

"Many years ago, Enchena was created by the goddess Minaeri. She gave the people tools and many healthy years so that they may make a happy life for themselves.

"So the story goes, many were blessed with powers to control the elements about them, though none could ever rival Minaeri's, of course. But one man was more powerful and more ambitious than the rest, he slaughtered any that held magick and proclaimed himself King of Enchena. He was King Ragoul the First. He was the one that designed the building of the great city wall that stands today.

"But he was a cruel tyrant, his only desires were expanding his kingdom and the funding of great armies; armies that were fabled to be invincible. Soldiers admired him greatly and began to see things his way. The world was blackened in their eyes and only they mattered. Yet the ordinary people started to hate him, they opposed his harsh, bloody ways and paid for it.

41

They were challenged to conform, or to die. Those that rebelled were hunted down; their blood marked the streets in public hangings and tortures. When the rebels saw this, some felt darkness touch upon their hearts and became as ruthless as King Ragoul. Thankfully many hid and gathered force. They called themselves the Gardyn – the protectors. They hoped to one day overthrow the King and bring back the old ways.

"When King Ragoul died, there was no peace, for his son inherited his powers, and his tyranny. It has been many years now, hundreds, maybe a thousand; but we know from the stories and biased histories, how we came about. It is a constant risk, our death is assured if we are identified as rebels."

"But what about Hrafn?" Samantha interrupted in a whisper.

Jillis smiled bitterly and continued. "Ah, King Hrafn has been the greatest threat to this land since Ragoul was upon the throne. When Hrafn was born, his father, King Naboar, ordered an oracle to See for his son. This is one of the few magical skills not abhorred in this land. The oracle told of a Lost Soul who would unite with Hrafn to restore the power.

"Now, King Naboar had no wish for the Gardyn to hear that his son might not have the power that is descended upon all Kings of Enchena, so that very night he had every person, save himself and his son, slaughtered so that word should never pass those doors. Even his wife, who he could not bring himself to kill, had her tongue removed so that she could not speak; and her eyes torched so that she could not write.

"But he failed in his secrecy, for our grandmother who was a housemaid of the palace, and a Gardyn spy, hid within the room as she did whenever there was a meeting of great importance. And so the Gardyn learned of the prince's frailty.

"It would have been better that we had not. They waited and kept quiet for years, until King Naboar died and his son ascended the throne. Then the Gardyn gathered their strength and came out in numbers not seen for many generations, thinking not to meet the magick of the ancient kings. But it was sending our largest army to be slaughtered. King Hrafn did hold the powers, as great and wielding as any other king. The Gardyn rebellion was flattened, whereas the King's army didn't lose a single soldier.

"At first the Gardyn leaders who survived did not understand. But after much research and debate on the subject, they came to the true conclusion: that King Hrafn stands to gain more than any other king, a soul from this world, grew in another, and shall come into their own when the powers combine."

David shivered at this, Jillis' words hitting a nerve.

"And so." Finished Jillis. "We have instead been searching endlessly for this Lost Soul; that we might persuade them to join us, and therefore overpower Hrafn. Or if he is black of heart, to kill him before the King has the chance to get even stronger."

For a while there was silence as David and Samantha slowly absorbed the tale.

Samantha was the first to speak up. "Why though? I mean, why didn't you all just leave, run away? You can't honestly tell me that you people have been fighting a war for a thousand years!"

The two Deorwines looked annoyed at their whole history being dismissed so lightly. Jillis, the kinder of the

43

two, decided to answer, although she spoke with a colder tone. "Once, perhaps people could escape. But do you think Ragoul or any of his descendants would stop while there was one inch of land not under his rule? There has not been a country free from the crown for nearly two hundred years. So – what would *you* do? Every previous generation and rebellion has failed – would you give up your very spirit and live by the King's law; or would you stand up and fight, in the hope that this may be the time that we are finally free?"

The young girl's spirit and fire shone through, making her beauty more alive. Neither Samantha nor David could meet her eye.

"And you think one of us could be the Lost Soul?" Samantha finally asked, taking a more apologetic tone.

"The King does." Tobias pointed out. After sitting quietly and letting his sister do all the talking, his low voice made Samantha jump.

David gazed down at his hands clasped around the mug. He didn't like where this conversation was going. Just because a crazy king had knocked him out and brought him to another world, it didn't mean he was anything special. David sighed, looking up and realising that everyone's eyes were fixed on him, he suddenly felt much older.

Jillis was looking at him curiously, her dark eyes glowing in the lamplight. "David?"

"I don't know."

Samantha yawned at that point; it had been a long and extremely exerting day. Tobias took the hint and showed them through a door to a back room where he quickly laid down padded material and clean sheets, making quick beds for the two guests. "I am sorry that we cannot provide something more comfortable."

The two guests lay down and were asleep almost immediately.

*****

Samantha awoke to find bright light pouring through an open window. Her first instinct was to brush it all aside as a weird dream, but as she turned from the blinding light, her heart skipped as she saw the unfamiliar room. She sat up to look for David; he was nowhere in the tiny room.

Samantha started to panic and threw off the cover, but relaxed as she heard the voices of David and that girl Jillis, in the front room. Samantha got up and took the single step towards the door, she reached for the handle and was about to open it when she found herself eavesdropping instead.

"We know that you are more likely than Samantha to be the Lost Soul." Came Jillis' voice. "Even if you aren't, why don't you stay and join the Gardyn? We need men like you."

"I can't." David's lower voice was harder to hear and Samantha leaned forward and put her ear to the door. "What about Sammy?"

"I'm sure she can stay too, we'll make room here. You can both help to fight Hrafn."

David gave a slight laugh at this. "I don't think so, I'm not a fighter. And Sammy's just a kid, we can't expect her to stay. And to leave… she can't go on her own."

Samantha's cheeks reddened at being called a kid, and the embarrassment of being discussed as such by David and Jillis.

"I wish you would change your mind, David." Jillis continued more quietly. "You might be the one, and if the Gardyn find out you are here, they may not willingly let you go."

"Then I'll go back where I came from. Make sure there isn't a chance that Hrafn can grow more powerful." David replied firmly.

At that moment there was a sharp bang of the front door. Tobias came in to find David and Jillis sat about the table, deep in thought. "Well? What are we going to do? If you stay, then our plans are simple enough, but any movement about the city will be hazardous. There are a great many more guards than we are used to, due to your escape."

"I'm going back to my own land." David informed him, trying to sound confident with his decision.

Tobias looked at him carefully. "Very well, but we will have to be careful, it is not just Hrafn that will wish to catch you." He glanced to the door which hid the eavesdropping Samantha. "And your friend, has she been in your councils?"

"I think she's still sleeping." David answered guiltily.

Samantha suddenly found the door wrenched open and stumbled forward. Tobias held out his arm and steadied her.

"I think our little companion already knows of the plans." He said with a smile, looking down at Samantha. "And are you wishing to stay here, or go back to your own world like David?"

Samantha looked over at David, sitting cosily next to Jillis. "I'll go home." She replied shortly.

"Very well, then I suggest we start out first thing tomorrow. Jillis and I can guide you as far as the forest edge, can you remember the route from there?"

David nodded, but Samantha butted in with a question. "Why don't we start today?"

"It is already past noon, miss." Tobias turned to the other two, and it seemed to Samantha as if they were already considered the better council than her. "If we go in the morning, we can blend into the market crowd. But I suggest that it is tomorrow we leave and no later. The guards and soldiers may be content searching the streets until then, but it won't be long until they search houses too."

"Tobias, I'm not sure about this." Jillis said gently, her pretty head lowered, not meeting his eye. "If the Gardyn council found out that we helped them leave, if Lord Mgair found out…"

Tobias grimaced at the name of the Lord. "Our guests want to go home, and I'm not going to be the one to stop them. The Gardyn will just have to never know. As for *Mgair*, we can deal with him."

Tobias looked back at David and Samantha, noting the confusion on their faces. "Oh, the Gardyn are just as dangerous for you as the King." He explained. "If they knew that you were here they would force you to join them. I'm not a traitor, but I don't believe the Gardyn should have any right over your life, as long as you don't want to join the King."

*****

The remainder of the day was spent talking of possible ways to escape the city without being noticed. This was made even more difficult by the fact that the only possible exit was the great golden gates and they

47

were sure to be watched. It was Jillis who eventually hit upon the simple idea of leaving in pairs, first David and Tobias would go, and then she and Samantha would follow later. It meant splitting up, but if the guards were only looking for a boy and a girl, they might just get away unnoticed.

David had quickly made friends with Jillis and Tobias, but Samantha hung back. Truthfully, she felt out of place and wished she had never come. David chatted easily and almost changed his mind about leaving; he felt as though he was finally in the right place.

"Where are your parents?" It was a while before Samantha built up the courage to ask her question, as the others had started to leave her out of their conversations. The silence was immediate, Jillis looked hurt and Tobias' face hardened.

"It's… it's just, I was wondering…" Samantha felt embarrassed, she hadn't meant to cause discomfort with her simple question.

Tobias sighed. "I suppose you have the right to be curious, you weren't to know." He looked to his sister. "Our mother died this winter."

There was silence again, before Samantha rudely interrupted it. "But what about your dad?"

At this, Tobias pushed back his stool and stood up. "I should get food for dinner, I'll be back soon." He mumbled, before quickly leaving the house.

David looked to Jillis for an explanation.

"He… he does not like to talk of it much." She began falteringly. "Our father was killed – I was too young, but Tobias remembers him."

The two guests waited for her to continue, and in her own time, she did. "Our father was a lieutenant in

Hrafn's army; he was not an outright spy for the Gardyn, but helped them because he loved our mother. They married in secret so that if trouble ever fell on him, we would not suffer. Sadly it was put to the test. My father was tried for treason and fell to the fate of all high status killings. I am glad that I do not remember my father dying, though sad that I never knew him. But Tobias…"

The room was silent again, and was for a long time after.

Five

In the centre of the city, King Hrafn paced across his throne room.

"Am I surrounded by imbeciles? Trained soldiers that cannot take control of two adolescents!" His face burned with rage as he glared at the solitary guard who stood stiffly in the centre of the hall.

"We didn't anticipate the rebel mob in the city, your majesty." Lieutenant Revill had lost all of his arrogance, and kept his eyes trained on the floor.

"You didn't anticipate that our enemies would come between you and delivering the one weapon that guarantees their destruction?" Hrafn turned and marched back to his throne on the raised dais, and sat on the gilt, high-backed chair. He looked back at the Lieutenant, his voice much colder. "Tell your men to dine well this eve, for they shall not taste again in the morning."

The Lieutenant bowed, then backed swiftly away from the audience.

Hrafn looked behind him. "Captain." He summoned.

A figure stepped out from the shadows of the hall. "My lord?"

Captain Orion Losan was a tall, stock middle-aged man whose scarred face was known and feared throughout Enchena, his name was respected and idolised even by his enemies.

"Dispose of those incapable fools. And the lieutenant, have his eldest son join him, then beggar his widow." The King said, pinching his nose to relieve the stress. "I should hang you alongside them, Losan. Your men lost the most precious thing to me."

The Captain crossed his arms, as disappointed as he was by his soldiers, the King could not inspire fear in him. "Then do it, your majesty. Your reign would end within a year, without *my* army."

King Hrafn grunted, his mood barely lightened by his old friend's attitude. "Set a garrison at the gate and another within the Great Forest. Take as many men as you need to search the city. We must recapture the Lost Soul as soon as possible."

Captain Losan watched the King, feeling a vague concern. He had known him since he was a young man, and the King a mere princeling. He had never seen him look so drawn as he did now. "Very well your majesty. Leave it to me, you should rest, your trip to the other land has taken more of a toll than we bargained."

"I do not need telling that!" The King snapped, waving a hand to dismiss his captain.

Left alone in his hall, Hrafn fumed. This had been in the planning for forty years, ever since that damned oracle had prophesied the existence of the Lost Soul. Over the years, he and his scholars had found the

51

location of the gateway. He then had to wait for the stars to align for the gateway to open.

Hrafn had been the only one able to draw the Lost Soul through from that other strange land, no one else could have physically survived the journey, though he was still recovering a day later from the physical drain it had on him. Even as weary as he had been, perhaps he should have completed the lowly task of escorting them back to the security of the palace, instead of trusting others.

"I know you're hiding somewhere." He muttered. "And I have waited too long for you to escape now."

*****

As the first dawn light flitted through the ragged drapes the next morning, David, Samantha and the two Gardyn made ready. David and Samantha changed into Enchenian clothes so they could blend into the crowd. Because his blond hair was rare in this region of Enchena, Jillis had also tried dying David's hair into a darker colour with tea leaves, and other items in her kitchen. The result was less than fantastic, and David hoped to hide the worst of it with the hat borrowed from Tobias.

Both David and Samantha had been given a small knife that could be hidden amongst the folds of their clothes. David took his gingerly, knowing what the blade was for and already imagining blood upon the steel; so it was with a mix of horror and awe David realised that it felt naturally comfortable to hold.

"Just in case." Jillis said quietly.

David and Tobias set off first. David had a rough rucksack of Tobias' to carry food and water, his broad shoulders taking the weight with ease.

Samantha and Jillis left ten minutes after them. Samantha got her first real view of the streets and poverty of Enchena, having previously been in a forced march, then a hasty retreat.

"Is all of Enchena like this?"

Jillis shook her head. "No, just near the great wall, in the centre of the city it is much more lavish. That is where the captains and people of Hrafn's court live. Here in the outskirts, it has gotten steadily over-crowded as the population grew. But it suits us well, we go unnoticed and have recently discovered tunnels that we think run everywhere beneath the city."

"Then why aren't we taking them? To get out of Enchena?" Samantha said, annoyed they hadn't come up earlier.

"Because they are derelict and unchartered."

"Of course, why didn't I think of that." Samantha stared at Jillis' back as she followed her down the streets of Enchena. Jillis seemed so perfect, Samantha had a hard time believing that she was as good as she pretended to be.

"But you do not know the town." Jillis replied, seemingly oblivious to Samantha's sarcasm.

When Samantha just snorted in response, Jillis must have got the hint, because she stayed silent from then on. She led down a narrow street, then left into a large square and on through the streets, leading steadily to the wall of the city.

Finally they reached the mighty golden gates that contradicted the stained city within. Guards were at their posts on either side of the gate, watching intently as the city folk moved in and out of the city boundaries, stepping forward to randomly question travellers.

Samantha started to worry, but Jillis walked forward undaunted.

A guard turned towards them and blocked their path. "Where are you going?" He asked Samantha gruffly.

"Er... to... to the..."

"To the marketplace in Talath." Jillis jumped in, a hint of impatience in her voice, as she grabbed Samantha's arm.

The guard glared suspiciously at them. "And what of your ware?"

"It's already there." Samantha ventured, as the guard stood, his face still showing doubt. "My cousin and I are going to relieve the people there."

Although Jillis looked calm and unworried, Samantha knew she was going to have yet another bruise where the girl was gripping her arm.

The guard grunted and finally turned away.

Jillis gave a sigh of relief and smiled at Samantha, but Samantha just grimaced in return, making a point of rubbing her sore arm.

Leaving the gates behind them they quickly made their way down the slope into the valley. Climbing the opposite bank they kept a keen eye, trying to spot where the boys were waiting for them. Further ahead, in a small copse, David and Tobias were just visible as they drew closer. The reunion was swift, and they were soon moving further within the forest, out of sight of the city.

"Brother, you should have been there! Truly, if all things were so simple, Hrafn would be defeated with ease." Jillis gushed as she recounted their exit of the city.

Tobias hugged his little sister, before turning to his former guests. "Keep off the track as much as possible, we don't know where the guards are posted."

54

"And be wary of forest creatures. You wouldn't want a mallus on your trail." Jillis added.

"Mallus?"

"Sister! Don't fill their heads with mythical nonsense!" Tobias warned.

"Well I think they exist." Muttered Jillis.

Tobias ignored his sister. "There are many dangers in the Great Forest, wildlife included. Be on guard."

There was silence for a few minutes, before they awkwardly made their farewells. Tobias solemnly shook hands with David and Samantha. Then Jillis, quite to Samantha's dismay, stepped forward and hugged David, who stood uncertain.

"Are you sure you won't join the Gardyn?" She whispered.

David shook his head. "No, I should go."

Nodding her agreement, Jillis turned to Samantha, but a cold, unfriendly look told her it was best to skip pleasantries. "Goodbye Samantha."

"Bye."

Six

David and Samantha kept well within the trees, in case anyone from the city looked in their direction. As time moved on, they found it increasingly difficult to keep parallel to the main track; the forest challenged them with impenetrable bushes and tangled thorns; or misleading trails that faded to nothing.

Pushing themselves uphill, they paused at the top, noticing that they were coming too close to the track, as they spotted the movement of black and red uniforms through the trees. They were close enough to hear the strained conversations of the soldiers, who milled close together and seemed strangely nervous of the forest.

David motioned for Samantha to stay quiet, and to move back into the thicker growth before they were noticed. David picked a route he was convinced led back to the portal, and marched on.

The trek was much longer because they were not directly following the track and progress was slower than when the soldiers had taken them to the city. The sun had risen high in the sky and through the thick canopy, they could just about tell that it was noon.

David decided that it was definitely time to stop for a rest and food, so the next time they came to a clearing, he sat down and shrugged off the rucksack Tobias had given him. Samantha followed suit, glad for the break. She was already worn out by the walk, but wouldn't admit it out loud.

Their snack was a meagre one – bread, apples and a few other items. But plenty for both. There were also two flasks, the small one had the same dark liquid they had drank with dinner the previous evening; the larger flask was full of water.

"So what's gonna happen. You know, when we get home?" Samantha asked quietly.

"What do you mean?"

"Well, we've been gone for days, how do we explain that?"

"Oh." David hadn't realised this problem existed. He couldn't think of any excuse that his parents would believe. "Don't know, what will you say?"

"Don't know." Samantha repeated. She sat quietly, even in her wildest fantasies, she never would have thought this is what an adventure to another world would be like. Running, hiding, and a painful need to just go home.

"Come on, we might as well keep going." David stood up and waited for Samantha to follow. "Sammy?"

She looked up at him; she was tired, but didn't want to admit it. She pushed herself off the hard ground and brushed the dirt from her trousers. "OK, let's go."

David lifted the lightened bag onto his shoulder and they set off again.

It wasn't much later when they stopped again. The horrible realisation finally dawned. They were lost.

David started to climb the thick trunk of a tree, swearing each time he reached higher. His head finally broke above the canopy, and he was bathed with sunlight. Once his eyes adjusted, he looked around, but the Great Forest wasn't giving away any of its secrets easily.

"David, do you see anything?" Samantha's voice came from the ground.

David took a deep breath and started to descend again. "Nothing useful." He admitted as he dropped the last few feet to the ground, and wiped his sore, grazed hands on his shirt. He'd forgotten how much tree bark hurt the hands.

"So, which way?" Samantha asked.

"How should I know?" He replied, loud and sharp.

"Well you're the superstar Lost Soul." Samantha shouted back. "And don't shout at me!"

"And you're the only reason I'm heading home instead of actually embracing that!" David shouted back, then bit his tongue. They didn't want Hrafn's men to overhear them. Although he silently admitted that would be one solution to their current predicament. When he spoke again, he kept much quieter. "Let's split up and find the damn track."

"Yeah, and lose each other as well." Scoffed Samantha.

"If only." David muttered. "Look, if you have a better idea, I'd love to hear it. No? Then let's get searching – whistle if you find anything."

Samantha watched him walk away, then started to march through a copse of trees in another direction. She went pushing branches angrily out of her way.

"It's all David's fault. He's the Lost Soul, he's the reason I'm wandering through this blasted forest." She muttered to herself, casually forgetting that she had followed him into Enchena of her own free will.

She had not walked far before coming to a small rocky descent. From here she could not see a great distance in any direction because of the thick forest, but directly below something caught her eye, some animal movement through the forest. Samantha stopped to watch and saw a glimpse of glossy hide, she was quite sure there were several animals milling at the bottom of the rocks.

She almost held her breath in anticipation, and bobbed down to keep hidden. As she gazed down, more of the animal was revealed, a lean, leggy frame that could be mistaken for a horse, before it turned in her direction. More moved into the small clearing, joining the first, grazing in the sun. From the forehead of each individual, a pearly horn rose and fell with the movement of the creatures' heads. Unicorns.

Samantha stayed, hypnotised by the sight, she could hardly believe her eyes; she never thought anything so beautiful could truly exist. She knew that she had to share this with David, no matter how angry she had been at him, he deserved to see this, too.

Samantha turned and hurried away as fast as she could, without disturbing the unicorns. Whistle, she had to whistle. She tried, but had never been able to do it the shrill, attention-worthy way. So instead she risked shouting his name as loud as she dare.

David heard Samantha call and turned back. He hurried through the trees, scared that something had happened to her. He heard her before he saw her, crashing through the branches without care. "What is it? Are you ok?"

Samantha just grinned and grabbed his wrist. "Come on." She said, pulling him back to her discovery.

When they got back to the rocky tor, David stared down in disbelief.

"But... that... they're... how?"

Samantha chuckled at his complete loss of words. "Want to take a closer look?" Her green eyes bright with the challenge.

David just nodded numbly.

Samantha started to move down the portion of the rock face that was shielded by trees, then made her way as carefully as possible towards the clearing. David appeared at her side, and they both silently watched the unicorns.

Samantha mused over the fact that these animals were not the pure and delicate white of the mythical stories, instead their hides showed colours of brown, chestnut, and all the colours of any ordinary horse, with the woody shades most common. Not a single white unicorn stood before them. Yet they were still a sight to be marvelled at, tall and majestic beasts, grace and power in every movement.

Samantha almost squealed when she saw an adorable foal stumbling into the sunlight, with its knobbly knees, and legs that seemed too long for its body. Before David could stop her, she had shifted to move closer to them. David staggered after her, his legs numb from squatting in one place for so long, and a fallen branch cracked underfoot.

The reaction was immediate. Horned heads were thrown in their direction. A horse-like call rang out, and from the far side of the herd charged a unicorn that was as black as night. It halted, wild eyes staring at the humans in disbelief, none had ever been seen so deep in the forest, and he was going to make sure none were seen again. The black unicorn lowered his horn to charge.

David gripped Samantha's arm and pulled her behind him, in a desperate act to protect her. He found his feet fixed to the ground with fear as the huge beast thundered towards him.

There was the flash of silvery hide and suddenly a pale grey unicorn stood in front of them, facing the black.

"Get on." Came a low, commanding voice that was more a thought in each of the humans' minds than out loud. "Now! Don't linger."

A darker, slightly smaller grey trotted up to Samantha and stood still, waiting for her to mount.

"Hurry." A high, beautiful voice pleaded.

Samantha leapt up and David helped push her on, then she turned and helped drag him up behind her.

The light grey and the black were now close and reared in warning. Neither backed down, and suddenly there was the flash of black hooves; pearly teeth and horns all tearing and thudding at the other.

The dark grey gave a worried whinny, then turned and galloped away, swifter than any racehorse, away from the black's approaching herd.

Riding a unicorn is a wonderful thing if, like Samantha, you'd had a few riding lessons. But even David found it easy to stay balanced on the swift and smooth strides. They raced so fast that the trees became mere green and brown blurs and David began to wonder how they dodged them all so quickly.

The dark grey unicorn finally slowed down and stopped. David and Samantha slid off and looked at the horse-like creature that stood before them.

"Thank you." David said, the first to find his voice.

The grey bobbed her head, catching her breath. "He should come soon." Came the singsong voice once more, obviously belonging to this unicorn, without explaining who was coming.

But sure enough, as fast and as silent as the wind, the lighter grey emerged from the trees, sweating and bearing a new cut along his fine neck that bled little. The two unicorns stood solemnly in the dappled sunlight. Both David and Samantha felt very much humbled and shy in their presence.

"You were unwise to approach that herd." Came the low, powerful voice that seemed to belong to the taller grey that had fought the black unicorn. "And I would not naturally come to your rescue, yet my sister Alina insisted that it was vital, though we do not know why."

David and Samantha stood speechless. The unicorns did not speak in any ordinary sense, they talked through shared thoughts and it was a strange and thrilling experience for the two humans.

"I am Nmirr." Continued the light grey male. "The afternoon grows late and the night-time forest has its dangers... If you wish, you may stay with my herd until morning. Then we shall set you on track again." With that he turned to his right and led off through the trees at a steady walk.

"Come." Alina invited in her joyous, singing voice.

David and Samantha could do nothing more than follow the mystical and shining creatures through the trees at a steady walk.

Eventually they reached their destination. Another large clearing, where the early-evening sun shone down on a rippling brook that splashed against a large rock. It seemed deserted, but then Nmirr raised his fine head and whinnied gently.

There was movement, as other unicorns emerged from the trees. Nmirr trotted to greet them, and after a welcoming look to the humans, Alina followed him.

The rest of the herd balked at the sight of the humans, but there was no anger in their eyes or movement. They all looked to Nmirr, and trusted his judgement in bringing the two young humans here. The herd was larger than the black's, and also consisted of many equine colours. In the herd there was a stunning black mare with a silver dapple on her rump, whom Nmirr had trotted over to first. She greeted the humans gracefully, introducing herself as Cassiopeia, Nmirr's mate.

Their son came up to them curiously, but shy at first. Sundance was a tall and handsome palomino colt, who truly deserved his name as the sun's flames danced on his golden coat.

David and Samantha agreed to stay with Nmirr's herd for what was left of the day and through the night, with no wish to hurry away. They remained mostly with the sweet Alina and her nephew, Sundance, who seemed to have an abundance of energy, playfully running to the brook and back.

Samantha spoke little with Nmirr, finding him too daunting as he stared wisely at them. David though, had told him everything about their journey and Nmirr had

63

listened thoughtfully, but did not speak his thoughts on the matter.

Alina and Samantha got on well, and Samantha found that they had been very lucky for the two greys to come along.

"Why did the Black attack us?" Samantha asked as she and David wandered alongside Alina and Nmirr.

"The Black?" Alina's thoughts expressed confusion.

"We call him The Dark Being." Nmirr informed them, his low voice murmuring in their minds. "He would kill you as soon as look at you."

"Why?"

Nmirr looked at Samantha, his brown eyes bright. "It is easy to tell that you do not come from Enchena. The Dark Being and his herd have the darkest and coldest of hearts."

"But… but unicorns are always good. They are where we come from." Samantha gushed, ignoring David's attempts to silence her on the matter of earth myths. "And they're all white, too. They'd never be evil."

Alina looked up at her with interest. "Then you must come from a strange and wonderful place. We have not known of a pure white unicorn since Praede. Hunters would catch such a light one easily."

Nmirr nodded his agreement. "Perhaps we once originated from your kind, but it is The Dark Being infecting the ill-will of the people of Enchena even within us."

"How do you mean?" David asked.

Nmirr snorted slightly and his feeling of sadness and regret could be felt by the small party. "He is older than I, so I only know what my father told me of the incident.

64

When The Dark Being was about 20 winters, only a youngster by our counts, humans captured him. This is rare, normally they only hunt us for our horns and hides; and when a unicorn is caught alive the fire within is put out and they quickly die. But The Dark Being somehow fought on, surviving around humans as he was paraded around fairs. I suppose being around all the anger and hatred that dwells in many human hearts, he saw the world in a different way, and the torture he endured as a caged animal… it is a terrible enough thing to turn the mind.

"When he finally escaped, he returned to his old herd changed. He challenged the leader and broke our lore by killing the old leader after he had defeated him. The herd were now bound to him, and he began to teach unicorns to behave more like men: fight first, stay alive. He turned many a good unicorn dark, and killed those that would not follow his commands. Thankfully our parents escaped and warned all other herds.

"He has caused us much trouble. Making enemies within our own species, something that has never happened before. He is getting old now, over 200 winters, but he is still strong, all the more for having his herd behind him. There are few that can match him." Nmirr sighed and hung his head. The new scar on his neck ached at the thought of his enemy.

Seven

The sun was dropping down to the tree line, turning red on the backs of the grazing unicorns.

Samantha shifted, hunger making her uncomfortable. A glance at David told her that he felt the same. David gave her a brief smile and jogged over to meet Nmirr.

"Nmirr, we were wondering if there was anything here that, um, humans can eat?" David asked hesitantly.

The unicorn looked thoughtful for a moment, remembering that these funny humans couldn't eat grass.

"Ask the trees." He said simply, then continued when he saw that David was still nonplussed. "Ask the trees to bear fruit."

David looked to Samantha and shrugged. Was this just one more magical part to this crazy world? Feeling more than a little nervous, David turned to a nearby tree and placed his hand on the trunk.

"Uh, can you... could I have some fruit?" He stared at the tree, aware of how stupid he sounded. "Please?"

Behind him, Samantha giggled. This was definitely the most ridiculous thing yet. But Alina trotted past her and up to David.

"Don't worry, I think they might ignore humans. But they'll respect a unicorn." She looked up at the tree and shared her amusement. "And we may wish to find another tree, rather than a fir."

Samantha continued to laugh as Alina turned and walked to a tree by the stream. She stretched out her silver head until the tip of her horn touched the bark. Within moments small, unripe fruits appeared on the boughs. After a few minutes the fruits had grown large and ripe.

"Eat." Alina sang happily.

David and Samantha, who had managed to stop laughing, walked over and reached up, gingerly pulling the ripened apples from the branches. The apples were crisp and fresh, more so than the fruit they had been given by the Deorwines. The unicorns munched delicately on apples knocked down by their horns, and though it was not a perfect meal, the humans enjoyed the food provided.

*****

The clearing was picked out by a bright, almost whole moon. David and Samantha were laying on the rough ground, using David's pack as a pillow. Nmirr was quite a distance away, sleeping as he stood beside a dark mass that was Cassiopeia. Alina was lying near David and Samantha, the warmth of her presence was pleasant as the air cooled.

All three were staring up at the navy blue sky, awash with glittering stars. With a pang of homesickness,

Samantha wondered if these were the same stars as back home.

"There's Praede." Came Alina's thoughts, as she pointed her horn to one of the larger constellations. "The first unicorn of Enchena."

"Was he real?" David murmured sleepily.

Alina nodded, before beginning the story she heard as a filly. "A long time ago the land of Enchena was barren, empty of all creatures. Then one day, with the rising of the sun, the Goddess Minaeri rode through the land on a pure white unicorn named Praede. In their wake, a forest rose up that stretched from sea to sea. Minaeri dismounted and turned to her faithful steed.

"'Praede, I give you the forest, in which you will always be safe.'

"And Praede replied. 'I thank you, O Glorious One. I ask only that I may always keep my sons and daughters safe.'

"The goddess nodded and gave her promise that would become Praede's Honour. Praede turned and called, his rich neigh singing through the forest and it was instantly full of unicorns. Praede bowed gracefully to Minaeri, then went to meet his own kind.

"The goddess journeyed to fill this new land, allowing humans to settle in the plains. And whenever Minaeri needed a steed, the noble Praede would always volunteer with a gracious heart.

"Years passed and the unicorns flourished, spreading far and wide, yet always knowing that the forest would protect them. Praede watched over his children with pride as he grew old. One night he disappeared from his herd to die alone in his forest. And as Minaeri had agreed, he rose to the skies to forever watch over us."

68

By the end of the story, David and Samantha had both fallen into gentle sleep, leaving Alina to stare up at the stars, consumed with her own thoughts.

*****

Samantha awoke with a start. A long grey face looked down into hers.

"You are awake, get ready." Came the low, almost throbbing voice of Nmirr.

She blinked in the hazy sunlight of morning. Overnight clouds had gathered and the sky was no longer clear. Samantha sat up as Nmirr turned away to continue grazing.

David was already up and talking with Sundance, but seeing that his companion was awake, he left the young unicorn and walked over to Samantha. "Decided to get up? Nmirr's offered to take us back to the portal, he's pretty certain where it is."

Samantha glanced around. "Where's Alina?" She asked, not seeing the pretty grey.

"She left before dawn to visit another herd."

They waited for an hour with the unicorn herd. The only option for breakfast was apples, and the humans were able to practice asking the trees for fruit. Samantha smiled as she finally found something she was better at than David, who failed and reluctantly accepted some fruit from Samantha.

When Nmirr had finished his morning graze, he found the two of them by the stream with Sundance.

"It is time to go." Nmirr whinnied gently, aware of the disappointment that emanated from his son. His two unusual guests seemed to be equally upset to be leaving.

Eventually, after fond farewells to the rest of the herd, David and Samantha found themselves astride the

69

mighty grey unicorn Nmirr, moving swiftly once more through the forest, the wind whipping tears from their eyes.

All too soon, Nmirr stopped and the two riders slid off his velvety back. His ears flicked back and forth as he listened intently to their surroundings.

"This is where I must leave you, the gateway to your own world is only a few trees away, but it is overrun with human guards. Wait until I distract your enemies before you leave the cover." He looked down at the two humans quite fondly. Alina was right, there was something about them. "Good luck."

Nmirr vanished into the trees, leaving David and Samantha surrounded by the dense forest. Even with the sheltering trees, the branches were bent by the fresh wind that constantly grew stronger. They shivered, drawing their Enchenian clothes tighter around them in the chill, and started in the direction Nmirr had gone. They walked silently, listening carefully as they went.

After a few steps they could hear the guards, so sank behind the nearest tree. They moved forward as quietly as they could, crouching in the rough undergrowth.

"Well, this is it." David muttered. "Back to reality."

Samantha looked glum. "Will we be, well, friends when we get home?"

David shrugged, keeping his gaze on the movements further on. "S'pose so. We've got this in common, though no one else will believe us."

Through the trees they could make out the small gathering of guards who huddled close, clearly uncomfortable in the Great Forest. The wild wind unnerved them and they muttered of myth and mallus.

70

Soon there was a crashing in the trees beyond the guards. The soldiers all ran to investigate, not wanting to split up, regardless of their Captain's orders.

David and Samantha moved quickly, but quietly.

"Whistle if you find it." Whispered David. "And remember, Hrafn said that it's difficult to see on this side."

They split up, not knowing exactly where in the clearing the portal stood. They rushed, in fear of the return of the guards, moving their arms in front of them, feeling for anything strange.

David cursed silently when he heard the approach of hoof beats. Too many for a single horse and too loud to be the return of Nmirr.

David quickly grabbed Samantha and pulled her behind the trees again. Samantha was about to argue, but fell quiet.

Two men rode past the tree behind which they hid. The first pulled up his bay mount in the clearing, and David tried to catch a glimpse of them. The men wore the same black and red livery as the rest of the soldiers, but something about them stood out as more important, more dangerous.

A sneer came to the scarred face of the first man as he looked about him, clearly furious.

The second man halted beside him. "Captain?"

"Need I have more disappointments." The Captain muttered to himself.

The guards that had run to Nmirr's distraction returned warily, one man ahead of the rest.

"C-Captain Losan." The lieutenant stuttered, his surprise quickly replaced with a composed and well-trained air. "There was a disturbance in the forest, sir."

"So you left your post unguarded?" Growled Captain Losan. "Your duty is to await the Lost Soul, if they try to get back."

"But Captain, surely they would have passed by now. Besides, their gateway no longer remains."

Losan drew his sword and with the hilt, gave a heavy blow over the lieutenant's head, making him stagger and drop. "Your duty is to do as the King commands. You and your men shall stay here as long as King Hrafn deems necessary. Disobey again and I will personally hand your hides over to the King for punishment."

Captain Losan sheathed his sword and barked out orders to the group, before he turned his horse around and picked up a trot down the forest track. His mounted companion followed suit, and soon the sound of hooves distanced themselves from the clearing.

*****

Cowering in the undergrowth, Samantha shivered. No way home… A tear ran down her face, and she quickly wiped it away. Someone tugged at her arm, and Samantha obediently followed David away from the guards, half-crawling, half-walking to what seemed to be a safe distance.

David turned to face her, looking pale and scared. "Maybe- maybe they're bluffing." He reasoned. He wiped a hand over his tired face. "The hell with this, I just want to go home."

Samantha felt swamped with thoughts from home, the faces of her family threatening to overwhelm her. Samantha took a deep breath then stood tall and started to move off.

"Where are you going?"

"If we can't get home, I think we should find Nmirr again. He might know what we can do." She answered with a shrug, surely it was the only logical option.

"Jillis and Tobias would know more." David replied.

Samantha shivered slightly. She hadn't really gotten on with Jillis and did not want to get stuck in the city again. "The guards will be searching about the city for us more than in the forest." She reasoned.

David sighed at the idea of spending more time in these blasted woods; but conceded that Samantha had a point. So it was swiftly decided that they would find the unicorn herd again.

Eight

Their first problem was where to go. They knew the rough direction of the unicorn clearing, but they had travelled so fast that they couldn't recognise any forest features as they tried to return to the herd.

The second problem, which was more of an irritation at first, was the weather. Up until now the wind had only teased and tugged gently, but it was starting to build up, whipping rain from the gathered clouds. It was not surprising to hear a distant roll of thunder as the two humans trudged through the forest once more.

By midday it was becoming impossible. The wind had intensified and even the forest didn't protect from the torrents of rain. David and Samantha had gone slipping through the mud and puddles for ages and rain plastered their hair to their faces, the chill wind cutting through their wet clothes.

Stumbling in the sludge, the wind whipped away Samantha's gasp as her ankle twisted beneath her. She shouted through the storm to David. He turned and staggered against the rain to reach her – there had to be shelter nearby. The way the wind twisted the rain, the trees might as well not be there. David then noticed a dip in the forest floor, above which hollow tree roots and moss had made a natural roof. David pointed it out to Samantha, then made towards it.

The hole in the ground looked like a den, belonging to some animal, further dug out by claws. It wasn't the most spacious, but they both wriggled in, before pushing dirt and rocks to block the bottom of the opening to stop rainwater running in.

Samantha wrung out her hair and squirmed uncomfortably, and even though it was only midday, she settled down to sleep through the storm. Even though the climate was warmer than in England, Samantha shivered in the wet.

David lifted his eyes to meet hers in the dimly lit den, he attempted to smile, trying to hide his own shivering. He moved round so they were sitting close together, his arm draped over Samantha's shoulder. Both of them suddenly eased in the other's warmth and presence, and David felt Samantha's breathing steady as she drifted to sleep.

David sat silently, unable to rest or sleep as the brunt of the storm moved directly overhead. He sat stiffly in the hollow, until the thunder shifted into the distance. The rain was still cascading down, but the wind had lessened.

David moved carefully, so as not to wake Samantha, and took the almost empty flasks that Jillis had given him, and placed them above the den to refill. Only then, did he finally settle down and slept.

They awoke several hours later. It was already dark, but the sun had not yet set. The clouds were still massing overhead, but the rain had stopped for a while.

Samantha's ankle had swollen, but she insisted that it didn't hurt too much and that it couldn't be broken.

David wasn't convinced, and insisted that they wait until morning to set off again.

For a meal they again had what they could beseech from the trees (or more rightly, what Samantha could, as David still hadn't caught up on that trick). This way of obtaining food had been a novelty yesterday, but already they were tired of fruit and craving real meals.

*****

The next morning the wind had died, but the rain was persistent as it trickled irritably on.

Samantha's ankle was still swollen, but after David strapped it up with a make-shift bandage torn from his shirt, it didn't hurt too badly and wasn't too difficult to hide her limp.

They trudged slowly, dejectedly through the drizzling rain and unfamiliar forest. Samantha couldn't help but be miserable, she wanted to be home, where she could curl up in her duvet, have a hot meal. She missed her mum; Terri and Malc; she even missed her stepdad.

David moved along, not allowing himself to think of what they were missing, he focused only on the forest.

A strange noise seemed to surround them, it was so quiet that David only just noticed it, but dismissed it at first as water dripping. A few minutes something later told him that it wasn't. Stopping, he listened closely.

"What's wrong?" Samantha asked, privately glad for the short break.

"Nowt." He replied. It wouldn't help to make her worry. He moved off again, more slowly.

It was like a tapping on hollow wood, a skittering of nails on the tree trunks, and it was coming closer. The forest seemed to darken, even though nightfall was hours away. The general noise of birds chattering and the rustling of other small creatures stilled, leaving an eerie and foreboding silence apart from the tapping that tracked them.

"My ankle's starting to ache again." Samantha whispered, only partly truthful as it had been hurting all day.

David jumped, he had been listening so intently to half-sounds that Samantha's voice seemed to shout through the silence.

Suddenly movement was all around them. David stopped, putting his arm out to tell Samantha to wait. He jumped back as a large thing ran across the tree trunks beside him, it was large, but too quick to see anything more than ruddy animal fur. David took a tentative step forward…

Something leapt down from the trees, to the ground in front of them. David rebounded with horror. The creature crouched before him, a nightmare prowler. It looked like something that should have been human, but reverted to the most basic predator; a deep chest and humped back were covered with a murky brown pelt, its spindly limbs were perfect for speed and travelling through trees. Its noticeably long claws made the noise as it skittered across the trunks. Its face, hair creeping in on remotely human features; slanted yellow eyes; flattened nose and wide mouth of pincer teeth that the creature now showed as it crept on all fours towards David and Samantha, as a cat before it pounces.

"What are you?!" David shouted.

Samantha edged forward, peering over his shoulder at the beast, tightening her grip on David's arm at the very sight.

The creature lifted its ugly head, emitting a call, a sound of hissing and growling from the back of its throat that made the humans' blood run cold.

To David and Samantha's horror, a wave of tapping and calls came in reply from every direction.

"What are you?" David repeated, with less courage. "A… a werewolf?"

The creature's eyes glistened, as it took in the speaking boy.

Samantha froze as she recalled everything she had heard about this forest. "Mallus…"

"We are mallus." The growling and hissing voice came. Even though it had some human-ish features, the fact that it could speak caused a stab of fear.

The mallus spoke again, eyeing them hungrily. "I am Sahr. My pack surrounds you, all be hopeless." The sentence was punctuated with calls and clacking of the surrounding mallus as they started to move into view. Sahr was scraping its claws into the ground, tensing to pounce.

David looked hastily about, wondering if they had an opening to run.

It seemed that Sahr read his mind. "We are hunters. If you run, we chase. We bring you down."

David noticed that the way was clear to Sahr's right for the moment. He looked at Samantha, her eyes wide with fear once more. But they both knew what to do. They ran.

It was only a moment's head start for the humans, before the noise of claws on wood echoed behind them. Samantha started to lag, the fear had briefly numbed her ankle, but now the pain seared through her leg. She stumbled once and pulled herself back up and ran after David. Samantha stumbled a second time, and the ground came up to meet her.

David glanced back as he ran and saw Samantha falling. Cursing, he turned back. The leading mallus was close, almost flying through the tree branches, it looked ready to jump down on the fallen girl. David flung himself down and both he and Samantha rolled away just as the mallus came crashing down to them.

David lifted his head, and Samantha struggled to sit up.

The mallus stayed still. The humans were mud-splattered and panting for breath, but they got to their feet and made for the trees as Sahr's pack closed in.

As Sahr led the rest of them forward, the mallus halted before the dark heap of the fallen beast. Sniffing suspiciously over it, Sahr hissed and backed away, fear burning bright in those yellow eyes. The other mallus followed suit and the dreadful noises faded into the dark forest as all the creatures took to the canopy.

David turned back, wary of the silence, yet saw no mallus following them. Samantha followed him as he made his way to the stationary beast. They edged closer until they were standing over the massive heap of grubby fur and spindly limbs. Its chest did not rise and fall in breathing, and its eyes were dull and staring.

"I think it's dead." Samantha stated as she nudged it curiously with her good foot.

"I don't understand. That leap wouldn't kill it." He shook his head. "Come on, let's get going."

Samantha watched him move off through the trees. She took a final, disgusted look at the dead mallus. A thought came to her as she followed David – what were the powers of the Lost Soul?

*****

Was it just the hallucination from their worn nerves, or was there still the terrifying sound of mallus travelling through the trees?

David couldn't stop looking behind him as they walked. "I don't like it. Do you think they're following us again?"

Samantha shrugged, concentrating on walking without hurting her leg, and throat too dry to speak anyway.

For the second time that day, a shadowed hunter sprang from the trees before them. Horror spread through the two humans as a single mallus stood panting in front of them.

For a moment that seemed to last an eternity, no one moved. Then the mallus took a wary step forward.

"Leave us alone." Samantha pleaded.

The mallus ignored her, staring at their pale faces. "You killed a mallus." Came the low, hissing voice.

David and Samantha moved closer together.

"It means you hold big power." The mallus continued, baring its teeth. It lowered its torso in a strange kind of salute, then spoke again. "I am Siabhor. I wish to come."

"Why?" Samantha was the first to utter.

80

"I am mallus." Siabhor went on. "You killed a brother. But we be creatures of opportunity. To defeat a mallus... you must hold great power. Siabhor is curious, and I will survive on right side of this power."

Moments of indecision passed, before David stepped forward, peering enquiringly at the ugly creature.

"If this is true, you are welcome." He greeted formally. He took a deep breath, his admission making him feel much older. "I'm David, I think that I may be the power that you speak of. The Lost Soul of Enchena."

The arrival of Siabhor seemed to set their aims. They finally had a reason and an action. The power of the Lost Soul was surfacing and if they could persuade a mallus, the most feared creature in Enchena to join them, perhaps they could fulfil a prophecy.

Perhaps they could defeat Hrafn.

*****

The journey was far from over. After a quick council the trio decided the best thing was for David to stay within the forest and find the unicorns again, while Samantha would go back to the city to gather and inform the Gardyn. Siabhor would go with David to show him the way, and to offer his protection if there were any of Hrafn's soldiers. Samantha felt quite rejected at going alone on the more hazardous task, but knew that it was David they had to keep safe. Besides, she had spent years perfecting being invisible and a nobody, it was time to put it to some use, slipping inside the city walls.

They agreed that they would begin tomorrow, as it was already midday and rest was needed.

As the day wore on, David and Samantha learnt much about mallus from Siabhor. The packs were always led by the strongest female and Siabhor was one of the younger males in the group, which along with his natural pride, made him an outsider of the pack. There weren't many mallus packs in this part of the forest, it was too close to the human city for comfort.

David and Samantha also found out why mallus seemed only a nightmare fable. Their stealth in trees and acute senses meant that any human who saw them never had a chance to tell his tale.

When the humans became hungry, they surrounded themselves with the usual bounty of edible, but dull, fruits and nuts. Siabhor looked on with interest and excitement at how they harvested the food, but would not eat it. He disappeared without a word, leaving David and Samantha wondering.

"Look, I'm sorry for shouting at you the other day, for giving you a hard time." David said, breaking the silence, and hoping to see a little forgiveness in those green eyes of hers.

Samantha turned briefly towards him, then blushed. No guy had ever spoken to her that gently before, and yes, she recognised that look. She'd seen it a hundred times before when a boy took a liking to her friend Lucy. She was completely lost, now that she was the recipient. "It's OK. I guess it's hard, knowing all you've got to live up to."

"And I'm sorry, that I implied you were useless when we got here; that I said you were a liability. You're not that bad."

Samantha was nodding along with his apology, but paused: a liability? "Um, no, you never actually said that one to my face."

"Ah."

The panic on David's face, after his smooth 'I'm sorrys' was too much, and Samantha laughed at his stress. She vaguely waved her hand to dismiss the whole nonsense.

Samantha sighed. "I still wish we could have gone home, had an easy end to all this; but it's all leading to something important, isn't it?"

"Not feeling homesick, are you?" David teased. "When you have the five-star luxury of a dangerous forest?"

Samantha smiled. "Sure, I'm missing home comforts. But – and I can't believe I'm saying this – I'm missing my family more. Not so much Terri, she's off at college at the moment; but my brother Malc? He's two, bless him, and he's the funniest little rascal... why are you looking at me, like that?"

David gave a tilted smile. "What can I say, I'm an only child. I'm jealous of the whole siblings thing."

Samantha smiled shyly; someone was jealous about an aspect of her boring life? It was unexpected, but felt quite good.

When she looked up again, she was surprised at how close David was. She hardly dared to breathe when he raised his hand and gently traced her cheek with the tips of his fingers; the skin felt like it was burning beneath his touch.

Samantha blushed and lowered her eyes, she thought that he was about to kiss her, and that was something she definitely had no experience of.

There was suddenly a bout of noise as Siabhor returned, claws scrabbling about the trees, obviously elated with his hunt. He had returned carrying a small

83

deer-like animal in his jaws, its dark blood staining and matting the hair about Siabhor's mouth.

"*This* is food." The mallus stated, as he tore at the raw flesh.

David and Samantha exchanged an awkward glance, then tried their best to avoid looking at the mallus eating.

*****

"...and a whole pack, working together, can bring down a unicorn." Siabhor was talking with pride about hunting again, having finished eating and cleaning his fur of all blood.

"You know when Sahr came, why weren't we killed straight away?" David asked.

Siabhor bared his teeth in a mallus smile, it gave a ghastly effect with his sharp, uneven teeth shining out of his murky face.

"Mallus are greatest of all hunters." He boasted. "But where be the fun in hunting, killing, if we do not chase? We meaning for you to run, or death would be too easy."

Samantha shivered at the callousness of his words.

*****

No one knew how they were found, or how long the soldiers had been there, closing in on them. Not even Siabhor, with the attention and smell of the two young humans, had sensed them until it was too late.

There was the crack of a fallen branch, making their presence known. Several soldiers with arrows on string, or swords drawn, moved stealthily forward, only a tree's length away.

Siabhor, the opportunist, quickly became the deserter as he alighted to the canopy. They jumped to their feet, and something zipped past Samantha. As the soldiers ran into the circlet of trees, Samantha spun around.

David had fallen to the ground, Samantha collapsed beside him, gasping as she saw the arrow protruding from his chest. Hot blood already soaked his clothes and he held her gaze, confusion clouding his expression. Through pain his eyes glazed, and he struggled to breathe.

The soldiers were upon them, grabbing Samantha roughly by the arms. David, looking up at her, gave a half-smile, his last apology. He moved no more and Samantha screamed.

What happened next was a mystery, with fresh death and with the screams of tragedy, there was an explosion of flame. Fire surrounded them, filling the air with suffocating smoke. Samantha choked and started to lose consciousness.

'This is it.' She thought, just before everything went black.

Nine

At first she wondered whether this was death and beyond. But as Samantha started to wake, the aching of her body told her that life went on. Though whether it would have been better to have died in the fire would often be a thought on her mind in the following months.

As she came around, she murmured to herself and turned onto her side. She lay on something soft and silky, quite different to the forest floor.

When Samantha tried to open her eyes, tiredness plagued her and the light momentarily blinded her. Slowly, she could make out the blurry image of a girl beside the bed. The girl seemed oddly familiar.

"Jillis?" Samantha tried to speak, but her parched throat stopped any sound.

Jillis looked at Samantha pleadingly as she set out fresh water and bread at her bedside. "Do not reveal me." She murmured, and then she stood up and rushed away.

Samantha suddenly became aware of her surroundings. She lay in a large bed with silken sheets in the middle of a greatly decorated room. She watched

Jillis rushing out through double doors at the far side; to Samantha's horror, she saw an Enchenian guard on each side. They followed the maid out and the doors closed, leaving Samantha alone.

Samantha took a moment to try and understand. Her confused mind slowly realised that she must be in the palace of Enchena, but why?

That evening in the forest: fire; death; where was David?

Samantha tried to understand as muddled thoughts and memories flitted chaotically. All that she truly knew was that David was dead, and now she was a prisoner (albeit a well-kept one) of King Hrafn.

Over that day Samantha found clean clothes set out for her and wandered listlessly within the room, her conscious self was almost encased and every action robotic and disconnected from her. The only person that entered her room was Jillis, bringing meals for the captive Samantha. But they were never alone, for there was always a guard present, which meant they couldn't talk no matter how much they longed to.

Samantha would stay in this room for a long time. She would sit in solitude, until time lost all consistency.

It was during the seventh night since she had found herself a prisoner that Samantha awoke, feverish and throat dry with thirst. Sitting up she reached for a glass of water, just visible in the light of star shine through her large curtainless windows. After drinking the cool water she lay down again, but felt uncomfortable. The stars seemed to burn too brightly and she felt as though she were being watched. But it was more than the heavens, someone was in her room.

87

Samantha sat up again, staring through the shadows, she felt more awake now than she had for the past few days. Then she saw the familiar face staring at her from the corner. He smiled and got up, walking slowly towards her, dappled in starlight. Samantha felt a great calm as David approached, she just gazed peacefully when he sat beside her on the bed. He was so close, but even in the darkness he seemed to glow with the ghostly light of stars silhouetting him. But he was here, his eyes dark with some new depth.

"It's time to sleep." He whispered, reaching out and gently stroking her hair from the side of her face. Samantha nodded and lay down, immediately being swept away to peaceful slumber.

*****

She was awoken by the bright morning sunshine through the large windows. Samantha lay still and sighed heavily, she missed the glorious morning chorus of birds in the forests. The dream had been strange and so real, but the vision of David had cleared her mind and she started to think how she could escape the palace.

Her thoughts were interrupted by the arrival of Jillis who entered unaccompanied.

Jillis looked bewildered and was nervous. When Samantha had arrived all the palace staff had been told that they were not to spend time with her alone. But now she was being sent in without a chaperone, and Jillis also suspected that she was being shadowed around the palace grounds. The only incident that could possibly explain this was that they had finally found out she was a Gardyn. Yet she was still alive, which meant some darker intent awaited her.

Jillis waited uneasily for the door to shut behind her before rushing over to Samantha, setting her tray down onto the table.

"What's wrong?" Asked Samantha in a hushed voice.

Jillis did not speak for a moment, then replied quietly. "I... I don't know. There have been whispers amongst the servants of the Lost Soul returning." She paused, wondering whether to share her worries. "And... I think they know that I'm Gardyn."

Samantha quickly worked out the implications. "Then you should leave, while you can."

The girls sat silently; Jillis glanced at the entrance then spoke. "I had better go. I'll return at midday."

The young maid stood up and walked quickly to the door. Samantha watched sadly as she left.

*****

Samantha waited anxiously as the morning dragged by. She wandered her luxurious prison, often staring out of the large window. The days were warming again since that wild spring storm. Rows of black and red uniformed soldiers were massing in the courtyard below her window, there was an air of impending battle.

Jillis came just after midday, she lost no time in asking Samantha what had happened in the forest. After Samantha rushed through the main details Jillis looked mortified.

"So David is dead?" She asked in a cracked voice. "I had hoped he'd escaped."

Samantha just nodded numbly in reply.

"Well, I do not work this evening, so I will go to the Gardyn and inform them. We may be bereaved of the Lost Soul, but at least we can save his friend." Jillis smiled kindly at Samantha, then to Samantha's surprise she found herself receiving a warm hug from the Enchenian maid as though they had long been friends. Jillis smiled once more then left. Samantha wiped a tear from her cheek and cursed her own weakness.

*****

There was nothing for Samantha to do but wait. Dusk was settling when she was next disturbed. A maid bustled in, older and more severe than Jillis. She informed Samantha that she was requested to an evening meal with the King. The maid brought out a dress of hunter green from the wardrobe and assisted Samantha in dressing. Samantha found it odd but dare not argue. Even for the slight Samantha the dress felt uncomfortably tight about the waist and the high collar made her hold her head high. The maid then dragged a comb through Samantha's hair, making it hang straight past her shoulders.

The maid ushered her through the doors and down a carpeted staircase. It was Samantha's first view of the palace and it was lavishly decorated with rich coloured wall hangings and items from past glories.

Samantha was led through a set of doors into a cavernous room in which stood a long table, candlelight flickered over the dishes that lay along the smooth wooden surface. At the far end King Hrafn was already seated, he looked up as Samantha entered and watched as she was shown to her place midway along the table. Samantha sat silently for a while, staring down at the swirling knots on the polished table.

The King started to eat slowly, his eyes flicking to Samantha who had not touched the food. "They have not poisoned your meal." He said in an amused voice.

Samantha ignored the comment. "Why am I here?" She asked, without looking up.

Hrafn sat silently as Samantha finally lifted her head. She smiled weakly. "David's dead. You've lost your chance to unite with the Lost Soul."

Strangely, the King smiled back at her, making her feel uneasy. "Ah, would it be so simple child." He replied, reaching for his goblet of wine. "But, sadly, you are wrong on both counts." He sipped at the cup, looking over the rim. He placed the goblet down and coughed gently. "Decided to join us?" He asked coldly to someone behind her.

Samantha turned as David was shown to his seat further down the table. David just glared in reply to the King's question and sat down.

Hrafn spoke once more to Samantha. "As you can see, your friend is quite well."

Samantha sat silently, staring at David. "David?" She murmured. Then scraped back her chair and ran breathlessly to him, flinging her arms about him. "You're alive! I can't believe it."

"Well, believe it, OK." David replied quietly, wriggling from her grip. "No thanks to you."

Samantha leant closer, keeping her voice low. "Don't worry, they're planning to get us out."

"And what if I don't want to leave? If I don't want to go hiding in muddy glades and damp forests anymore?" David made no effort to lower his voice and fixed his gaze on the table in front of him.

Samantha stood back, wondering what David was saying. A cough sounded at the other end of the table and Samantha was once again aware of the King. She looked back suspiciously at David. "How *did* you survive anyway? I saw that... but you died."

David clapped slowly and mockingly. "You always were slow. I did die." He stated, then fell silent.

"But..."

"He will tell you no more." The King spoke up. "For even he does not fully understand how it came to be."

Samantha stared open-mouthed, looking between the King and David. Slowly realisation dawned, David had received help from Hrafn, and the Lost Soul had been found.

"No, no." Samantha's throat felt dry and the words hardly formed. "No. I saw you die." She started backing away from the table. With one last dry cry she turned and fled through the set of doors. Hrafn did not move to stop her, but outside the guards restrained her and she was escorted back to her room.

Back in the grand dining room David sat silently, not touching the food as Hrafn ate and talked.

"Remember our agreement David." The King said threateningly. "If you wish to stay alive this time you will help me find out everything."

David shuddered, he had been through death once, and that was enough for anyone. But Hrafn had brought him back, he vividly remembered the tearing feeling, it was as real as the scar on his chest from the arrow. That had been the first time. David did not know whether he had died or not as his body had been beaten to the brink of death several times over, as the King's men brutally ensured his service, each painful encounter followed by the healing power of Hrafn so that the torment remained fresh.

It had taken three days of this for David to finally disconnect from all his old ideas of right and wrong and to realise that he was free from the morals and conscience that held down every mortal man.

Now he looked up at Hrafn, the one who had enforced the violent teachings and grimaced as he felt his one sense of duty.

"Look, you need me more than I need you. But fine." He paused, and looked in the direction of the doors. "In fact, I'll start now." He stood up, threw down his napkin and marched out.

*****

It was late, the moon had risen beyond sight of the window in Samantha's room, but she still lay unable to sleep, on her bed in the growing darkness.

The door opened slowly and someone entered carrying a candle that flickered insignificantly in the shadows. Samantha hardly moved, she felt so mentally fatigued that she scarcely noticed the intrusion.

"Sammy? You awake?" She recognised David's voice. He moved forward, he couldn't see her face, but he knew that she wasn't asleep. "Why'd you leave at dinner?" He asked innocently.

"I thought you were dead." She mumbled without turning to face him.

David let out a short, harsh laugh and sat on the bed next to Samantha.

"I was." He said simply. "To tell the truth, I didn't expect you to understand. I'm surprised Hrafn thought he could reveal everything at once. Perhaps he assumes you're able to comprehend it all."

David paused, glancing at Samantha who remained motionless, then helped himself to some of the water on her cabinet. "You know, the funny thing is how everyone made such a fuss over me, and how you were always ignored."

Samantha finally looked at him. "I don't understand." She said slowly.

"No. You always were a bit clueless." David, replied drily. "I'm not the Lost Soul. Never was. I was only brought here as a tool to get to that person." David stared at Samantha with darkened eyes, he smiled slightly as she finally worked it out.

Samantha just stared at him for a moment. "Why are you alive?" She asked breathlessly.

"Hrafn brought me back from… from Death…"

"Why?"

"That's of no importance." David snapped, suddenly angry. "Tell me Sammy. How long have you known about Minaeri, what do you know about her and the Lost Soul?"

"O… only what you do." She stuttered, taken aback and suddenly feeling quite afraid.

David stood up and grabbed the candle, with a look of disappointment he walked out of the room. After the door was closed he turned to the shadows of the corridor.

"She knows nothing." He said quietly. "Or at least she wouldn't say."

Hrafn stepped out. "Very well. I hope you did not tell her any more than was necessary. Keep it quiet until we are ready."

David nodded glumly and followed the King down the corridor. With Samantha so confused, it would be easy to keep her from the full truth.

Ten

Days went past slowly, and a change came over Samantha. She was not allowed to leave her room, but that did not matter because she had no wish to. She could usually be found by the largest western window, gazing out past the city to the forest that stretched to the horizon. Samantha hardly noticed as time slipped by, the warm sun shining onto her pale face which showed her uncertainty of reality.

David would visit her, but didn't try to help her out of this daze. Samantha's only other visitor was Jillis, but the maid rarely talked to her now, sensing that in her bewildered state Samantha might let anything slip to Hrafn. Jillis had, however, found out that David was alive but she was unable to go to where his quarters lie.

*****

It had been nearly two weeks since Samantha had been brought unconscious to the palace. David had come to talk to her again as the King had told him that it was time to finally tell Samantha everything.

When he entered he found her sitting by the open window, the soft, light wind lifting her hair from her thoughtful face. David smiled as he walked slowly up.

"Sammy." He called gently, but she did not respond. "How are you?"

Samantha closed her eyes for a moment and sighed. "I hate this, everything happening around me." She looked back at David, who moved round and stood beside the window. "Sometimes... sometimes I think you're still dead and wonder how you're here. Then sometimes I'll see you and think we're still in the forest, or even at school." Her eyes glazed over with unshed tears and she looked away.

David leant against the wall, staring out of the window, smiling. "You know, it could all change." he said softly. "Everything can become clear again. Hrafn can make it so."

Samantha looked up at him, waiting for him to continue.

"He helped me. Brought me through death to a place you can hardly imagine." David no longer looked at Samantha but stared away with brightened eyes. "It's clearer now than it ever has been. There's no sadness, no fear, only truth. He can help you too, Sammy."

Samantha sat silently thinking. "But they thought you were the Lost Soul. They won't help me."

David laughed coldly. "Lord! Sammy, can you be any slower!" He knelt beside her and whispered quietly. "You are the Lost Soul of Enchena, Hrafn was always aware of that."

"The Gardyn. I can't... how could I go against them?" Samantha muttered as she started to level everything in her own mind.

David grunted with contempt. "The Gardyn? What do you owe them? We were escaping them as much as Hrafn when we ran to the forests, you remember what the Deorwines said - the Gardyn would rather have us dead than undecided." David shrugged. "Besides, they are the rebel group that instigate all the rumours and trouble that the empire has to fight against. It's time to join the real good guys."

Samantha sat silently, still staring out over the city.

With a smile David stood tall again. "Think it over, yeah?" With that he left. He knew he couldn't get any real answer from her this morning.

*****

That evening, Samantha was made ready to dine with Hrafn again. She'd had time to think over the offer, but was still unsure. She was escorted down to the dining room again, her borrowed dark crimson dress rustling as she moved. Along the large table seven figures already sat. King Hrafn, David and five that Samantha had not yet seen. A cold and graceful lady of immense, yet unusual beauty, white-blonde hair and pale skin that years ago had enchanted the King so greatly that he took her as his queen. Next to the woman was a young boy, hardly ten years of age but glancing warily as she entered. Further along sat three girls, slightly older than the boy, all with dark brown hair and plain, pasty features that were similar enough that Samantha guessed they were all siblings.

Hrafn beckoned Samantha to be seated. "I don't believe you've met my wife, Arianne, nor my son, Tagor. Oh, and my three daughters." He waved a hand to the assembled family, showing no intention of honouring his daughters with a full introduction. Samantha sat down nervously, aware that they were all watching.

"Have you had time to consider my offer?" Hrafn asked.

Samantha thought through her reply. "I'm the Lost Soul aren't I?" She asked. Hrafn nodded in answer.

"How long have you known?"

"I was unsure at first, but I knew the moment you were able to step into Enchena unaided. Only those blessed with Minaeri's powers can pass through the gateway between worlds. Anyone else who tries is lost to the abyss." The King replied softly.

Samantha bit her lip. "If... if I agree to help you, everything will be put right? I mean, I won't have to worry, and I can go back home afterwards?"

The King smiled and nodded. Again the room fell silent. Samantha looked over at David, surprised that his expression was dark and troubled.

She pushed back all doubts and thoughts of the Gardyn and spoke up. "What do I have to do?"

King Hrafn's smile grew. "We shall leave that 'til the morning. For now, let us feast." He replied.

Queen Arianne looked solemn, yet nearly happy. The children kept quiet, uninterested in what had happened. David glanced towards the King uneasily, but quickly hid it away and turned to converse with the eldest daughter who sat beside him.

The eight diners began to eat and talk, Samantha found it pleasant finally sitting with people who could talk freely, but something challenged her confidence, the joviality and discourse of the others was like water sliding over ice and this doubt quietened Samantha. But her desire for this nightmare to end won out, the King of Enchena would receive any help she could give.

*****

Over the next few days, Samantha was free to move as she wished through the palace and its grounds. She had been shown the lay of the palace, from the torture chambers to the treasury. She would often sit with Queen Arianne or her daughters, with whom she would converse formally, but would never hold as friends.

Her other frequent companion was David, they would wander through the gardens as the days grew hotter. David would talk quite happily with Samantha, but often turned pale and would stare into the distance when he thought she wasn't looking. Samantha seldom liked being alone with David, he had changed, he always looked as if death were to return to him and he would do anything to stop it.

The only other thing that made Samantha worry was Jillis. They saw very little of each other and never spoke, but when Samantha did see the young maid, she remembered all that she had turned her back on in her selfish desire for everything to go back to normal.

It was when Samantha was sitting in the gardens with David that he finally revealed the thoughts that plagued him.

"When will I have to help Hrafn?" Samantha asked. She felt a distinct lack of usefulness, having been asked nothing more about being the Lost Soul.

David seemed to come out of a daze. "What's that? Oh I don't know. As soon as they find out how to get your powers I suppose."

"But I've never purposefully shown powers. I... I don't even know how to use them."

99

"All the better." David muttered. "We don't want to end up dead like that mallus. You just keep yourself safe."

Samantha looked quizzically. "Do you want me to give my powers to Hrafn?"

He shrugged. "Doesn't bother me, my time's nearly up." He glanced at Samantha. "I'm only here 'til Hrafn gets your powers; then I've got no further use." He scowled, feeling almost scared, the nearest he had come to an emotion since he had died. "I'll just be killed again."

"But that's not right! The Gardyn." She hissed. "They'll get you out."

"Our wonderful allies? They are as doomed as the unicorns."

"What?"

David turned to look at Samantha, curious how she would react. "Hrafn's hunters came back one morning, bringing the horns as trophies. They cut down the whole herd, every last one."

Samantha's breath hitched and she began to tremble. "You're lying."

David shrugged. "Hrafn didn't want to risk them helping the Gardyn. One price of many, placed on me staying alive – I had to tell him where the unicorns were."

Samantha stared at him, tears stinging her eyes. "Nmirr? Alina? *Sundance*? He was only a baby!"

"If you're looking for remorse Samantha, I'm sorry to disappoint you. This is a world at war, sacrifices have to be made."

Samantha started to cry, and didn't want to stop. Not only had she lost the unicorns, who had never done

100

anything but help them; but the David she knew was gone.

"No need to get emotional, Samantha. You have made your choice to support King Hrafn; how can you get so worked up when his enemies die? First the unicorns, then the Gardyn - they'll be gone as soon as Hrafn is at full strength." He paused as a shout of mirth came from another garden where Prince Tagor had just hit his manservant with a wooden broadsword. David smiled, he might have a death sentence hanging over his own head, but both Tagor and his eldest sister, Helena would help him. Even if they did not know it yet.

"I can take care of myself. They'll find me worth keeping." David stood up and brushed dirt from his trousers, then glanced back at Samantha. "See you at the big party tonight, Sammy. You might want to stop with the tears, red eyes don't suit you."

With that he stood up and left, walking slowly back to the palace doors.

*****

Over the past few days the palace had been a bustle of activity in preparation for a ball. It was held annually by the royal family and everyone of importance was invited. This year it would be more than a celebration of the Enchenian empire, it would be the King openly regaling the possession of the Lost Soul.

For the rest of the day the poor Lost Soul had been instructed and drilled on how to act at a ball, on what to say to certain people and what not to do and say. By the time a maid came to get her ready Samantha was already exhausted, but agreed to dress and be made ready. A dress was chosen of lightest grey, which seemed to shine silver in the candlelight. The maid busied about

101

Samantha, brushing her hair so vigorously that it hurt. When she was ready Samantha looked in the long mirror, the change was startling. No longer was the reflection a pale and scared schoolgirl, but a lady of great power. Which was soon chased away with the irritating thought of which side did that power belong?

*****

In the dining room the atmosphere was expectant. Samantha found the room decorated grandly in royal colours, and many coats of arms adorned the walls. The room was quite full with many lords and ladies all talking amongst themselves with a detached air. As she entered everyone turned to face her. Samantha glanced around nervously.

"Samantha Garrett, guest to our King." Her presence was announced, which made her blush from the unwanted attention. Samantha moved as quickly as she could to mingle and disappear within the crowd.

"David, Royal Prince of Leeds." Samantha looked back at the doorway as David walked through, looking very regal. He saw her in the crowd and made his way over to her, smiling in a lop-sided way.

"Prince David?" Samantha asked scornfully. "Of Leeds?!"

David shrugged. "What did you think, that Hrafn would admit to housing a nobody in the palace? His council decided it would be easier to pretend I was the prince of our home country. How else do you think I've been treated so well?" David looked about the room with a casual interest. "Ah, there's Helena. Please excuse me."

David quickly melted into the crowd in search of the princess and Samantha was left alone again, trying to be invisible in a room full of strangers.

Over the next half an hour there was a steady flow of entering guests… "Lord and Lady Odrium of Telka"… "Sir Mihal of Goum"… until…

"His Royal Highness, Hrafn, Lord beneath Minaeri, King of Enchena and Emperor of all known lands."

Everyone turned to the entrance and bowed or curtsied to the King and his family. Samantha made a pitiful effort and she saw a flickering smile as the King glanced over her.

Hrafn bowed his head, then lifted his hand to allow his people to rise. "Please be seated." The King's voice rang out over the silent, waiting crowd.

There was a low rumble of murmured conversation as the guests moved automatically to their places about the three long tables set out. Servants rushed out, bringing elaborate dishes. Samantha glanced around her, the only people she recognised were the King and Queen and David. Seated close to the King was the Captain with the scarred face from the forest, who was obviously more high-ranking than Samantha had guessed. All the other guests were dressed in a royal fashion, they were later introduced to Samantha as the greatest of lords and ladies from other lands who all paid homage to Hrafn.

The meal ended and Hrafn stood, wine glass raised. "I thank you all for attending, as you know we have long searched for a way to finally defeat the insufferable Gardyn." He nodded to Samantha. "And we have discovered how. By this time next month all of our enemies will be gone."

Applause filled the room.

"But tonight is not a war cabinet, it is a celebration. And if you follow me, we shall continue to the dance hall."

There was a scraping of chairs, and the low chatter rose up again as the lords and ladies made their way out of the dining hall. Already music flowed out of the dance hall doors, drawing them on.

David approached Samantha and bowed his head before offering his arm. Samantha took it and, looking about nervously, followed his lead onto the large polished floor. Shuffling along slowly to the music, Samantha decided to ask David something that had worried her since their conversation that morning.

"David, does Hrafn know how to obtain the powers of the Lost Soul?"

David took a moment to mimic the movements of the other dancers, then replied quietly. "Yes."

"So, he's going to kill you soon?"

"No, no I have found a reason for him to keep me alive."

Samantha moved back to look him straight in the face, but seeing he meant to keep this reason secret she asked another question. "Will Hrafn kill me? When I have no use?"

David didn't answer. King Hrafn made his way through the dancing partners towards them, he bowed his head respectfully.

"May I steal your partner David?" He asked, laughing.

Samantha found herself being passed over to the tall, handsome Hrafn.

"You seem so sombre, Samantha. This is supposed to be an occasion for celebration." Hrafn looked down at her with his dark eyes, his arm encircling her waist as he pulled her about the dance floor.

Samantha purposefully looked away, refusing to meet his gaze. "David told me about the unicorns today, your majesty." She said quietly.

Hrafn's hold on her tightened for a moment. "A necessity my dear. But remember, you have sworn to help me end the conflict we find ourselves in."

Samantha felt heavy on her feet and stayed quiet. As David had said, this was her choice. Surely, if she had chosen the Gardyn, it would simply have led to the deaths of other people.

"You have been wondering when we need your help." Hrafn murmured to her. "Well, the time is soon. A ritual is involved and it will begin with tomorrow's dawn."

The rest of the evening passed like a daze; before Samantha was aware of it she was already moving tiredly up the stairs to her room. Feeling exhausted she collapsed down on the bed, and thinking she must get up and change, she fell into dreamless sleep.

Eleven

Back in the forest, on the same day that Samantha had awoken to find herself in the palace of Enchena, Alina was trotting slowly through the woodland, the joy of spring in her veins.

She had just been to visit Autumn, a fine male chestnut unicorn of a nearby herd. Alina's happy thoughts hung in the air around her and the day seemed fine.

But as she moved further on, she could smell something on the breeze, it was the acrid scent of ashes. It unnerved her and she moved cautiously forward, before her was a strange sight indeed. The ground and foliage was scorched in what must have been an intense fire, but it only reached to a twenty metre circle, beyond it everything was green and fresh, as one would not expect so close to such a blaze. There was another, fainter scent which disturbed her, but she could not discern what it was.

Alina whinnied gently with uncertainty, then started as she heard a sound from the unscorched canopy. A hairy, murky face bent down, it seemed to be searching for something in the burnt area. As it dropped down Alina nearly gave a cry of fear. It was a mallus, with the sight of the singular nightmare prowler the undertone scent came clear. Death had happened here, and human blood had seeped into the baked ground.

She did not linger anymore but turned and cantered swiftly on silent hooves, ears strained for the sound of a chase. The thought came to her as she ran, that she had never heard of a lone mallus, so why was this one unaccompanied...?

Alina started to slow as her fear ebbed, she snorted with unease. The day was fine when morning had broken; yet now signs of death and misery loomed, following the silver mare like a shadow.

She halted again as she heard the sound of pounding hooves, she was close to her home valley and wondered what had caused such a disturbance.

A loud, throbbing neigh rang out through the forest, she recognised it as Nmirr's and felt scared once more as his voice held the command for the herd to flee. Alina was uncertain and skittered across the forest floor, moving nervously towards the valley.

Suddenly the pale form of Nmirr burst through, galloping along the forest tracks, he skidded to a halt and looked with surprise to find his sister there. "Alina, dear heart." His thoughts passed, conveying his sadness and distress. "Flee, we must. There are humans. We did not hear them approach and now they are shooting us down. Cassiopeia…. Cassiopeia…."

The unicorn reared in anger, in his strength he looked the image of Praede. "Go, now." He drove his sister before him.

They travelled as two silver flashes through the trees, but their path was ill-chosen and soon they struggled through thick vegetation, going no faster than a walk. But as they heard humans, thrashing about the bushes for escaped unicorns, they pushed harder until sweat beaded their grey coats.

"It is vain for us to continue." Nmirr's thoughts betrayed him. He halted and looked at his beloved sister. "Go, to Autumn's herd. Warn them that men are hunting us again."

He turned back to the sound of men forcing their way through the tangle of trees.

Alina let loose a whinny of fear. "You will not be made a martyr."

Nmirr turned back to her, horn lowered angrily. "Go now Alina."

She stood uncertain for a moment before following her brother's command. She daren't look back, but the horrifying sounds of an angry and desperate creature resounded through the forest.

The area cleared and Alina ran as fast as she could without making any noise. She did not know where she went, nor how long her flight would last. But eventually she slowed and stopped, far from her usual territory. Overwhelmed with sadness she wandered idly until she lay beneath the leafy shade of a tree and fell into fitful sleep.

*****

When Alina awoke, the sun was setting, blood red streaks marred the darkening sky and the lonely unicorn did not dare to look up for memory of the tragic day. Standing up stiffly, Alina started to walk steadily onwards, involuntarily moving back towards her old herd's valley. In her desperate flight she had covered much land and now the return took many hours. The silver unicorn walked dejectedly through the forest, hardly a shining beauty in her grief.

The stars had travelled right across the inky sky and to the east the horizon was fringed with faint dawn light. Finally the silver unicorn approached the tree-tangled area where she had last seen her brother. The rising sun was just visible now through the trees, strong rays of dawn light fell upon a silver mass in the long grasses.

Alina moved cautiously up to her brother's body, then lay down by the bloodstained corpse, large, crystalline tears dampened his grey coat as she leant over him. The humans had removed any arrows that might have pierced him, and had sawn off, and taken his horn. There were gaping red sores where spears had gored the mighty unicorn, but the blood no longer ran.

Alina waited in mourning close to Nmirr's body, forgetting about warning other herds. She stayed there, alone, for another day before her peace was intruded. The sun was setting when Alina was aware of the presence of others.

"So, it is true. The mighty Nmirr has been killed." Came the thoughts of another unicorn, oily and seeping across the darkening air.

Alina staggered up to face the unicorn, whose black coat made him merge with the shadows. "The Dark Being." A thought of fear flickered, she suddenly felt very alone and vulnerable.

About this fearsome stallion stood a choice few of his herd, all obscured by fading light. The Dark Being lowered his horned head, not hiding the amusement from his thoughts.

"I have not forgotten that you bore away those human foals, nor that Nmirr dared to wound me." He threw up his head for a moment and a glistening scar could be seen across his neck in the gathering dusk, almost identical to the one he had inflicted upon Nmirr. "It is well that this herd was destroyed, you were all a disgrace to our kind. Harbouring *humans*." With this last disgusted thought The Dark Being charged forward.

Alina dodged swiftly, but found the members of his herd encircling her. The Dark Being had charged so hastily that he had to jump the mound of Nmirr's carcass, giving the discourtesy of one last kick at the lifeless silvery hide.

The stallion turned to face the silver mare again and he snorted, in the evening dusk she shone like a star herself and another idea came to him as he approached more slowly towards the beautiful mare. "But you cannot help the misfortune for having such a fool for a sibling. You now have the chance to renounce your naïve past, join my herd."

Alina became more scared and shivered slightly, sweat-stained ears flicking nervously. "No, I am no betrayer of my blood."

"Then you share the same fate as your brother."

Without warning The Dark Being suddenly reared, Alina felt his scything hooves come down to her flesh and rushed back out of range of the flailing feet but found cruel teeth nipping harshly at her hindquarters. She kicked out, then moved swiftly to an open space. Alina lowered her head uncertainly, she had not been made to fight before and she could not match this stallion's strength.

The Dark Being walked slowly forwards, horn down in challenge, the members of his herd moving like a shadow behind him.

Alina shifted back gradually, but found herself against the trunk of a large tree and no escape. The dark-hearted unicorns seemed to realise this and teased their helpless pray behind their leader.

A slight breeze blew, on it came a scent that made Alina tremble more than any thought of these sinister unicorns, it held the smell of death for forest creatures. The Dark Being halted and lifted his head, his lip curled back in disgust at the scent of mallus.

Above and behind Alina he could see two eyes gleaming dimly in the nightfall, long claws rattled slowly on bark and breath hissed gently through sharp teeth.

Suddenly it leapt down onto the bared back of The Dark Being. The stallion reared up and roared a horse's scream as the creature tore into his hide. Twisting violently The Dark Being managed to throw the mallus off.

The nightmare prowler crouched defensively between Alina and the angry stallion and The Dark Being snorted as dark blood seeped from the wounds, pain clouded his thoughts. He looked back at Alina. "You have some strange, dark magic."

With the mallus spitting and growling at them, The Dark Being and his herd turned and fled.

Alina was left staring at the hideous creature, it turned its hairy face to her, then leapt back up to the canopy. Its claws could be heard tapping against the wood as it travelled.

Alina whinnied a soft call to it. "Wait."

Her curiosity had been stirred. This mallus had not attacked her, indeed it had saved her. She knew that mallus were cunning creatures, a pack of them had once brought down a cousin of hers years ago. But something told her to trust this one, the same instinct that had told her to trust the humans.

Using the sound, rather than sight, to guide her through the forest she followed the mallus all the way to the burnt area she had discovered before. The mallus had left the trees now and was snuffling busily across the arid ground.

Alina trotted cautiously up to it, sending nervous, but peaceful thoughts through the air.

The mallus turned and snarled at her before returning to his business.

"What do you seek?" Alina ventured her question timidly.

"Humans. Little humans, I think you know them. You be Nmirr's sister?" His rasping voice startled the unicorn slightly.

Alina nodded, sadness seeped into her mind as she thought of her brother. "But you knew David and Samantha? How? They went back to their home."

"No, they found the gate closed. Then we… well, we meet." The mallus went on to tell Alina of how he had journeyed with the humans and they had decided to find the unicorns and join the Gardyn to fight King Hrafn.

"And so." Finished Siabhor. "We rested, then the guards came. I managed to escape, but now I am searching for sign of the human children."

Alina looked quite coldly at Siabhor, trying to hide her feeling of anger at this pitiful creature that had deserted her friends.

Siabhor sniffed the ground again. "There is blood soaked into the ground here." He sniffed again, looking thoughtful. "I am very sure it is not adult blood, but which of David and Samantha has bled I cannot tell, and it has been days since it was spilt."

The mallus glanced up at the unicorn, finding this experience disconcerting, he knew a unicorn was deadly to singular mallus and he shifted round slightly to further himself from the glinting horn. "I am thinking this trail cannot be followed. But, the humans had said you and your herd would help them." Siabhor's yellowy eyes flickered over the silver unicorn.

"My brother can aid no one. But... but there is another herd." Alina's sad feelings echoed. She continued, remembering Nmirr's wish for her to seek out Autumn, she glanced up at the starry sky. "Their herd is not far, we could make it by sunrise."

*****

Such a strange pair had never been seen running through the wilderness, as this silver unicorn and shadowed mallus swept fearlessly through the forest trees in the night.

The final star before dawn was dimming and the sky was tinted with sunrise as they approached a dense thicket of trees. Alina halted and looked hesitantly at the mallus.

"The herd is close but, no offence, you are regarded as foe by them."

Siabhor bared his teeth grimly, it was only his desire to make amends for abandoning the humans that held him to this loathsome situation. "I understand. You go find your friends, I wait here."

113

Alina flicked her tail and followed a hidden path through the thicket, uncomfortably aware of Siabhor's grief, finding her own pity for the creature a disturbing experience.

Within a matter of strides the silver unicorn had pushed through the grove to find herself in a familiar clearing. She lifted her head and whinnied quietly to announce her presence.

Immediately a tall and handsome chestnut trotted forwards, the rising sun shining both gold and silver on his coat and mane.

"Alina!" Autumn's thoughts held relief. "We heard what had happened to your herd, to Nmirr. We thought that you…"

Alina nuzzled him with consolation, then stepped back and peered up at his face questioningly. "How did you find out? Did any of my herd escape?"

Autumn's kindly eyes smiled, and for an answer he threw up his head and called. From the far end of the Valley came a reply and, trotting nervously, a young palomino led a small band of unicorns. There were only four of them, but they all squealed with delight at the reunion.

"Young Sundance here remembered the way to our herd after you last brought him to visit. He told us that the herd had been killed and that he found some of the others that had managed to escape on his way here. Of you there was no trace, living or dead. I had hoped that you were not back from travelling when the slaughter happened."

Alina stood silently, the thoughts of her escape marred the happiness of finding Sundance alive. Then she suddenly remembered why she was here. "Autumn, do you remember I told you of two humans, the ones we saved from The Dark Being. Well, we think they are in trouble and we came to you for help and advice."

"We?" Autumn looked confused, wondering if Alina had been taken by another herd.

Alina sensed his confusion and looked nervously into the peaceful valley, wondering what right she had to disturb it.

"I met someone called Siabhor." She replied. "He's waiting beyond the thicket, I did not think it wise for him to enter."

Autumn started to the border of his Valley. "Well, show him to me." His troubled thoughts murmured.

Alina moved past him and pushed through the dense copse. When they emerged to the forest again, there was no one in sight.

Autumn moved about uncertainly. "Well, where is he?"

A rustling noise came from above and a hairy shape hung down from the bough of a tree. Autumn immediately swept between the hunter and Alina, horn lowered defensively.

Alina whinnied with amusement. "Peace, Autumn. This is Siabhor, he saved me from The Dark Being... he won't harm you today."

Siabhor scowled down at the glittering unicorns with intense dislike. "This be the Autumn you told me of?" His voice hissed. The mallus dropped down and squinted up at them.

Autumn looked disgusted, he did not understand what Alina was doing with creatures that had killed their kind. "Well, what plan have you arranged?" Asked Autumn, warily eyeing the mallus.

115

"None of yet, other than to find you and to seek your help." Alina replied yawning, she shook her head and looked hopefully at Autumn.

The chestnut unicorn stood undecidedly, but he was fond of Alina and knew to trust her. "I think we should go back into the Valley for now, I suppose you have had little sleep over the past few days." He led the grey mare back to the thicket, then stopped and looked back. "You, O hunter, if you promise not to approach any of my herd, or to keep the way in to memory for future hunts then I will allow you sanctuary for as long as Alina wishes."

Grumbling quietly Siabhor followed the unicorns through the thicket. The herd were watching for the return of Autumn, but spooked at his hairy companion, the chestnut stallion narrowly avoided the flight of his herd, promising the mallus was to be under Alina's care. Siabhor still wasn't happy though, and kept at the edge of the Valley, hiding in the shadows.

Twelve

Alina was left all that day, safe to sleep with Autumn grazing nearby. By the following dawn she was well rested and moved through the herd, meeting those she feared she would never meet again.

Siabhor stayed in the tree line, avoided by all but a bay stallion set to guard him. He watched the movement of unicorns uneasily, something like conscience flickered at the sight of prey socialising. But still he wished to be elsewhere.

A young golden palomino was moving furtively towards where the mallus rested. It lifted up its horned head and looked inquisitively at the beast. "Do you really kill unicorns?"

Siabhor hung down from the tree branches and snarled at the youngster. The palomino shuddered but did not run. Siabhor's eyes narrowed as he tried to fit this one into the humans' story. "You are Sundance, yes?" The unicorn nodded his head in reply. "Then have fear of me, because I am a hunter of any creature that crosses my path."

Sundance ignored this, with a flick of his pale tail. "Are you going to help save David and Samantha?"

Siabhor looked bemused. "You… you do not fear mallus?"

"Autumn told us that as long as Alina befriends you, you would not harm us, even though he doesn't like you." He replied. "Are you going to help? How did they get captured? Were you there?"

Siabhor let out a strangled bark. "Silence!" He shook his head at the questions. "Why do you care so much?"

"David and Samantha are my friends, I do not want the evil humans to hurt them." Sundance lowered his head and thoughts of sadness quivered in the air, so that even Siabhor felt almost sorry for the young unicorn.

"Alright, I be helping get them free, then I am hunter once more." Siabhor turned and moved away as silently as he could, so the over-inquisitive Sundance could not follow.

*****

No plans were set until Autumn called the herd and Siabhor together mid-afternoon the next day.

"You have told us that Samantha was to seek out human help when you and David came to find us." The mighty stallion quizzed Siabhor. "Now I see no other way forward but to find them ourselves. Do you remember the names of these humans?"

Siabhor shifted nervously amongst the horned beasts. "Yes, they were Tobias and his sister Jillis."

Alina stepped forward. "But Autumn, we cannot possibly go into the city. Even if we *could* be disguised as horses, a loose horse would draw attention."

Autumn nodded his head wisely. "This is true, but by Praede's grace we have one who, if fully cloaked by

118

human attire, covered so that none would see an inch of his true self. One that may pass relatively unnoticed through the city." His large, liquid eyes fixed onto Siabhor.

The mallus realised what he was implying and hissed his disagreement. "No, never. Siabhor will not be humiliated by this plan of yours." He turned and ran across the flat ground back to his trees. The herd readily parted to let him through, their fear of mallus still beyond their control.

The only one who followed him was Sundance. The young unicorn felt lonely now that all the older beasts were congregating and disregarded him completely.

Sundance trotted quickly over and whinnied lowly. "But I thought you were going to help David and Samantha."

Siabhor came into view again, scowling. The palomino's thoughts held great disappointment.

"I say I would help them. I not say I be made foolish, Siabhor never be made more ashamed."

"I do not know much of humans in general." Sundance's thoughts slowly formed. "But, David and Samantha were not a breed to be ashamed of. Did you not say you would help them? It seems you are too scared to carry out your oath." Sundance turned, and with a flick of his silver tail cantered back over the green grass to the others. Siabhor watched him go and felt strangely respectful to this one.

Perhaps it was thanks to Sundance that not much later, the murky shadow was seen crossing the open space towards Autumn. "Siabhor been thinking. This plan will do. But we be needing the humans' cloth. And, you think of more plans, so I may not have to be disgraced."

Autumn bowed his head to the noble mallus. "Well done, Siabhor." Came a murmuring voice of praise, and the chestnut left the mallus feeling, not quite friendly, but a little less hostile, towards his natural enemy.

*****

That very same afternoon, Siabhor along with Billan and Tân, the two fastest unicorns of Autumn's herd moved to the edge of the forest. Across the valley the city wall loomed, with the western shadows of the trees reaching out, clawing across the glen.

"How am I meant to get disguise?" Asked Siabhor as they stood in the last reaches of the forest before the land of men.

Billan, a gentle and handsome brown stallion, looked across to him, pale horn gleaming. "About the other side of the city, that is where humans cultivate the land to feed themselves. We are sure to find human belongings there."

"But, O tree-climber, you will have to show us your gait over open ground." The second unicorn stallion exclaimed, none too kindly. "For it will be nothing but open fields from now on."

Siabhor snapped angrily at this bay-coated creature. Then moved to make himself comfortable in the bough of a tree. "We wait until night, you two be standing out too much in sun."

The bay and brown unicorns rested too, taking it in turns to watch not only for any human danger, but not trusting the mallus.

*****

When night settled in, the three travellers moved out again, moving like shadows down into the valley. The fastest, and surest way to the farms was to travel alongside the wall. This was daunting for the entire trio, but it meant they were more in the shadow, and guards along the top of the wall would find it very difficult to see the dark-coated individuals in the fortunately overcast night.

The three swift creatures didn't take long to get to the rural area beyond the main city. The low-lying buildings were spaced out across the dark fields. The growing cornfields swayed like black water as the trio moved down towards the closest farmhouse.

Pushing through the cornfields, they approached the small house. "What now?" Grumbled Siabhor.

"Why, O hunter, gather your quarry." Tân snorted callously. Then nodded over to a fair-sized window.

Siabhor scowled. "If I not be under oath not to kill you…" The mallus said no more and moved over to the house, leaving the unicorns standing in the shadows. He stood upright to see through the grubby glass, his nails scrabbled on the pane slightly as he forced it open.

There was a small noise from inside the house and Siabhor could hear the gentle breathing of several humans. Dropping lightly into the dark room Siabhor could smell strong traces of an animal, and sure enough as he turned a large dog stood a few paces away, hair bristling and teeth bared. Siabhor crouched down, then growling quietly he shot out a claw, swiping at the brute. The dog quickly backed off and scrambled under cover with its tail between its legs.

Siabhor shook his head, knowing the dog wouldn't bother him again. He crept along in his usual style,

121

moving towards the sound of sleeping humans. He could tell from the breathing that the oldest of the family were through a thick wooden door. It made no noise when he pushed it open. Siabhor had no real knowledge of human habit, so started to scurry through the whole room looking for garments.

A snort came from behind and Siabhor froze as the father figure stirred, but then fell into deeper sleep. The scent of the mother and father humans made Siabhor question what he was doing here, helping humans and unicorns when he should be hunting them instead. He shook his hairy head again and picked up what ragged clothing he had found, wanting to leave. Moving out through the door he snapped once more at the dog, catching its hind leg. And, with the taste of fresh blood in his mouth, Siabhor jumped up and clambered through the open window.

The unicorns started as he threw the clothes at them for they had not heard the stealthy hunter approach. "I got the clothes, now you carry stinking rags." Siabhor swore, then loped of through the fields back towards the forest.

The unicorns snorted at the scent of the dog's blood, but dutifully followed when they had managed to lift the garments onto each other's backs.

*****

The journey back to the forest took only as long as the initial journey, and though weary, the trio made it back to Autumn's hidden Valley before the sun had rose too high behind the cloudy sky. They were welcomed by the herd and bid to rest. Siabhor sloped off to the fringe again, where, grumbling to himself, he fell into fitful slumber.

The next day, Siabhor moved stiffly over the grass to see Autumn and Alina. They greeted him with a simple nod of their horned heads. "We had best see how this would look." Alina suggested, prodding the bundle of clothes with her pearly horn.

Siabhor sat up uncomfortably, then raised the rags. With a sneer of resentment he lifted the tunic over his head and let it fall over his torso. Then picking up the trousers on his claws, he looked at them questioningly before attempting to put them on using teeth and paw. Unfortunately, human trousers are not made for the mallus physique and Siabhor ended up falling to the ground, ripping the torn materials from his legs.

"They won't do." He growled.

Alina, who had been containing her amusement, looked down at the fallen mallus with bright eyes. "Then use the cloak and hope it covers you completely."

Siabhor followed this suggestion and draped the heavy cloak over his shoulders.

"Stand up like a human." Commanded Alina.

Siabhor did so, his spindly limbs straightened, making him stand taller than any mortal man, though perhaps unbalanced. Alina whickered at the sight, eyes wide open with a hint of fear. The cloak, made for an average man, now hung about Siabhor's calves, revealing the long, murky hair about his legs.

"You will have to crouch slightly." Suggested Autumn.

Siabhor bent down, knees flexed comfortably. The cloak skimmed the ground and covered the Mallus completely. Siabhor flicked the hood up and Autumn slowly circled him. "You will pass for a mis-shapen human. Hopefully no one will look too closely."

123

Siabhor looked down at his attire, it seemed strange and confining. "We not be going to the city today." He argued. "Siabhor can hardly walk."

Autumn agreed and they planned to wait for another couple of days so Siabhor would be back to full strength.

*****

At dawn a few days later, Siabhor left the herd to go to the city. He was accompanied by Autumn and the bay and brown unicorns again. Alina had stayed behind to make sure Sundance, who was growing restless, did not follow.

When they reached the edge of the forest they could see down the valley, where roads congested and people were already moving in and out of the city gate.

Autumn's far-seeing gaze could see that the guards were stopping most individuals at the gateway, undoubtedly a higher state of security was in and about the city.

"That will not do." His thoughts stayed to himself, then he looked contemplatively at the high, smooth walls. "Could you scale something so high? It appears to be the only way in."

Siabhor looked swiftly at the wall. "Aye, I can." He replied proudly.

"Then this is where we will wait for your return." Autumn bowed his head respectfully and watched from the safety of the trees as Siabhor went down the slope and mingled with the crowd. Siabhor kept with the flow of people, body hunched down to stay overlooked. It was terribly strange to walk along disguised like those who had occasionally become his prey. He shrugged his wide-set shoulders, fearing his hood, or cloak might slip to reveal what he really was. Thankfully none knocked into him; the townspeople, put off by his hunchback appearance and foul stench, gave this cloaked character a wide berth.

He continued up the opposite slope and around the wall as if he were heading for Talath, the market town. Siabhor left the throng of morning travellers as the path veered away from the city of Enchena. It was not long until he was alone again, he crouched down, travelling like a true mallus now none would see him. Moving swiftly around the edge of the wall, Siabhor quickly deduced that there was no low point at all. Staring up he started to feel uncertain. The wall rose high and smooth. But taking a deep breath he leapt up, claw-like hands and feet designed to grip even the tallest and smoothest trees scrabbled on the pale stones before finding their hold.

As a black shadow, Siabhor scurried up quickly, hesitating at the top he glanced down the walkway that ran along the top of the wall where guards patrolled. The section was empty and Siabhor clambered over, then climbed down the other side. Fixing his slipping garments, he took his time to look about. The turrets of the palace rose dramatically from the low buildings in the very centre of the city. Siabhor pulled his clawed hand back beneath the cloak and stood up again, then moved from the shadows of the wall into the small streets.

It was with amazement that Siabhor witnessed the city. People crowding together, packed into unnatural trails. He barely understood the humans' reasoning for such ways of living. The mallus had to stop himself from growling as groups of people walked close to him and hurried on with his task.

The further he went, the wider the streets became, and the busier they were. Keeping his hairy hands covered he twitched the edge of the cloak about his nails to draw it close, fearing someone would knock him. Siabhor glanced up, then made towards the palace because in their brief encounter David had told him that one of the Gardyn, a girl named Jillis, worked up at the palace as a maid.

Moving along the increasingly busy roads Siabhor made his way unnoticed to the more grand area of the city. From here crowds dispersed and more guards stood at their posts, protecting the people of the King's court. The palace still rose high above the rooftops and Siabhor paced towards it.

"Halt." A voice called across the street. Siabhor stopped and instinctively crouched slightly as he heard the tap of boots stride towards him.

"What are you doing here?" The voice implored, a youngish man stepped in front of the disguised mallus, and he peered suspiciously into the shadows of the hood. "Who are you?"

Siabhor's eyes flickered about the area, it was empty and a short distance from the main road. "I be nightmare." Siabhor growled, then leapt forward, the cloak parted and the mallus' strong arms clawed and pushed the guard away. The guard struggled to draw his sword as he fell backwards, but soon found the mallus perched heavily on his torso, talon foot pressing on his sword hand. At such close proximity the guard could hear the raking breathing of the creature, and could just make out a strange dark face.

"Now, you help me, or you die." Siabhor hissed. With great difficulty the guard managed a nod. The mallus stepped back and crouched, before remembering to stand like a human.

The guard struggled up, then turned and ran. But Siabhor was on him in an instant. Catching the man's legs Siabhor growled over him. "Do not run."

The man turned his head. "I am of the guards of King Hrafn, you cannot hurt me." The guard sprang up, having released his sword and lunged at Siabhor.

Siabhor's movements were quick and the sword rang as it hit the floor. The guard was left clutching his arm, stemming the blood from three deep cuts. The guard finally felt fear.

"Now." Siabhor barked. "I be shown where the servants get to your palace."

Grudgingly the guard walked stiffly to the left of the palace, Siabhor followed, cloak wrapped deftly about him. It did not take long before another high wall rose before them, the only entrance on this side was a rough wooden gate large enough for a horse-drawn cart to pass through.

The guard halted and looked warily at Siabhor. "Well, you are here, what of it?"

Siabhor glanced around, thinking quickly. "You be knowing the maid Jillis? She is thought beautiful by you humans."

The guard's eyes narrowed. "I have seen her before, yes."

"Then you will show her to me." Siabhor answered with a snarl. The guard dare not do otherwise, so after informing Siabhor that the work shift would not end until midday, he was made to wait, hidden away in the shadows so that none could see him or his fetid captor.

127

Time went slowly for this poor, young guard, but eventually the wooden gate opened and palace workers moved out into the city. A very pretty maid with black hair shrugged away from the crowd shyly.

The guard pointed at her. "That's her, Jillis." He mumbled to Siabhor.

The mallus shoved the guard in the back. "You take me to her."

The guard grimaced and walked out, with Siabhor behind him. "Jillis." He called out.

The young maid spun round at the call of her name, dark eyes wide with apprehension. "Oh, Derren, it's you. Look, I've told you I'm not interested." Jillis looked over Derren's shoulder at the cloaked and hooded figure. "Who's that?"

Siabhor leant to the guard and whispered in his ear. The soldier, Derren frowned and repeated his words. "He... er. We have to go somewhere private. He needs.... He needs to speak with you and your brother. He says that he knows... knows what you are."

Jillis looked startled. "I have no wish to-"

"It is about David and Samantha." Came Siabhor's growling voice.

Jillis looked more bewildered than ever, and the guard's hand twitched to his sword again, suspicious of the maid. Jillis quickly weighed her options, then motioned for them to follow. She walked slowly through the town, conscious of Derren, and this stranger following her. She knew of an inn that was owned by a Gardyn who would give them a place to stay and talk safely. It was not far to this inn and Jillis made a sign that the stressed-looking soldier, and the cloaked stranger should follow her inside.

128

Jillis walked up to the barman. "I'm looking for the uncle of Bern." She mumbled the old Gardyn pass-phrase and the barman nodded. "We need somewhere to talk privately."

The barman showed them through to an empty room, far at the back of the building without question. Siabhor waited until the door was fully closed and the sound of footsteps had gone before turning to face the maid.

"You are Gardyn. Is he one of you?" Siabhor motioned to the red-faced Derren.

"No, but-"

Jillis did not get to finish what she was saying, in a flash, a hairy, clawed hand shot out and cut across the young soldier's throat. Jillis let out a strangled scream as Derren's body hit the ground, blood already soaking into the wooden floor. The poor maid was close to fainting when Siabhor finally lowered the hood of his cloak, the smell of blood and sight of the nightmare prowler was almost too much for even Jillis to stomach. She switched back the flap of her bag and drew out a small dagger that she took everywhere with her.

"What are you?"

Siabhor scowled, he had not gone through all this trouble to be hassled by a young human. "I be mallus, I travelled with David and Samantha in the forest."

"I knew mallus existed, but when Samantha told me what happened, how you ended up deserting them... But what are you doing here, inside the city?" Jillis looked sceptically at the mallus' effort of garments, the tight tunic across the wide chest and cloak clasped by brown-coated arms.

"I come to help David and Samantha escape. I be sent to find you and your brother." Siabhor replied.

129

Jillis was about to ask who had sent him when they heard a commotion in the corridor. "What right have you to search my inn?" The barman's voice thundered.

"The soldier Derren is missing from his post. He was seen coming in here with a palace maid. Now move out of our way, we have orders to find the deserter."

There was noise enough for several guards to be within the inn. Jillis blanched at the sound.

"The door, where is it, where is it." She murmured, glancing about the floor. The mallus looked with confusion at the human, but Jillis knelt down and fingered a loose floorboard, pulling it up as quietly and as quickly as she could.

"Get the body in." She ordered, hearing the guards searching every room down the corridor, growing steadily closer.

Siabhor dragged the heavy corpse across the floor and let it drop into a dark hole Jillis had uncovered, then leapt down beside it. It was a tight fit and Jillis was left looking nervous, but she replaced the floorboards and sat down on a chair just as the door opened.

"You, maid. Where is Derren?" Three guards stood at the doorway.

"I rejected his advances for the tenth time this year, he stormed off in a mood. I don't know where he went." Jillis replied sternly. Her eyes flickered to a patch of blood-soaked wood where the body had lain and suppressed a tremor of fear, hoping they would not notice it. Still the guards remained. "What, do you think I am hiding him in thin air?" She challenged.

The guards backed off and closed the door behind them. Jillis waited until their footsteps receded into the main room, before she opened up the trap door again.

A miserable Siabhor clambered out and stretched. "What be that place? It is all blocked with earth."

Jillis stood wondering whether to leave Derren's body down there. "It is the beginning of a tunnel, a passage underground, but it caved in. There's lots, all over the city; the Gardyn know most of them." She answered distractedly.

Siabhor snorted. "When is your brother here?"

"My brother? He will be at our home, you shall have to come with me." Jillis walked to the door as Siabhor refitted his cloak and hood.

"Strange humans, why have places that you do not live in?" He grumbled, but he obediently followed her out onto the city streets towards her house.

Once inside Jillis turned to him. "You'll be safe here. You can even take off that tunic. I have to go get Tobias, my brother. I won't be long." And with that, the mallus was left alone.

Thirteen

When Jillis returned with a very bewildered Tobias, her heart leapt to find the house seemingly empty, but then the mallus moved out of the shadows to meet them. Tobias immediately leapt back, struggling to release his dagger from the leather clasp. Siabhor growled at him, his opinion of humans very low at this point. When Jillis managed to calm her brother the whole story came out and Siabhor told again that he had been sent to find them so they could rescue David and Samantha.

"Who sent you?" Tobias asked.

"Autumn and Alina, Siabhor hides better in the city than them." Noticing the humans' blank expressions, he added. "They be the unicorns. The ones that did not die."

Siabhor decided to stay until nightfall, and then to scale the wall again with whatever plan the humans could concoct. The mallus found out that it was David's blood that marred the forest floor, but he had been brought back to life by the King so everyone was unsure where the boy's loyalties now lay.

"We was always thinking it was David who had all the power. But it is Samantha?" This was also a revelation to the mallus.

The trio pored over ideas and plans all afternoon, it seemed agreed that Siabhor could climb the wall to get Samantha out of the palace, but they could think of no way to safely, and secretly leave the city. Then Siabhor remembered the tunnel mouth that he hid in, under the inn.

"Where are all the tunnels?" Siabhor asked suddenly, eyes bright with enthusiasm. "Maybe there is being one close to the palace, that leads outside the city!"

"It's a long shot, but there might be. In fact..." Tobias stood up and paced the small room. "In fact, I think I know where an original map is. I'll be back as soon as I can." He grabbed his cloak for the cool evening journey and made his way out of the house.

"But Tobias, it's getting late." Jillis pleaded him to stay, since Samantha had gone into the palace the hunt for Gardyn had increased. But Tobias just smiled grimly, then left.

Siabhor's plans to leave the city that night were cancelled and he grudgingly spent the night curled up in a dark corner of the humans' house. Tobias did not return until mid-morning the next day. He placed something on the table, before going to wake his sister. Siabhor snuck forward, sniffing at the piece of parchment, it smelled old and fusty.

Tobias came in, followed by a sleepy Jillis. "Here, I found it." He said breathlessly, delicately holding up the parchment.

Jillis immediately woke up when she saw it, it bore a faded map of the city. She gently traced dark green lines that ran about it, showing the labyrinth of tunnels long forgotten. "By Minaeri!" She exclaimed. "How ever did you get something like this?"

Tobias sat down, exhausted. He had been travelling all night. "I heard about the map ages ago, Rian told me about how a cloaked stranger turned up at a Gardyn Council meeting and used this to buy himself a seat. It *was* put into Lord Mgair's care, but I don't think he'll notice it's missing for a while – you'd think that pompous arse would have better security."

Jillis looked worried at how keen her brother seemed to upset the leader of the Gardyn. "Oh Tobias, you didn't. You can't give him another reason to distrust you."

Tobias smiled bitterly, and gave his younger sister's hand a comforting pat. There were bigger concerns than a few past grievances.

Siabhor was nonplussed to the human problems, and crouched by the table like a large expectant dog. "Tunnels? But are they safe, are they your Gardyn tunnels?"

Jillis shook her head, still staring at the map. "No, they were made along with the city wall, by order of the King so he and his people might escape easily, but were forgotten from being unused. It was the mouth of a caved-in tunnel that you hid in at the inn. They are safe enough if we can move discreetly."

"Yes, I thought of that already. You see this line here." Tobias pointed out a green line that led well out from the city wall to a rocky outcrop near to the forest. "And it brings you closer to the palace than any others."

Jillis followed the marking, looking at it dubiously. "It does look close, in fact it looks as if it goes inside the palace walls, the gardens perhaps. And how are we meant to scale the walls? Samantha is too high up for us to climb, and it would be too dangerous going inside."

"There is someone who has already shown his climbing abilities." Tobias replied staring with meaning at Siabhor.

The mallus backed away and hissed his displeasure. "Why is it always Siabhor that must be used." He grumbled.

"You said you were here to help Samantha." Jillis reminded him.

"Very well. But now this poor mallus has to run about like a messenger and tell unicorns."

"Oh, do you think they'll help too?" Jillis asked excitedly. "If we can stay in the forest with them we'll never be found."

So it was arranged that Siabhor would leave at nightfall and tell the unicorns everything. They planned to act during darkness, the sooner the better, but the earliest chance would be in two days to allow for travelling. So Jillis would camp at the outcrop to wait for the creatures' arrival.

Siabhor was loathe to wait in the human city, often he had hunted wanderers in the forest and the temptation rose inside him to kill again, making him wonder what on earth he was doing here, being a messenger for his prey. So he curled up in a dark corner and slept for the rest of the day, uncomfortable and ill at ease. He praised Minaeri when the sun finally sank below the horizon and walked stiffly on his hind legs to the city wall. He scaled it quickly, without difficulty, then removing the abhorrent garments he loped into the forest like a true mallus.

135

At first Siabhor thought he was alone, but on the air came the scent of unicorns, and emerging from the darkness came two gleaming horns. Siabhor halted and waited for their approach.

"Greetings, mallus. We have waited for a long time for you, Autumn had to return to the herd, there were rumours of The Dark Being in the area." Billan communed. The bay, Tân, just snorted, finding no kind greeting for the creature.

"Very well, then we will go back to your herd now." Siabhor replied and leapt to the trees, finally content with his style of travelling.

It did not take too long to return to Autumn's herd, but as the sky turned to dawn pastels, the travellers were left to sleep away their weariness. Siabhor was allowed to rest until mid-afternoon before Autumn pressed him for news. Siabhor relayed the information and plans to the chestnut, then left to hunt in the forest.

The unicorn stallion called together a small council. "So the question is, do we give these humans our aid?" He asked, once all had been told.

Alina stepped into the circle of unicorns. "I say that after what we have done already, we can hardly turn away now."

There was a general nodding of horned heads, but Tân burst forth, coat gleaming red beneath his long black mane. "There is never any point where we cannot turn back. I remember when we lived like true unicorns, not servants of mallus, and bearers of humans."

"We cannot choose against what Praede has sent to us." Alina's thoughts became low and angered, then she looked over to Autumn. "Please, if they wish for a

136

unicorn to accompany them, even if your council does not agree, I will go."

Autumn looked at the beautiful grey mare and his heart went out to her, but his response was interrupted.

"A mare? You count yourself too highly, sister of Nmirr." Tân looked callously at Alina.

Autumn cried out, a horse's neigh rang across the Valley and the unicorns were silenced. "If it pleases you not to argue Tân. It seems that the general agreement is to send one of our kind to help the humans. This meeting is dismissed." All the unicorns dispersed, except Alina who stood close to Autumn in the warm afternoon.

*****

That evening, Tân moved like a shadow towards Autumn. "Can I speak to you, sir?" He asked, his displeasure seeping into every fragment of thought.

The two stallions walked away from all the others. "What is it Tân?"

"What do we owe these creatures? First we allow that mallus into our Valley, to roam among us unchecked. Now we are to be the steeds of people? I am starting to think that your heart rules your head."

"Alina is of a well-respected lineage." Autumn replied firmly. "We will go through with this task, and there is no argument to that."

"Well, if it is to be done, I wish to accompany the humans, after all I am the fastest and strongest. Next to you, of course."

Autumn looked wisely at the bay stallion. "Tân, for many a year I have trusted you, if you are not opposed to working with humans I would be honoured for you to go."

Tân bowed his head respectfully, then trotted away.

137

The next morning the bay stallion trotted over to the trees. He lifted his head to the sleeping mass in the boughs and let out a shrill whinny. Siabhor jumped and barked with surprise, then scowled down at Tân.

"Good morning monster." Tân greeted coldly. "I have been chosen to go get the girl. I hope you will keep those claws sheathed."

"You be keeping away your sharp thoughts from Siabhor. Shame on mallus for putting up with nasty unicorns." Siabhor snarled in return, his harsh words the only threat the once feared predator could offer.

They then parted and avoided each other until the afternoon. No one was close when the fight started so no one knows why it began. There was an almighty scream of fury from a wooded end of the Valley, Autumn came galloping up to the source to find Siabhor crouching on the ground with blood on his flexing claws and Tân, horn lowered and a splash of blood across his flank and hind leg.

Autumn rushed forward and came between the two just as they moved to attack again. They cowered back from the mighty chestnut that seemed to burn with fiery glory in his anger. "What is going on?" Sharp thoughts commanded.

"That... that thing attacked me." A snort accompanying Tân's furious thoughts.

Siabhor growled menacingly. "I would kill you, you lying... *cureta*!" He swore in mallus tongue.

Autumn turned to the mallus. "I let you stay in my Valley, but you have betrayed me by injuring the best of my herd." He lowered his horn, but his deadly charge was hindered by a silver flash racing up.

"What is happening?" Alina asked, eyes wide at the blood staining Tân.

"Your hairy friend has tried to kill me." Came Tân's sharp thoughts as he limped towards the mare. Alina looked at Siabhor with shock, feeling betrayed beyond thought.

"Siabhor did not, Siabhor did not." The mallus mumbled, shaking his head sadly. Then he turned and loped to the cover of trees, away from the angry and accusing stares. He was not alone for long. A silver-fringed, golden glimmer passed beneath his hiding place.

"Siabhor, is it true? Did you really attack Tân?"

Siabhor hung down from the tree, looking into Sundance's innocent face. "Why, how does it matter to you? Nobody believe the hunter."

"Well, I believe that you would not break your promise. Tân never did like you." The young unicorn replied. "You are still going to help the humans aren't you?"

"They cannot do it without mallus." Siabhor answered, suddenly feeling important. "But now they have no help from your kind."

"I will-"

"No." Interrupted Siabhor. "Irritating Sundance is still too young."

*****

Across the Valley, Alina stood close by as Autumn spoke with Tân and assessed his damaged leg. Then he turned and came over to Alina.

"I should never have let that creature into the Valley." He sighed.

"Will Tân be alright?" Alina asked anxiously.

139

"Yes, but he won't be travelling tonight. We will wait until tomorrow to see if he's fit and then…" The chestnut trailed off.

"I will go in his place, Siabhor can show me the way."

Autumn looked worriedly at Alina. "You must not put your trust in that creature. But if Tân is not healed quickly, you may go to the humans."

*****

The next afternoon, the air was tense. Tân could be seen hobbling to the stream. Alina was excited and nervous and went to find Siabhor. She began to become more worried as she trotted along the tree line and there was no sign of the mallus. Seeing a golden glimmer ahead she moved up to Sundance.

"Have you seen Siabhor?" Alina asked kindly.

Sundance looked quite upset. "He left, he said he had to be a mallus. What does he mean?"

"I don't know." Alina replied hurriedly, then went back into the forest. She did not have to search for long, Siabhor had, in fact, just camped down a short walk from the Valley borders. "Sundance said you were leaving."

"I am." Siabhor replied, without looking at her.

Alina looked about the forest. "I know you are feeling torn, Siabhor. But we still need you to help Samantha. You can't turn away now when you've done so much."

Siabhor finally looked into the familiar grey face. "Alright, but I not be going back to the Valley. I be here when it is time."

Fourteen

Samantha lay on her bed, still wearing her silver dress, she had been so exhausted after the ball she hadn't even bothered to change. Perhaps it was the fatigue that left her with unsettled dreams, the rattle of skeleton fingers made her jolt awake, her pulse beating erratically. Samantha lay with her eyes still closed, she was unsure whether the noise that woke her had been a dream or reality. But there it was again, the insistent rattling against the glass. It reminded her of dead branches scraping against windows, but no trees grew high enough to trouble her.

She opened her eyes but could see only darkness. The tapping came again and as her eyes grew accustomed to the shadows she could see the window lit by the distant starlight. Samantha knew the noise wasn't her imagination, nor was it a tree branch against her window.

The scrabbling stopped, but Samantha was fully awake now. She sat up, then slowly made her way across the room to the largest window. She could make out city lights far below, receding down the hill to misty darkness.

Suddenly something shot into view, Samantha recoiled as a dark hairy creature scrabbled at the window pane once more.

"Siabhor?" She mumbled, then hastened to open the latch. Her hands fumbled with the metal clasp as Siabhor's eyes gleamed in the darkness.

The window swung open and Siabhor perched on the wide frame.

"What are you doing here?" Samantha hissed.

"We be getting you and the other one out." Came Siabhor's husky, hissing voice.

Samantha glared at him. "Decided to help us now?" She said spitefully, not forgetting how he had deserted them in the forest.

There was a noise so quiet that it was a half-noise, or a noise half-heard down below in the courtyard. She leant out of the window, a silver glimmer was in the shadows far below. "Is that Alina?" She asked breathlessly, tears forming. "I was told that she was killed."

"The evil humans lie, Samantha." Siabhor looked at her with bright eyes. "But come, we take you from this place - back to forests."

Samantha stepped back, shaking her head slightly. "No, I have sworn loyalty to Hrafn and the crown. There is nothing for me out there, I have betrayed everyone and cannot return." Her voice faded.

"You seem to forget that the people who need you would still forgive you. That is why we fight for them." Came Alina's sweet thoughts faintly from below.

"Now." Hissed Siabhor. "You come willingly, or by force."

Samantha smiled weakly and agreed to climb onto the mallus' hairy back, hitching up her skirt and wrapping her arms around Siabhor's thick neck.

Siabhor climbed nimbly out of the window and down the side of the palace wall. Only a mallus' claws could have found purchase down the vertical stone tower. Samantha stifled her fear as they made their way to the ground.

It was a happy reunion between Samantha and Alina, but tinged with sadness over the loss of Nmirr. From the shadows, Jillis stepped forward, looking strangely timid.

"I am so sorry." Samantha mumbled.

Jillis smiled forgivingly. "One day all the Gardyn shall be in your debt. But now it is time to flee to the forests."

Alina carefully nuzzled Samantha. "I would gladly carry you once more."

With a murmur of thanks the two girls clambered onto the silvery back of the unicorn. Siabhor stared up at them uncomfortably for a moment before sliding a long object towards Samantha.

"Here. You may need it, the guard no longer does."

Suspiciously, Samantha received Derren's sheathed sword, tying the leather about her waist. "Let's go home." She simply said.

Alina walked as silently across the cobbles as she did across the forest floor. A silver rider on a silver steed, Jillis and Siabhor were no more than shadows. The stealthy group slipped from shadow to shadow, looking anxiously up at the dark windows when suddenly there came a piercing scream. The girls looked to the palace windows as candlelight flickered behind the glass, they did not know what had occurred, but they knew it would not be in their favour.

Moving more cautiously, they made it to the palace gardens, then beyond to the stables. Horses could be heard snorting from their sleep, obviously aware of their majestic cousin in the shadows. A shiver of horror went through the group as a night-guard stepped out of the stable boys' room, wondering what disturbed the horses so.

"Now is the time to use that sword." Siabhor's husky voice whispered in Samantha's ear.

She looked terrified but slipped obediently from Alina's back, then, creeping forward she struggled to keep her hand steady. She now stood at the very edge of the nearest stable, ready to strike down on this guard when he came close, but a voice interrupted her plan.

"All soldiers are to report to the palace now." Came the man's harsh command.

"Yes Captain." The reply came.

Samantha could not help peering about the corner. The night-guard was moving quickly to the palace, and Samantha recognised the newcomer as Captain Losan, the head of Hrafn's army. Losan stayed momentarily, glaring into the shadows before striding off.

Samantha was thankful for whatever magic veiled the silver lady and star-bright unicorn from his sight, but could not help but wonder what tragedy had happened for the Captain to become a messenger, collecting his men. Her three companions came quietly up, making her jump. Siabhor then loped off in front of them.

"Where are we going?" Asked Samantha.

"Do you remember that I told you of secret passageways beneath the city?" Jillis replied. "Well, we have found one in the palace stabling area that leads outside the city wall."

They followed Siabhor to a far part of the stables, the horses started in their boxes as the creature went past. Finally, the mallus stopped, his long claws scrabbled about a small crack in the wooden floor and with a mighty heave several thick planks came up to reveal the entrance to a dark, uninviting tunnel. Working quickly Siabhor moved enough wooden boards for even the unicorn to fit down. The two girls and unicorn climbed down uneasily, followed by the mallus who carefully replaced the disturbed planks. As the last wooden block came down the four were in almost complete darkness, even Siabhor, who had the sharpest sight, could only just make out the pale form of Alina. He grunted and rushed ahead of the others who were left to stumble after the sound of his nails against the rock sides of the tunnel.

The dark journey took over an hour and when they emerged from their black passageway Samantha was surprised to find the faint light before dawn tingeing the night sky. They had come out of a rocky outcrop perhaps half a mile from the city wall and a short distance from an overhang of forest. Jillis looked longingly to the city that had been home, but it was no longer safe for her to return. All four moved towards the trees, tired but joyful.

"I'm sorry you could not get back home, Samantha." Jillis looked up to the young lady beside her.

Samantha gazed ahead, while Alina and Siabhor conversed comfortably as they walked in the wild forest. For the first time in weeks, Samantha smiled.

"I'm starting to feel this is home." Then she gathered her skirt and ran forward to join the unicorn.

Jillis watched happily, everything was finally falling into place. Then she remembered the pack on her back and called out to Samantha. "I brought you some clothes to change into, if you want them." She said almost shyly when the silver lady came.

Samantha grinned and took the package behind a thick screen of bushes. Returning with the gown neatly folded she declared. "You have no idea how uncomfortable it can be, being a lady!"

They kept walking until they reached the passage to Autumn's Valley. The trek was long and when the two girls were tired, Alina graciously carried them once more. When they arrived at the seemingly impenetrable bush they dismounted and followed Alina closely. They looked with wonder at this large valley, secluded from the rest of the world. Jillis curtseyed when Autumn, the living flame, approached.

While introductions were being made, Alina sidled off and made her way to the forest again. As she had guessed, Siabhor remained within the trees, looking thoughtful.

"What is the matter? Why do you not come?"

Siabhor looked across to the grey sadly. "I only stay to rescue Samantha. That is done now and it is time for Siabhor to leave."

Alina lowered her head, the mallus had almost become a friend. She looked up again. "Very well. Perhaps we will meet again."

Siabhor snarled. "No." He snapped. "May us never meet again. I am mallus, the hunter. Too much strange things have passed - because of you I be losing my place

146

in the forest. I go now and make myself of Sahr's pack again."

"You can always stay here. Autumn might let you, and Sundance and Samantha would wish you to stay."

The mallus remained torn. "Perhaps, perhaps not. No! I leave now and be mallus again."

He raised himself and leapt from tree to tree, and Alina stayed until the sound of tapping wood receded, now missing the sound that once drove terror through her heart. Turning back to the herd she thought how right Siabhor was, how everything was changing and all she could do now was go along with it. She trotted slowly to where the unicorns gathered with curiosity about the two girls. One threw his head up, then moved to intercept Alina.

Sundance's big, sad eyes glanced up to his aunt. "He's gone, hasn't he?"

Alina's heart stilled. "It was time for him to go back to his kind. Do not go looking for him."

Fifteen

Samantha and Jillis were disappointed to find that Siabhor had already left. But the rest of the herd were very relieved, they had never fully trusted the creature, and the incident with Tân had done nothing for the mallus' reputation.

Autumn and Billan left the herd to wait for sign of Jillis' brother at the edge of the forest. They returned with the tired Tobias late the next morning, who was relieved to find both Jillis and Samantha safely with the unicorns.

After grazing until midday, when the grass started to wilt in the summer sun, Autumn sought a council with the three humans.

"We would wish to know what you plan to do next and how we can help."

Jillis looked wide-eyed up to the chestnut stallion. "Oh, but we couldn't possibly expect you to get involved in the wars of men."

The unicorn's usually warm gaze fell cold. "Aye, and neither did you expect it of Nmirr. We have become involved now, none of us have a choice anymore."

The humans were humbled by this, each murmuring their thanks and apologies.

Tobias was the first to speak his mind. "I am not sure what will happen, eventually or immediately. A Gardyn council has been considering setting up a camp away from the city, and bringing the King to war. But it would have to remain secret, otherwise we would be attacked before our numbers are ready. The problem is finding a large space, difficult for the larger King's army to get to; and about a day's trek from Enchena."

Tobias and Autumn stood looking at each other, as if they were communicating even more subtly than a unicorn's shared thought.

Then came the powerful voice of the chestnut. "I know what you ask of me, human. Gladly I will let you three stay as long as you wish, but to let the possible hundreds invade my land is unthinkable." Autumn shook his head, his light-coloured mane flicked across the chestnut neck. "But, when we decided to help Samantha escape we knew we would be involved from then on. I will speak to the herd." He turned and walked away, head heavy with thought.

A tall bay trotted over to him, swift, even with a savage limp. "Autumn, what do the humans say?"

Autumn looked across to Tân, already knowing how his old friend would react. "They speak of setting up a camp for their army. The boy thinks this valley would be ideal."

Tân threw his horned head up in surprise and anger. "But that is out of the question. Autumn, I say what I have from the beginning, let us have no more to do with them."

"And I say that our course has been set by Praede himself." Autumn repeated. "This human war will be troublesome for us, even if we refuse, because the whole forest will undoubtedly be caught up between the armies." He looked away, beyond his herd. "Tân, I want you to take the mares, younger stallions, and anyone else who wishes to leave, down the river to the *Wentra*."

"You mean to stay here?"

Autumn nodded sadly. "Tell Billan and Alina that I wish to speak with them. Then gather the others, you leave tomorrow at dawn."

Tân peered enquiringly at his lord. "But sir, I am to stay also, am I not? I would not leave your side."

"No Tân, your place is to take care of the rest of the herd and warn other herds that the forest is unsafe. You are injured and I would not suffer you to die needlessly."

Tân bowed low, then headed over the grassy valley to the gathering of the others. Autumn was left once more to contemplate what he was about to do.

*****

In the palace of Enchena, King Hrafn was in a terrible fury.

"How could this have happened?" He roared, the anger flooding his body, making him itch to throw his sword through the nearest person. He paced ceaselessly to and fro across the throne room. The two men in his private council remained silent, not wanting to receive the brunt of the King's furious outburst.

"Orion, explain to me how that pitiful girl even got out of her room, never mind the rest." Hrafn demanded, spinning round to face the Captain.

"My lord, I cannot say. We had the door heavily guarded, my men say they heard and saw nothing, and I believe them."

"Your men are fools, have them killed!" Hrafn shouted.

Captain Losan frowned, not wanting to lose more loyal men, but willing to follow Hrafn's every order.

"Maybe she went out the window." A bored voice said quietly.

The two older men turned to look at David who sat on the raised dais. The lad looked stubbornly away from them, his face dark with anger and fatigue, his hidden eyes filled with tainted amusement.

"What did she do? Fly? That wall is impossible to scale and the drop is deadly." Captain Losan replied sharply.

"Enough!" Hrafn barked. "Orion, go, find what you can. Clamp down on the city in case she's still here. Have scouts dispatched immediately, don't let them return 'til they have found her."

Captain Orion Losan bowed his head in consent, then marched out of the room, leaving David alone with the King.

"Perhaps she did fly." David said quietly, lifting his gaze to the King. "After all, she is the Lost Soul, she may have magic and powers that we can only dream of. How else could she have done all the sins of last night?"

Hrafn's anger faded and he suddenly appeared weakened. The King stumbled over to the throne and collapsed into it. "So you believe she did it too?"

Hrafn tried and failed not to think of what had happened last night, but his wife's screams could still be heard and in his mind he could still see the small, still body of his son. Prince Tagor laid with his eyes and mouth wide open, forever more in surprise in a grey face. There had been no sign of a wound, no blood spilt, yet the boy was dead.

"Of course I believe Samantha killed him." David replied softly, with his back to the King, Hrafn could not see his smile. "She has a foul magic about her and can cause death, like she did for the mallus. But perhaps it would be better that no one knows she killed your son and escaped, sir." David kept his voice sympathetic, but secretly thought to make sure that very same rumour was spread.

"How can it be hidden?" Hrafn muttered to himself. "I must bring Tagor back, it is the only way."

The King stood up, already searching for his powers to restore life.

"You already tried it, it didn't work." David sniped, then tried to sound humble again. "Sir. I doubt Samantha's sins can be undone. Your majesty, let me help you."

At this David stood up, his hand reaching out to support Hrafn's arm, playing the sympathetic son. "You gave me life, you are like a father to me now, your majesty. Let me help in any way possible."

Hrafn felt himself suddenly relax, tension released. "Ah, David, be a model of loyalty. Now, I think I shall see to Arianne."

Hrafn walked away from David, taking a different door out of the throne room than Losan had. The King thought of his wife and frowned, the death of their son had been the first time she had shown emotion and he hated it, no longer was she a shining beauty. But what alternative was there to her giving him another son...

152

David watched the disturbed King leave, waited until the door was fully closed before he laughed out loud. His eyes watered as the triumph within him threatened to burst out. He leant against a large open window, feeling the warmth of the summer, the city lay sprawled before him, and beyond it the dark fringe of the Great Forest. True, Samantha was making things more difficult for herself, and he had been surprised by her impossible escape, but perhaps it had added to the effect. Regardless of the war that would soon start, David had his own plans.

*****

The unicorn herd left the Valley in the cool of the new morning. They moved down the open glade silently, then into the dark forest. It was a long trek to the area Autumn had mentioned, Wentra was a place used by his herd in hard winters, or when fire drove them from the Valley. The entrance was difficult to find and precarious, the forest became dense and rose on a steady ascent; you had to keep slow because at the top of the hill was a sharp drop of a rock cliff to a deep lake. A nimble unicorn could pick out the path down to a narrow tunnel in the cliff. The natural tunnels and caves were dark, but safe from the outside world.

Autumn went with the herd for several miles, before turning back with Alina, Billan and two more unicorns who wished to see the war through. When they got back to the Valley, Autumn wandered away, seeking solitude in this time of stress.

The humans however, had their own travelling to do. Tobias would go back to the city with their news and arrange for the Gardyn families to leave at a safe rate.

The girls would wait inside the forest to show the groups where to go.

Tobias entered the city wall, trying not to appear nervous. The gate-guard had doubled since Samantha was whisked away to the forest, the same fateful night that a murder had taken place. Neither his sister, nor Samantha had known that as they escaped the body of young Prince Tagor had been found in his chamber. Rumours had been flying, most involving the Lost Soul seeking revenge, or a Gardyn that ignored their morals and assassinated the young heir. Tobias knew that Samantha had not killed the prince, but many believed the rumours. The problem was now some of their followers were beginning to question everything about the Lost Soul, some seemed darkly excited by the powers she must hold, but mostly the Gardyn feared the morality of their saviour. After all, they didn't want to risk their lives in the deposing of one tyrant to make way for another.

Tobias reached the inn where Jillis had taken Siabhor, he went inside and approached the bartender. "I'm looking for Bern's uncle."

The man grunted and pointed to a thickset man who was out collecting mugs. Tobias walked over to him. "Are you Bern's uncle?" He asked discreetly.

The man looked up at Tobias wearily. "Bloomin' passes and such. Aye, I am if you say I am. What is it now?"

"My name is Tobias Deorwine, and I'm meant to be meeting our friends."

"Deorwine? Aye, they're expectin' you." The man said gruffly, then led Tobias to the back rooms. He was about to open one of the doors, but hesitated, looking back at Tobias. "Deorwine, eh? Got a problem with your sister. She the one that left a dead body in me trap door, didn't she? Still got the blood stains soaked in!"

Tobias just smiled apologetically and pushed past. The door swung shut on the barman's moaning. In the room, sat around a small table were three men. They stopped their conversation when Tobias entered and stared up expectedly at him. Tobias bowed before them and waited.

"Well, Deorwine." A man spoke up, looking very self-important in his lordly, bright garments and a clean trimmed beard about a hardened face. "We hear that the valued Jillis Deorwine, your sister, was the one who helped the Lost Soul escape King Hrafn's clutches. For that we are thankful, but, perhaps escape is not the way. We have heard rumours also that this Lost Soul is a cold-blooded killer and we cannot allow such a person to influence the Gardyn."

Tobias stood tall again, staring at the man as unemotionally as he could muster. He doubted Mgair realised that one of his prized possessions had been pilfered. It definitely made it easier to face the arrogant Lord. "Lord Mgair, I can say, on my honour, that Samantha is no killer. She was in the tunnels when Tagor was murdered."

A much older man, whose beard was long and grey and wise eyes shone from his rugged face, matched only by his rugged attire cleared his throat before speaking in a rather wheedling voice. "Your honour is questionable, Tobias; we know all about you. But as both your mother and sister have been so valuable to us, swear by them that what you say is true."

Tobias glanced towards the second speaker, a look of disgust crossing his face. As if his life wasn't hard enough, he had to put up with everybody doubting him. Oh, his mother and sister were the revered Gardyn spies, Tobias was left to be the unappreciated messenger under the disapproving stares. Like now. One day past grievances would be left behind, but for now, Tobias lowered his eyes and replied humbly. "I swear it."

"I am not completely convinced, but we shall resolve that later." Continued the lordly gentleman, the Lord Mgair whose family had infiltrated the King's courts generations ago and remained there, all the while standing as the acknowledged leader of the Gardyn. "Now we must decide what we are to do, can we really gather an army in the forest?"

"I believe we can, sir. We have a valley there which is large enough for any number of folk, and is completely secured from the rest of the forest." Tobias informed them.

The third gentleman was sitting at the far end of the table, his features hidden in shadow under a dark cloak. The same man that had brought the maps of the tunnels to the Gardyn. "Hrafn isn't going to stop, you know. Already the number of guards have doubled. When they find nothing here, more soldiers will be called to the city and they will start to spread out, searching further and further." He warned in a heavy voice.

"What are you trying to say? Unless your only point is that Hrafn and his men are a detestable infestation!" Lord Mgair cut in sharply.

The cloaked man turned to face him, but nothing more than a black space in his hood could be seen. "I am saying that if anything is to be done, the sooner the

156

better. We should stop bickering, trust this poor lad and flee to the forests." His voice held an edge, growling slightly.

The other two men murmured their jaded agreements in lowered tones. Tobias was permitted to leave with the knowledge that Gardyn would start moving that afternoon.

He decided, in the meantime to take some food up to the girls in the forest. Walking up to the dark trees he began to wonder how everything would end. Jillis stepped out to meet him, and the provisions were shared.

"There is something that I cannot understand." Jillis said to Samantha as they ate. "How did you find enough food and water in the wild?"

Samantha blushed. "Oh, well the unicorns showed us how to get trees to bare their fruits. We lived on what we got."

Tobias sat a small distance from the chatting girls. He started to think it was a bad idea for Samantha to be here and finally spoke out about his troubled thoughts. "Samantha, I want you to go back to the Valley, now."

"What?" Samantha exclaimed. "But I thought…"

Tobias sighed, running a hand through his dark hair. "At the meeting I was told- well, there are rumours and maybe it would be best if the Gardyn didn't meet you until they were settled."

"What rumours?" Jillis asked.

He wondered whether to withhold his information, but looking into the determined young faces he sighed again.

"That Samantha murdered Prince Tagor." Tobias looked at their stricken faces. "So maybe you should stay at the Valley, or maybe even Wentra at least until we can sort out the misunderstandings." He added before they could argue back.

Samantha stood up suddenly. "Fine. It's not as if I've got anything to do. Lord, it's like being back with David!" She said sharply, before storming off into the now familiar forest.

Jillis looked at her brother disapprovingly.

"What?" He demanded curtly. "I don't want her being interrogated when the others come."

"Sure. You'd rather she went back unprotected..." Jillis retorted airily.

*****

Late that afternoon there was a gathering of about fifty Gardyn, mostly women and children who would be the first of many to move to the Valley. They stayed in the covering of the forest, they waited until the lordly gentleman, Mgair, came along the track on horseback.

"Well, what are we waiting for, let's go." He said gruffly.

They set off at a slow pace, hindered by younger children. Tobias and Jillis walked at the front of the procession, the Lord Mgair would ride alongside the group, sometimes stopping to hurry along stragglers, sometimes trotting off to see what lie ahead. By dusk they had stopped, perhaps a quarter of the way to the Valley. It was unsafe to start fires, so supper was cold, then all were asleep even on the rough ground after their trek.

The night was cool, and unknown to the sleeping Gardyn, another was travelling from the direction of the Valley towards them. It was with the breaking of dawn that everyone awoke, some had heard a beautiful and melodic equine call in their dreams, some merely felt someone, or something, important was coming. It was in the first bright golden rays that the Gardyn saw them.

A silver goddess astride a proud star-bright unicorn cantering lightly through the dark trees. People who were standing fell to their knees and the Lord Mgair gasped as he tried to restrain his own horse. The Silver Lady glanced about the group with a solemn face, then rode forward to the brother and sister who led the Gardyn through the forests. Tobias stared up at her, stunned, but Jillis smiled for she had seen this silver lady somewhere before.

"It seems..." The youthful lady began to say, her quiet voice carrying across the silence of the travellers. "That the murderous rumours are stopped." She smiled and dismounted, leaving one hand resting on dear Alina's grey neck.

Lord Mgair had now pushed his way across to the newcomer. "Whether you are our Lost Soul, or Minaeri herself we ask your forgiveness." He removed his hat and bowed low.

"I am Samantha, Lost Soul of Enchena, if you please. You're forgiven, anyone would be wary in such circumstances." She replied, smiling at her own attempt at sounding sophisticated.

Mgair seemed satisfied and went to fetch his horse so that he might ride close enough to associate with the silver lady.

"I thought you said the dress was uncomfortable." Jillis said teasingly.

"But it worked." Samantha replied with a laugh.

"Brilliant. Absolutely brilliant." Tobias laughed. "Sometimes I could kiss you!"

159

Samantha blushed deep red and turned to Alina to hide it. "Well, Alina thought of it." She said shyly.

Alina whinnied lightly, which drove the Lord's horse quite mad, and her sweet thoughts filled the air. "When Samantha arrived last night she told me what had happened. We thought it would convince them of her innocent nature if she arrived like Minaeri to the Gardyn."

The group moved happily, and were less footsore with the accompaniment of Samantha and Alina, they made good time and even managed to reach the Valley by late afternoon. Although Samantha would prefer not to encumber her friend and was willing to walk, Alina insisted that the girl stay astride her for effect. Alina and Samantha went ahead of the group as they neared the Valley's borders and they were trotting up to the thick hedges when Alina suddenly started, nearly throwing the girl from her back.

"There is something close that does not worry to travel in complete silence." Alina's senses were high, ears strained to the forest. They stayed for nearly a minute in silence before catching a golden glimpse in the trees. A young unicorn came skittering towards them.

"Please, please, he is hurt." Distressed thoughts emitted from the troubled palomino.

"Sundance? What is happening? Why aren't you with the herd?" Alina questioned.

"I wanted to stay with you, but I came back and saw him; he is hurt and I cannot carry him into the Valley." Without waiting any longer Sundance moved swiftly away again, leading them back through the trees.

"Jillis, Tobias. Get the others into the Valley, we'll be back soon." Samantha shouted, then bent down and put her hand to Alina's neck. "I'm coming with you."

Alina followed quickly after her cousin. The trio went along the borders of the Valley at a quick pace. A terrible and unmistakable scent came to the unicorn's nostrils and soon they halted beside a dark heap of bloodied creature.

Samantha slipped down from Alina's back and knelt down to it. Its chest rose and fell in laboured breathing, so they knew it was still alive. Alina delicately rolled it over with her pearly horn. Siabhor had a deep gash across his front and several smaller wounds over his body,

"Oh no, what happened?" Gasped Samantha.

Alina didn't answer her, she was looking about them, senses straining. She was not entirely sure, but she thought that other mallus might be close. "We should take him into the Valley, he'll be safe there and we can help him."

Sundance moved nervously beside the grey. "But Autumn, he will not like that."

Alina had already lain down and Samantha was dragging the dead weight of Siabhor onto the grey's back. Then Alina stood up and walked slowly back to the entrance with Samantha holding Siabhor steady and Sundance flitting nervously about.

Sixteen

When Siabhor started to wake, his muscles jerked as though he were still running. Then his eyes opened to darkness and he struggled to rise, fearing he had already died. A stinging ran across his chest, telling him he was still alive. His sharp bark of pain disturbed a sleeping mass near him. In the dark the silver-grey unicorn walked slowly towards him. "Siabhor, are you okay?"

He looked up, his sight blurry at first, then the grey blur became sharper. "What am I doing here?" He growled.

"Sundance found you, you were nearly dead." Alina replied, as Siabhor tenderly inspected his wounds. "What happened to you?"

Siabhor grunted. "Siabhor was not welcome." He replied shortly, wincing with pain and with memories of his old pack chasing him down, then added. "But Siabhor be fast, yes, I managed to get away."

"Well, you are safe now. The wounds are healing." Alina added, it had been a tentative moment when they carried the mallus into the Valley. People had crowded about them, trying to see what they had brought.

162

Autumn was furious when he saw the creature here again, but after a persuasive conversation with Alina, he had warily agreed to let the mallus stay under the grey mare's protection.

*****

Further down the Valley, the Gardyn families had set up camp and most were fast asleep under canvas, or open air, but one fire still burnt to dimly throw light on several shadowy figures. Samantha was almost falling asleep on Tobias' shoulder, and Jillis' head would keep nodding, but the Lord Mgair had insisted upon this late night council to privately discuss their immediate plans. In the flickering circle of firelight, they were joined by those of importance or their representatives.

After a very long-winded and overly-important introduction to the council, Lord Mgair continued straight into the first line of business.

"Now, one big problem is transport, for messengers initially, and then for battle. We have very few horses; and carts cannot move through such thick forest. It would be a slow process to get horses honestly, and more expensive than we can currently afford. But, there is an outpost for soldiers about fifteen miles from the main city, the Gardyn will raid there as soon as we have enough trained people to go. But for now..."

"Why don't we go now? I'll take a couple of others, then the unicorns will help round the horses once they're loose. If we wait too long the whole Enchenian army will be assembled." Tobias interrupted in a low voice.

Lord Mgair glared at Tobias, disgruntled that the boy not only interrupted him, but that he dared to speak at all in such a council.

163

"Yes, you may be right." A solid-looking man on Mgair's right said musingly. "Speed and secrecy will be our greatest weapons. We should act now."

Mgair sat, looking thoughtfully now the idea had been backed by someone worthy of respect. But he would not sway to Tobias willingly. "Yes, yes, your point is well-made. Rian is already here isn't he? Well, he knows the layout of the place, if he takes his cousin... Bring him immediately."

"What! I thought I would lead this one." Tobias hissed angrily at the Lord, as a messenger jumped eagerly away to bring Rian. "You still don't trust me."

"Merely a precaution, we cannot have you around such a base. Anyway, Rian is our best-" Mgair replied in soothing tones, a false smile on his lips.

Tobias was not comforted and rose suddenly, jerking Samantha from her doze, then strode into the shadows of night.

"Wha's 'appening?" Samantha asked groggily.

Lord Mgair was still staring after Tobias. "Nothing." He murmured, then stared into the embers of the fire. "But soon, perhaps this coming day, or the next, we are raiding an outpost for horses. Will the unicorns, and yourself, help?"

"Yeah, sure. Should we go back to camp now?" She mumbled, glancing around the council anxiously. It was supposed to be an honour to sit amongst these Gardyn leaders, but it seemed nothing more than a dull audience for Lord Mgair.

"Not just yet, I want you to meet - ah, here he is now." Lord Mgair stood up to greet an individual that had just arrived to the council, the young messenger breathless with awe beside him. "Rian, I am sure you know the rest

164

of the council.   These two young ladies are Jillis Deorwine, I am sure you are aware of her work; and Samantha, our 'Lost Soul'."

Samantha looked up at the introduction, the young man nodded briefly in acknowledgement. Samantha eagerly returned the gesture, glad that she didn't have to trust her voice - she had never considered an older guy attractive, but Rian undoubtedly was and now she felt the unease of something silly and girlish in this serious meeting. It was hard not to, Rian, whom Samantha guessed to be in his mid to late twenties, was tall, his frame noticeably lean and muscular, even beneath the heavy fabric of his clothes; he was undeniably handsome, with his dark brown hair naturally tousled, his skin tanned from being outdoors and (when Samantha dared to look) his dark eyes staring out intelligently, often mixed with an amused gleam. Samantha felt even Jillis sit up straighter as Rian joined them.

"You summoned me?"   Rian asked, his voice betraying the question that he should be summoned for anything as trivial as meeting new members of the Gardyn council.

"Yes, Rian. We need you to lead a discreet raid on a certain outpost to get more horses. With the help of the unicorns, when will you have enough men to carry it out?"

Rian glanced away at the dark camp, he was known amongst the Gardyn for carrying out seemingly impossible missions swiftly and with little casualties, an undefeated warrior and hero for these people. As skilled as Rian was, he would always be only as strong as the men under his command. His trusted 'gang' were of course already in the Valley, eager to do their part for the Gardyn, and Rian could think of no reason to linger now a challenge had been set. "Rinar and Philip are here - they are all I need if we are guaranteed the help of the unicorns. We will leave tomorrow - the sooner the better, right?"

Mgair smiled and nodded his head in agreement, as did the rest of the council. The two girls had the idea that no one would say no to Rian, and even they were captivated by his very presence.

"Very good, and Samantha will accompany you." Lord Mgair replied. Both Rian and Samantha were shocked by this decision - a defenceless (and quite useless) girl joining a small elite team, it didn't make sense. But Mgair just held Rian's gaze firmly, as though conveying something more. "She will act as representative and go-between for you and the unicorns; a sign of good faith, Rian." The lord now glanced at Samantha and Jillis. "You two may go now. Samantha, see to it that Autumn agrees to our plans."

Lord Mgair excused them with a nod of his head. Samantha roused Jillis and the two girls walked tiredly to the camp.

*****

When the morning finally dawned, Autumn was watching the unnatural sight of his Valley filled with humans. His attention turned to a tall girl running up to him. He inclined his horned head in greeting. "Hello, Samantha. Your kind are settling well."

Samantha pushed her hair back from her face and glanced down the Valley. "Yes, I suppose. I'm still thankful you have given your home to us." She watched the stallion uncomfortably. "Mgair, he says we've got to get horses."

Autumn just stared into the distance, waiting for the inevitable.

"And, well, we were wondering if you and the others would help us?" Samantha looked at him, green eyes wide in hope.

"I have no council now to debate this, but how can I say no." Autumn looked to Samantha with his soft eyes. "What is it you require from us now?"

Samantha quickly informed him on the plans Mgair had covered that night, then waited once more for the great stallion's answer.

"Tân was right, we are to be fanciful steeds..." Autumn's regretful thoughts seeped out, but the trace of emotion was swiftly recovered. "What you ask does not sound dangerous, or arduous, but I leave Alina here for the mallus. I shall go with Billan, and it is about time Sundance acted like a stallion instead of a colt, running with monsters. He shall come also. I have one request - no matter what the Gardyn think, this is still my Valley; therefore at least one member of my herd should be present at all human councils. Our voices must be heard."

"That is all we ask." Samantha replied uneasily to his agreement. "I shall tell Mgair and we'll leave as soon as possible, and of your request - I doubt he will deny you that."

"We should leave today, then stay overnight close to this outpost. So we can get the horses back here in daylight." Autumn informed.

Samantha nodded, and went running over the grass again to tell Lord Mgair.

167

They left before midday. Samantha and the unicorns led the way through the forest, knowing it better than the other humans in the small party. The other two, chosen by Rian, were both young men, but trusted deeply for Gardyn deeds. Rian knew the layout of the outpost, and Philip and Rian's cousin, Rinar, both excellent with horses and good riders. The group headed to the north of the city, which meant they could travel for many miles within the trees. Eventually the forest opened out to grassy plains and the odd section of farmland.

The unicorns offered their strong backs to carry the humans quickly across this open land, and at length, the men in the group nervously agreed. Samantha giggled as she gladly clambered onto Sundance's golden back. Rian and Rinar both sat astride Autumn, who looked untroubled by the extra weight. Philip mounted Billan and looked very nervous indeed, sitting on his own, but Billan was extremely kindly towards him and Philip relaxed, and soon the two of them were chatting away like old friends.

They travelled steadily on until the sun sank low in the sky, rests were often, but brief. They did not hurry terribly, for there was no use in arriving at the outpost that day. When they eventually came to settle for the night all were ready for sleep, but Rian decided to go over the details for the following day.

"Now, it's simple enough. We'll set loose some horses as a distraction, then herd about ten to fifteen more from a different area. That's all we really need for now. When we get them, you and Billan." Rian nodded to Autumn. "Come down if you can do so without being seen and help us get them back." He now looked to the

168

palomino. "And Sundance, you stay up here to show us our route at speed."

After this briefing, Rian took Samantha aside, looking at her seriously for once. "Look, hopefully this should be simple, but there's always the chance that it will become very dangerous very fast. Personally I think it was stupid for Mgair to insist you come, but he has his reasons." Rian drew out a small knife in its leather scabbard. After a brief hesitation, he handed it to Samantha. "Here, take this. Make sure its hidden - the rest of us won't even be carrying anything, but... just in case. It's a bit late to get your fighting up to scratch, so if anything goes wrong, don't do anything stupid or heroic - get yourself out and back to the Valley."

Samantha's hand trembled slightly as she reached up and took the small blade. This was only the second time she'd been given a weapon; and the first time she felt she might need to use it. But as for leaving Rian and his gang behind if trouble arose - Samantha glanced up, looking at Rian's frowning expression - no, she didn't think she could turn away from danger now.

*****

The night was thankfully warm, for no one knew whether it would be safe to light a fire, but still all were restless. The moon had risen long ago, yet still Samantha could not sleep, she sighed as she rolled over again. Whenever she closed her eyes she could see a ring of fire that held all fear and a path of moonlight that led to something that Samantha would never admit... But eventually all the travellers slept 'til the break of dawn to begin their journeying again.

This time the humans went the rest of the way by foot the short distance to the outpost. Sundance stayed close to where they had camped that night and Autumn and Billan followed Rian to a copse of trees closer to the range of green pastures where warhorses were put to graze.

It was easier than the small group had expected, there were no high walls or heavy guard because this outpost was, as Samantha discovered, designed for the training of new soldiers and cavalry. So the four humans were able to enter the compound and, picking up head collars and ropes, they were indistinguishable from other stablehands. Their plan was to set loose a good number of horses at one end of the base. Billan and Autumn would ignore this first outbreak because it was intended solely as a distraction. Then they would round up the horses they wanted and get out as fast as possible.

The four humans moved surreptitiously beside the paddocks until Rian signalled a particular group. The horses looked nothing special but appeared sure-footed and able to carry a good weight. There were over twenty steeds in the enclosure, more than they were anticipating, but they could always cut out what they needed.

"Rinar go. Get another group loosed, then get back here as fast as possible." Rian said to his cousin, then led Philip and Samantha into the musty stable block. On one side, hay and straw were stacked high, and on the other were a row of horse boxes, some empty and some with equine heads looking at them with lazy interest. Rian kept walking until he came to a doorway that led to a long room bordered with rows of saddles and straps of leather.

It all looked a mess to Samantha, but Rian and Philip brought down four sets of tack.

"Why do we want that?" Asked Samantha.

"We'll get a few tacked up, that'll get us away faster and we'll herd the loose horses." Rian answered hastily, moving out of the door.

Already there were orders being barked and the sound of running feet and hooves. Rinar had done his job. The other three were leaving the tack room laden with the leather gear when they were aware of someone approaching fast. They scrambled behind the stacked bales and waited. Rinar came jogging into view, then stopped and looked around keenly.

Rian got up again and sighed, greeting his cousin. "Well, done. Now get this and get tacked." He handed over some tack and moved out again.

Samantha was going to follow, but stopped, looking into the stall before her. An intelligent pale head stared back at her. She reached up with her hand to gently stroke the almost white coat of the stallion.

"Hey, what are you doing?" An unknown voice came. A grown man was moving down the aisle to her, Samantha could tell by his uniform that he was a captain. "Who are you anyway?" The man peered irritably at her.

"I- I'm Lucy." Samantha blurted out the first name that came into her head, then she continued, thinking as quickly as she could. "I was told to get this horse tacked so that it could be used to round up the loose ones."

"And who's orders-?"

Samantha struggled to breathe and think straight enough to give her answer, but her hand trailed instinctively up towards the knife that was strapped beneath her loose top...

"Hey, hurry up. The captain out here is waiting for his horse." Rian shouted out, coming back and catching

171

on quickly as he saw Samantha reach in panic for the knife he knew was hidden.

The captain still stood looking wary. "Well... I suppose you had better hurry."

Samantha smiled meekly and let herself into the creamy-white horse's stable. The captain turned and marched back down the aisle, shouting at another group of stable hands on his way.

Rian came running up to Samantha. "What did you think you were doing?" He hissed furiously, entering the stable. "I told you not to do anything stupid."

"I don't know." She replied with a scowl. "It's just I saw this horse and... well, he's nice. Sorry! I'm sorry, I just stopped for a moment, it wasn't my fault."

Rian shook his head. "Why Mgair thought it a good idea to bring you, I don't know. Fine, get him out." With skilled hands, Rian quickly fitted the leather tack to the pale creamy horse, then ran off to the paddock. Samantha left the stall, pulling gently on the horse's bridle, he followed willingly with ears perked and eyes bright. Samantha smiled and looked at him, before setting off to go outside. She saw a brass name-plate on his door: "*Legan.*" She murmured before mounting with ease and nudging the horse onwards.

Already in the paddock Rian and his cousin were rounding up the small herd and Philip held open the gate. As Samantha approached, Philip spoke out to her in hushed tones. "Go in and get the horses to follow you out."

Samantha nodded and, biting her tongue in concentration, she picked up her reins and walked Legan into the paddock. The horses were well trained and were easily persuaded to follow on, but they were also a herd

172

and refused to be separated so the four riders were obliged to take the lot. It was still quite simple taking them though, and soon they all felt comfortable moving along at a steady jog. They knew that it would not be long before this horse-knapping was noticed and were eager to be clear of the place.

Two unicorns, one almost camouflaged in his brown coat and the other looking as though the plain was on fire, trotted down to meet them. The horses perked up at the sight and followed willingly after Autumn and Billan. As they drew nearer the tree line, a third, smaller unicorn emerged and joined them also. All were relieved and elated by this small victory over Hrafn and his army and gladly knowing that they would be home by nightfall.

*****

Moving at a steady pace throughout the day they managed to make good time, and within the trees where the horses may have scattered they followed the unicorns docilely and the humans' job was easy.

Drawing close to the Valley there was a rustling and two men emerged, one armed with bow, the other with a short sword. They glanced up to the riders. "Aye, Rian. You're finally back." The man greeted, lowering his bow.

Rian nodded to the horses. "Give us a hand with these, we need to get them through the hedge."

The men obeyed and walked before them, helping hold back the brush and waited until all horses, riders and unicorns were through. They gawked at Samantha's steed that stood out beneath the dusky forest trees, but went to take their post again.

The Valley was noisier than normal and Alina could be seen trotting frantically about. Autumn automatically ran up to her, but Billan and Sundance helped herd the horses into a makeshift paddock. Samantha and the others untacked their horses before adding them to the paddock also. Samantha was carrying away her tack when Tobias came walking up with a bemused look on his face. "Let me guess, you chose your horse?"

"Aye, she did and nearly got us all caught." Rian replied before Samantha could say a word. "Too bad you couldn't have come, Deorwine."

Tobias scowled slightly. "Yeah, well, can't be helped." Then he looked to Samantha again. "Oh, and you might want to help Alina. The mallus friend of yours is scaring everyone."

"Oh no!" She exclaimed, passing her saddle to Tobias and taking off in the direction of the grey unicorn.

"What's happened?" Samantha asked breathlessly when she drew close.

Alina looked at her with a worried expression. "The people, they saw him and wanted to kill him. He's taken off, I have calmed down the humans, but Siabhor is still recovering from his injuries."

"Where is he?" Asked Samantha, eyes scanning the borders.

Alina snorted gently and walked towards the edge of the Valley, Samantha followed on. In the dark boughs of the tangling trees which made the impenetrable fence of the Valley, Samantha's sharp eyes could see the movement of a large, long-limbed creature.

"Siabhor? It's Samantha, are you coming down?"

A gloomy face protruded from the foliage, the creature snorted slightly and withdrew again, before shouting out. "It is bad for mallus here. Where do I go?"

Samantha looked at Alina with bewilderment. "What does he mean?"

"His old pack drove him out when he returned. They'll kill him if they come across him again." Alina's sombre thoughts emerged.

"Oh." Gasped Samantha. She looked up into the trees again. "Look, Siabhor. I can't help you about your pack, but please, we'll talk with the others and they won't harm you."

Siabhor appeared again, "You means it?"

Samantha nodded, and with a small thud the mallus dropped lightly to the ground. He peered up to the human and unicorn and a foul, sharp-toothed grin cut across his face.

Seventeen

Samantha landed on the ground with a heavy thud. Rian had just disarmed and tripped her again and now held his sword steadily at her chest.

"You're dead." Her instructor told her calmly, then held out his hand to help her up. "You think too much. Try to be aware of everything around you and react accordingly. And we need to build some muscles on those skinny arms of yours – it looks like you're about to fall over every time you raise your sword!"

The Gardyn army, which grew every day, was left to their own motivation to practise fighting with weapons and bare-hand, but it was well known that Rian would stalk the camp with the ethic that if you still had the energy to lift a sword you hadn't spent enough time on the practise field! And now Samantha, an absolute novice with any sort of weapon, had the unhappy privilege of private and unrelenting tuition from the famous Rian.

Samantha ignored his hand and got up by herself, trying to minimise her gasping breath. She was already exhausted, but Rian hadn't even broken into a sweat.

"Look, I know the basics now, why do I have to learn fancy tricks and mind over matter rubbish?" Samantha asked irritably, her backside and hip hurt from the trips and she used her question to gain a few minutes break from another humiliation.

"You think the basics will do?" Rian asked back. "The soldiers in the King's army know more than the basics, there are no second chances in war." Rian looked at the exhausted girl and felt slightly sorry for her, but stubbornly persisted. "Samantha, I am teaching you this to keep you alive, even those who are not on the war front may need to protect themselves. Now, are you ready?"

"Hey, give her a break. You've been working her all morning, and she hasn't had to grow up with all this stuff." A male voice called protectively from the sidelines. Jillis and Tobias were sitting in the grass watching their friend's progress.

Rian glared at Tobias, he was not used to people questioning him, he was about to give a harsh reply but thought better of it. "Fine. Samantha, sit down and rest. Instead, let's see how the infamous Tobias Deorwine fares against the famous Rian."

Samantha walked thankfully towards Jillis, handing Tobias her sword. She settled in the grass beside her friend and watched as Tobias swung the sword expertly through the air, getting the feel of it.

"Go easy on me." Tobias said, only half joking as he took his position.

"Not a chance." Rian replied.

Suddenly there was a flashing of steel and the two swords met with a clash. The two men broke away again, their blades moved with such speed and accuracy,

Samantha watched with wide-eyes, amazed. Then Rian performed an obscure movement in which he came in extremely close to Tobias and managed to knock the sword from his tight grip.

"You're dead too." Rian smiled triumphantly as Tobias rubbed his wrist.

There was a pause as Tobias picked up the sword again.

"Round two?" Rian challenged.

"Definitely."

*****

Among her training sessions of the usual Gardyn fighting techniques, Samantha was subjected to a more unusual session that was carried out in secrecy - not even Jillis or Tobias had been allowed to accompany her.

She had gone alone with Rian to the far end of the large Valley where there was still open space. She knew nothing of what was to follow and looked curiously at a small pile of dry wood that Rian had collected in preparation.

"Now, your ability to control fire would be a huge asset to the Gardyn, but only if you tune it perfectly, or we would have a problem." Rian nodded to the heaped wood. "Use that to focus on."

"But - but I don't know how." Samantha pleaded. "I thought the fire started because David…" Her voice trailed off as she refused to revisit those memories. "Back then, I still thought that he was the Lost Soul."

Rian looked apologetically at the girl. "I know this is going to be difficult for you, both physically and emotionally. But Samantha, we must work this out, if not as a weapon, then at least how to stop accidental combustion. If the council are right, then you will only

178

grow more powerful - you must begin training for it now, or you will become too dangerous." His gaze was intense, he was being as truthful as possible with the girl, but even he could not bring himself to reveal that the council had already decided that if Samantha proved too hazardous she would be permanently removed, so much so that her flesh would rot in several corners of the earth so that even the King would have no use for her.

"But where do we start? I don't even know how I did it before." Samantha said exasperated, looking away to the forest to avoid her tutor's gaze.

"*You* start by thinking about the last time." Rian said, watching the girl look back at him with a pleading horror. "I know it won't be easy, Jillis filled us in on your tale shortly after we came to the Valley. I want you to picture the night that David died, relive it. The trigger may be anything, an action, an emotion, words - anything."

Samantha shut her eyes, the terrible memory was recalled far too easily after being suppressed for so long and she opened her eyes again quickly to see Rian looking back at her with uncharacteristic sympathy. She nodded gently, the slight movement awakening her stubborn streak and Samantha closed her eyes to concentrate.

Once all light was blocked from her gaze, the prickly darkness blurred into a memory, vivid and stored away 'til now. The scene played itself out, the forest surroundings, the mallus and David sat beside her. In her mind's eye everything was clear and sharp, but try as she might, David's face remained a blur, a sin to see.

She remembered standing up suddenly when the guards approached, the arrow shot past her with a zip.

Samantha could clearly see David's blood seeping out onto the ground. A rush of emotions passed over her, a mix of fear of the moment, anger at all that pursued them; and sorrow, most of all, uncontrollable sorrow.

The heat of the fire as she screamed suffocated her once more. Her knees gave way and Samantha collapsed onto the grassy area, sobbing. Rian knelt down beside her, arm wrapped about her shoulders. He hated himself for putting her through this. Yet he knew that this session would have to be repeated over and again. But it occurred to him that future sessions should be carried out in secrecy, so that even Mgair wouldn't know. Rian would tell the council her power was inaccessible, Samantha would be safe from them.

As Samantha calmed, Rian helped her up and back to the tents, both of them ignoring the flickering bonfire behind them.

*****

The fated day came. The Gardyn were unaware of the day's significance as they rose and went about daily chores and training. The atmosphere was light-hearted, with friendly competition as a row of Gardyn men stood in a row, bows in hands and a supply of arrows at their feet, each taking aim at five targets set up forty metres away.

Rian and his captains moved up and down the line, barking corrections to all but the last two individuals that were all but ignored.

Jillis took a sure stance and drew her bow and effortlessly let fly an arrow that thudded into the centre of the target. The maiden smiled cheerfully and glanced over to her companion who sat in the grass beside her.

Samantha grimaced, thinking ashamedly of her own archery attempts. "That's not fair." She mumbled.

Jillis shrugged. "I've been practising for longer than most people realise." She explained, then looked about almost slyly. "I bet I could beat any man in this army in a challenge!"

Samantha was going to dare her to challenge Rian when her attention was diverted by one of their scouts entering the Valley to the far right and running at full speed to the collection of tents. Samantha and Jillis shared an intrigued look, then decided to follow and find out what was so urgent.

They weren't the only ones to break away from practice. After a few brief instructions to the other captains, Rian made his way to the council area.

Already at the main camp were the Lord Mgair and a stormy-looking Tobias. The scout stood, panting for breath having delivered his message. The Lord Mgair looked gravely towards the approaching Rian, Samantha and Jillis.

"It starts." He said in a weary voice. "Our scouts have seen a massing of soldiers to the east. They have already begun felling trees and making camp."

Samantha looked troubled by this news. "They are close? They know where we are?"

Tobias glanced over to her. "All we know is that they're settling, so they roughly know our whereabouts. I would have led a party to find what we could about the army but it seems I am here for no other reason than a link to the Lost Soul." He added with a sharp glance to Mgair.

Rian sat down, close to Lord Mgair who had evidently become the leader of the Gardyn army. "Lord, what else is there to do but wait and prepare."

Mgair sighed. "I would have the families to somewhere safe, but nowhere is safe anymore." Then he nodded resolutely. "Fix every man with light gear, we will plan an ambush."

This order marked the end of this rushed meeting as Rian jogged away to an area designated for storage of bows, arrows and the few swords, shields and such things.

Jillis was clearly scared by this news, she gripped her wooden bow so tightly her knuckles were white. She excused herself to return to the archers, wanting to do what she could for the army.

Samantha was left to walk slowly away with Tobias, children were running about playing games in the sunlight, but Samantha stared ahead in an unseeing gaze. It would be so simple if only she could create some unease in the enemy.

"Oh no you don't." Tobias' voice interrupted her thoughts.

"What?"

He stopped and turned to face her. "You're planning something. Don't bother, you'll just get yourself into a trouble that we'll have to get you out of."

"Oh, but I'd never-" Samantha's innocent reply was cut short by a nervous tug on her sleeve. She looked down to the bright face of a young boy, no more than seven years, who smiled up at her.

"You're Lady Samantha, aren't you?" He said in a quiet voice. "I've seen you with the unicorns. Is it true you will make us a castle with the trees for us to live in?"

Samantha blinked. "Um, I'm not sure what you mean."

The boy looked about nervously, then added in a meek voice. "I saw it, they twisted when you said and we were all safe."

Samantha did not know what to say. A harassed looking woman rushed over and grabbed the young boy's hand and looked across to Samantha apologetically. "I'm so sorry Lady Samantha. He don't mean no harm, he just don't know who he's talking to."

"Um, it's okay." Samantha mumbled as his mother led the young boy away. She looked up to Tobias. "I'm going for a ride with Alina, I'll see you later." And she ran off to the paddock before he could object.

She spent the rest of the afternoon leisurely riding on Legan to Wentra and back with Alina to visit the rest of the herd. The kindly grey knew something was on her friend's mind, but did not mention it until they were almost back to the Valley.

"I've just got this feeling that I should do something after all that's happened, all that I might be." Samantha revealed sadly.

Alina glanced across at her. "Like you have some part to play in disquieting Hrafn's army?" She stopped and shook her silvery mane. "I feel that way also. I had a dream of Minaeri last night where I was her steed."

Samantha reined in her horse. "You know Alina, you might be onto something." She sat quietly, thinking for a moment. "Will you meet me tonight? Make sure Sundance doesn't follow you."

"What have you planned, Samantha?"

The girl just smiled in return and pushed Legan into a smooth trot, riding back to the Valley.

When Legan had been put with the other horses Samantha returned to the small canvas shelter she shared with Jillis and Tobias. Outside there was a small fire crackling with dinner cooking above it. Tobias and Jillis were both sitting close by and looked up as Samantha approached.

"You've been gone a while." Tobias chided. "What if Hrafn's men had caught you."

Samantha sighed and sat down. "I was with Alina, we went to see the unicorns at Wentra. Any trouble and I could jump on her and be far away in a moment."

Jillis handed her some food, hot from the fire. "Don't worry about him, he's still upset that he's not trusted."

Samantha smiled her thanks to Jillis and withheld from asking why. The trio sat by their small fire until the dusk had become darkened to night. Jillis and Tobias had fallen to sleep easily, but Samantha lay awake, anxious of what she was planning. By the time that all the small campfires across the Valley had been extinguished, she silently arose and dug through her things. She finally found what she was looking for and, as uncomfortable as it was, she slipped the silver dress over her head and tightened the bodice, then fastened the sword that she had kept of the murdered Derren and sneaked out of the shelter.

Samantha could make out the grey image of Alina moving like a silver wraith, silent across the grass. Without a word Samantha vaulted onto the grey mare's back and Alina made to leave the Valley by the eastern pathway.

"Are you sure this will help?" Alina asked with nervous thoughts.

"No." Samantha replied. "But surely it can't do any harm... we'll just have to wait and see."

The stealthy mare and rider continued eastward, unseen by any. Alina followed her senses in the dark forest and it was not long before a large camp of hundreds lay before them. Samantha gasped at the sight, she had not truly known how outnumbered the Gardyn were, and if this was a mere contingent of the whole army...

Alina shook her mane out. "Shall we go back?"

"No. No, we're here now." Samantha replied in a shaky voice.

The ghostly unicorn and rider rode to the very edge of the encampment. The army's security was lax and it seemed no man remained awake in this dead hour of the night. They continued forward until they were very close to the tents.

"What now?"

"Get the horses to notice you; that might wake some of 'em up." Samantha whispered to Alina.

Alina flicked her tail unhappily, she did not want to be in the middle of an army while it was awake, but she did as Samantha instructed. She nickered lightly, the gentle sound holding all her love of being the breed of Praede, of running free with Autumn by her side.

Even this, the softest of sounds made an impact and the horses were whinnying in desperate reply and straining at their ropes to be with their majestic cousin. At first Samantha thought nothing would happen, but then out from the tents stumbled several men coming to find what had disturbed the horses. At the sight of the ethereal unicorn and silver rider the men stopped, they did not even go for their weapons and two even fell to their knees.

Samantha gazed about at the thirty or so young men whose faces showed ever so clearly the fear of the forest. For it was true that rumours were going about the guard, that the very trees and creatures that made the Great Forest obeyed the Lost Soul, and now they were confronted with the very image that had kept them awake while the older (and possible wiser) men slept.

"Minaeri, Minaeri. You come to us, have we done wrong?" One young fellow asked in breathless voice.

"No, brother. Not yet, but there is time for you all to change your ways." Samantha replied in a soft voice, for once not worrying about her choice of words. "If you follow my envoy, the Lady Samantha, all will be well."

Then, as if Samantha had learnt to communicate like the unicorn, Alina obediently reared and backed into the darkness, disappearing as strangely as they had come. The soldiers were left baffled and most crept back to their tents and would, in the following days, cause great unrest in the army. A few, pausing momentarily to collect their swords and shields, left immediately, following the western trail with the imagined goddess riding ahead.

As a safety precaution, Alina had purposely deviated northwards in case anyone followed them too closely on the straight trail west.

Samantha was almost dropping to sleep now that the excitement and adrenaline rush were over. Her head started to nod and she became unaware whether her visions were real or part of a shallow dream, but it seemed the trees moved in the darkness. Not just the branches, but whole trees parting to make way for them,

186

and then up above, branches and boughs entwined stretching high to claw the starry sky. It seemed that the trunks of mighty trees drew together to form a wall of living wood.

Suddenly she lost her balance as dozing changed to sleeping and Samantha found herself falling off Alina's smooth back.

Alina snorted. "Are you okay? Perhaps we should hurry on back."

"No." Samantha replied as her head started to clear from the fall. She stood up, tripping on her long dress before she caught her balance again. "No, there's something I've got to do."

"But we've already been to the camp Samantha."

"I don't mean that. There was something a little boy said to me earlier." She began to explain, striding off northwest. "He said the trees would protect them. I didn't understand until now, but I've seen it. Come on, there's still time before sunrise." She picked up her skirts and started to run, with Alina following curiously.

Samantha kept on running through the forest, she did not trip or stumble, and for some reason, when only a quarter of this midnight journey would have fatigued her back home, she never felt tired or out of breath. The sky was beginning to pale when Samantha finally stopped, she glanced about, the trees were spread out, but as she walked between them, in the rum light they moved and bowed to the Lady Samantha as she came. She laughed lightly and murmured words that came unbidden.

Alina watched as curious as ever, and was startled by what was happening, the very forest was contorting by this young girl's murmurings. The unicorn's sharp hearing caught very few words, even fewer did she understand, but within them *Minaeri* was repeated so many times. As though in a great dance the trees pulled together, then apart forming what seemed a great wall.

Then all movement stopped. Alina walked cautiously forward, softly nudging Samantha from her daze. Samantha turned and smiled, then walked straight towards the solid wall of living wood, the boughs lifted to allow her through and the unicorn followed quickly. Within the boundary there was a large open space, the wall of trees ran all the way around it, tightly packed so that none could enter unbidden.

"What is this place?" Alina asked nervously.

"It's where the children can be safe." Samantha replied, looking with wonder about the area, then up into the lightening sky. Dawn was not far off. "Come, let's get back to the Valley." She said and ran to the wall of trees, they parted to allow her and the unicorn out, then thudded shut behind them.

*****

They arrived back at the Valley as the sun began to peak over the horizon. Samantha could see outlandish gear by their own weapon stock and guessed that some soldiers had already converted. The second thing she saw was a livid Tobias standing at the near end of the camp. Samantha slid off Alina's back and said goodbye to her friend, finally feeling guilty about their dangerous little excursion.

"Where have you been now?" Tobias demanded. "You went to the enemy camp didn't you?"

Samantha walked past him, wanting to change from the restricting, and now quite muddy dress. "Yes, so? I did what I had to do - now Hrafn's army is a nervous wreck."

Jillis came out of their shelter just as Samantha approached; she was pale with fear, but when she saw Samantha she understood and smiled. "Tell me everything." She begged.

Samantha changed her clothes then came back out, she was starting to feel drowsy after a sleepless night but couldn't wait to tell her story. Jillis and her brother listened enraptured and were amazed by the tale.

"We'll tell Mgair straight away about the tree-fort. We can get the children and their mothers there as soon as possible." Tobias said when Samantha had finished.

"Perhaps we best let our adventurer sleep first." Jillis replied softly, Tobias looked to Samantha who had fallen into a deep sleep now her immediate worries were over. Jillis held open the canvas flap as Tobias picked up the sleeping girl and carried her to her bed.

*****

Samantha was wakened in the afternoon by someone shaking her. She opened her bleary eyes to see Jillis.

"What time is it?" She asked groggily.

"Past noon." Jillis replied. "I would have let you sleep longer, but Mgair wishes to meet with you."

Samantha struggled up. "Fine, fine. Is he by the usual meeting place?" She stumbled out of the shelter and the warm breeze refreshed her.

Around the unlit hearth, the usual council gathered, including the familiar faces of Lord Mgair; Rian; Tobias; Autumn; and also a mother who represented the families. Samantha sat down quietly next to Rian, she could just see a small group of men that stood out as soldiers of Hrafn, with their red and black uniforms.

189

"Ah, Lady Samantha. I was just wondering whether you could add any light to the strange tale of these soldiers." Lord Mgair asked politely enough, although Samantha could tell that he was very displeased.

Samantha tried to reply, but her words stuttered hopelessly.

"I vouch for their truth." Rian added, ending Samantha's discomfort.

"Very well." Mgair nodded gravely, then turned in his seat. "Set them loose, but keep a close watch." He instructed to the soldiers' captors, before looking back at the small assemblage of the Gardyn council. "So, I hear that we have another safe hold?"

"Yes, it's about as safe as you'll get. I'll lead the families there first thing tomorrow." Samantha informed the council. The rest of the meeting covered briefly their plans of attack. A small contingent, mostly of archers, would go to investigate the enemy the next day.

Eighteen

The next morning broke with a fresh breeze and pale blue sky and already an argument had broken out between Jillis and Tobias.

"You are going with the other families." Tobias demanded.

"By Minaeri I won't! I'm one of the best archers we've got and you know it!" Jillis retorted, standing defiantly before her older brother.

"I'm not having you getting into trouble." He explained irately.

"This coming from someone who can't be trusted by Mgair. I've got more respect in this camp than you'll ever have. You might as well run back to Hrafn's army before you make me hide away from this war!"

Samantha jerked her head to look at Tobias. "What?"

Jillis pushed past her, leaving their little hut.

"What does Jillis mean you should go back to Hrafn?" Samantha asked, turning to Tobias.

"I'll explain later. Get your horse ready we're about to go." Tobias also left the shelter, looking to help organise the families for the short journey.

Samantha got her horse, Legan, tacked up and ready. The Valley was a hive of activity about them, families were gathering all their belongings as they travelled on once more; those that were staying prepared for fighting; and some were already leaving to scout the enemy camp. There was a group of perhaps twelve, all armed with short bows, Jillis stood out as the only girl in the group of men, and she had swapped her usual work skirt for a pair of hardy breeches.

Samantha led her horse over to the congregation of families.

"Samantha!" Someone called her name, she turned to see Tobias striding over to her with a large bundle in his arms. "Here, I got you this."

She accepted the large sheet of webbed material, grimacing slightly at the dank colours.

"It's for your horse." He said with a smile. "If you insist upon having that pale nag at least you should cover him up." He then helped her fit the thin rug over the horse, Legan looked strange but his white coat no longer shone out.

It was not long before they set out. Samantha rode at the front with Alina, and Tobias was just behind on a borrowed horse. The families strung along on the forest paths.

"What is that on Legan?" Alina had asked when they had set out.

Samantha laughed. "It's to stop him showing up, Tobias insisted on it. Careful Alina, or you'll have one next!"

Tobias came beside Samantha at that point. "Laughing at my expense are we?" He accused, only half in jest.

"Well, I promise to stop teasing if you tell me what Jillis was on about earlier." Samantha answered quickly.

All sign of amusement quickly left Tobias' face. "It was a long time ago. Or at least it feels like it."

He stopped and didn't say anymore for a while as they rode through the forest. "It was when I was thirteen, the age I became an adult. I wanted to be like everyone else, and to be like my father." He glanced over at Samantha. "Jillis told you about him? I wanted to become an important lieutenant like he was, so I disobeyed my mother and went into training. I went to the same camp that you got the horses from, that is why Mgair would not let me go there."

"What happened? What changed?" Samantha asked quietly.

Tobias looked behind him before replying, checking no one else was listening; then he gave a bitter smile. "They kicked me out of the army. I guess I held back a bit because of my family, because of my betrayal to the Gardyn." He sighed and shook his head. "I ruined it for myself, lost everyone's trust."

Samantha bit her lip, gazing silently at him for several long moments. Very much used to the judging stares of people, Tobias sighed and looked straight on.

"Is that it?"

"What?" Tobias snapped his head around to look at her.

"I thought it was going to be something actually terrible, like you'd eaten a baby, or set fire to Mgair's house." Samantha broke off, smiling. "Although that last one could definitely be a positive."

Tobias just continued to stare at her, completely lost for words. He'd suffered many jibes over the years, but no one had ever made light of his betrayal.

At the continued silence, Samantha blushed under the growing discomfort. "Oh well, I mean, what you went through was awful. I'm sure it has emotional repercussions and everything..."

Tobias finally chuckled, shaking his head at her nonsense.

Alina whinnied gently, trying to bring a little more sense and maturity to proceedings. "The past must not be forgotten, but do not dwell on these thoughts. Perhaps Minaeri has something in store for you yet."

*****

The whole group moved steadily along, led by Samantha, whose thoughts were fresh and the memory of the place brought them safely to the new Treefort.

All were in awe when they saw it, huge trees compacted tightly to form the living wall. Samantha rode up to the border and the mighty trees creaked as they drew slowly apart. The other horses balked and strained to flee, but Legan walked calmly through the passage into the large space inside. The people followed, tripping over themselves with fear and wonder in equal measure.

"But how...?" Tobias' voice trailed off and he stared wide-eyed at Samantha. "How did you find this?"

"I didn't." Samantha shrugged, she dismounted and looked calmly about. "I took the unicorns advice on asking the trees and took it one step further. The trees agreed to keep all the Gardyn safe as long as no one keeps an axe. They can detect whether the person entering is good or not, so I guess there's nowhere safer!"

194

'Asked the trees?' Confused thoughts spun in Tobias' mind, he couldn't believe that this simple girl they had sought to send home could do such a thing.

Alina was also mystified, not even a unicorn could completely control a tree like that. It was rumoured that Praede had set up the barrier of the Valley an age ago, but that was just a myth to tell foals.

A small child came running up to Samantha. "You did it, you did it." He cried with delight, tugging on her sleeve.

Samantha smiled, recognising the young boy. "Yes, thank you for telling me how." She watched as he ran off again, before turning back to her friends. "Well, that's done. I suppose we had better head back."

After a brief consultation with the head mother, Samantha, Tobias and Alina left the happy refuge and trotted gently back to the Valley. The excursion had taken until early afternoon and the trio were glad to be back, but arriving at the Valley reminded them what else had been planned today.

Tobias and Samantha loosed their horses in the makeshift paddock, and went back to their shelter to find Jillis.

The younger Deorwine was rooting through the supplies to find a suitable bandage. Her face was even paler than normal and blood soaked the top of her left sleeve. When she saw them approaching, Jillis sat down and let Samantha find the length of material, meanwhile Tobias cut back the sleeve.

"It's okay, it's just a nick." Jillis said as Samantha securely wrapped the bandage about her arm.

"What happened?"

195

Jillis shook her head. "We didn't keep a good look-out. On the way back we collided with one of their scout parties."

"We didn't lose anyone, did we?" Samantha asked.

"No, thank Minaeri! We managed to take down a couple of their guys as we retreated though."

Tobias had been pacing back and forth by the entrance, but stopped. "What's the army like?" He asked.

His sister sighed. "It's not too bad at the moment, but they still outnumber us. I think they're having problems getting their men and equipment into the forest, and there's sign of cowardice, there had been a recent hanging at the camp, I think this place is scaring them."

"Well, that is good enough, for now." Tobias tried and failed to sound optimistic.

*****

Everything remained calm for only the briefest time. A messenger came running to their shelter with the urgent request that the Lady Samantha would come to the main council ground immediately. Samantha did so curiously, and found the Lord Mgair hovering by the meeting place, waiting for her.

"Our scouts found him not long ago. He said he comes as a messenger of the King, but will only speak to the Lost Soul."

Samantha nodded, then entered the large hut. Standing in the middle of the room, hands bound tight was David. His face had grown darker and seemed to have matured greatly since Samantha had last seen him.

"Nice to see how you treat your friends, Sammy." David forced a grin, holding up his hands.

196

"She is addressed as Lady Samantha, now." Lord Mgair growled.

Samantha gazed at David, before turning to Mgair. "Leave us. It's okay."

Mgair reluctantly left the room, shooting a dark look towards his Lady Samantha.

Ignoring the Gardyn Lord, Samantha walked slowly over to a chair to sit down, taking the time to compose herself. "They say you're Hrafn's messenger now. Nice reward for killing his son and heir."

"So you knew that it was me." His words came out plainly, in neither question nor statement. Behind his emotionless front David felt the surge of triumph return again, the adrenaline that had flooded his veins as he held the pillow over the young prince, suffocation masked as a magical death.

"Actually, I'm more than a messenger. I'm now the heir of Hrafn unless another brat boy is born, which I doubt - Tagor took long enough to come along." David simply shrugged at Samantha's surprised look. "Oh, a lot has happened since you left. I'm engaged to the Princess. When Helena fell pregnant Hrafn thought it better to have her marry the 'foreign prince' rather than further court scandal and upset. The ceremony will be next month, it's gotta be rushed, before she starts to show, of course. I'd invite you, but I don't think it's your scene. So the main point is, unless another son comes along, I get the throne. Not bad, eh?"

"Or, unless the Gardyn win this war and remove Hrafn and his court forever." Samantha replied coldly.

David's eyes softened. "Look, Sammy, can we skip the formalities. Get these ropes off me, they're starting to chafe."

197

Samantha looked suspiciously up at him, but finally agreed and untied the knotted cord.

"Ah, that's better!" David rubbed his wrists and sat down quite leisurely. "Now, Hrafn wants to know what it'll take for your lot to stop all this rubbish?"

"How about giving up the throne for a start?"

The cold glint came back to David's eyes, but he kept his anger restrained. "Now, Sammy - or is it *Lady Samantha* these days? Yes, we've had lots of rumours going round about you. How you summon silver ghosts, control beasts of good and evil, and the newest one - how you manipulate the trees into crushing your foes!"

Samantha just stared dully back at her old friend, and this seemed to infuriate him.

"Maybe some of it's true; after all, we did make friends with mallus and unicorns, and pledge fruit from trees. But don't think you're anything special Sammy, remember these stories are only exaggerations. You're still just that quiet, silly little girl from school who no one cares for."

Samantha bolted up, fists clenched.

David smiled, pleased that he could actually rile her. "Stumbling over whatever task they give you. You're nothing but a performing freak for this army aren't you? Be honest, they don't care for *you* - friendless yet again Sammy."

Something in Samantha seemed to spark and a warm breeze rustled through the open door, but still David goaded her.

"But then you did have friends, didn't you. The unicorns. Funny, they're dead now. Honestly Sammy, you're a first-rate tragedy! Maybe you'll wake up to find all of this a deluded dream of a sad little girl."

198

"Shut up!" Samantha screamed. Flames shot up in front of her, she gasped and grabbed the water cask, tipping it out until all that was left was a smouldering patch on the ground.

David walked behind her, leaning in close. "It feels good doesn't it, to know you've got that strength within you." His enticing voice murmured in her ear. "If you hadn't have left us you would have mastered it."

Samantha was trembling. "No! David, it's over. If you've got nothing more to say…"

"I have plenty, but you won't listen." David replied calmly.

She turned and looked him straight in the eye. "You look like someone I once knew, and for that I'll let you walk out alive. Back to Hrafn if you want."

She turned and left through the open door. David stood frowning, his hand reaching to his back where a dagger had been secretly bound. In one swift movement he unhooked it and jumped forward to drive the blade down into the girl; but a soldier had been standing guard outside the door and reacted quicker, he knocked the dagger flying from David's hand and drew his own sword to slay the treacherous lad.

"Don't." Samantha ordered, glaring down at them. "I'm not hurt, let him live, but take him away from the Valley immediately. Make sure he doesn't know of our location."

The Gardyn soldier bowed and obeyed, roughly pulling David away.

*****

David arrived back at his King's camp in the early evening and was escorted straight to the royal base. Hrafn looked up, candlelight flickered on his sinister

199

face, just as these past months had caused David and Samantha to mature; they had made the King age.

He had crushed many attempts of rebellion during his reign, and he swore that this was simply another, but this was the first time Hrafn had felt fear. True, he had the power to bring fallen soldiers back to life and make his foes believe his army was invincible, but how would his strength clash against this new Lady Samantha's.

"What did you find out?" He asked in a quiet voice.

David collapsed down onto a chair and sighed. "The army's small, but they are too well concealed in the forest. If only we had them on open ground."

"That isn't an option." Hrafn growled. "But what of Samantha?"

He shook his head. "She's not going to be swayed again. She is a bit nervous, and she hasn't learnt to control any real power yet, but she has matured a lot and I think she's gonna cause us trouble." David looked away, deeply disturbed. "The rumours are true though. She didn't confess it, but I could tell. She has brought unicorns, at least one mallus, and even the trees to her control. I should have killed her."

"You are a worthless assassin David; I wonder why I still let you live."

"I'm your only link to that girl and you know it." David retorted in an equal tone.

*****

Back at the Gardyn Valley, there was a hive of activity. The coming of a messenger marked the beginning of this dreaded war and everyone was kitted out immediately as far as the stores could. Samantha didn't see much of Jillis for the next few days, because the dear Gardyn maid was summoned to the bowmen.

Samantha was designated to be with the other mounted swordsmen, along with Rian and Philip.

As dusk fell on the eve of the first battle, the chaotic preparations calmed as everyone settled down to try to sleep, knowing that with dawn came death. Samantha was too restless, so she sneaked out of the shelter and went to find the unicorns. They were right down the far end of the Valley, but the walk was refreshing after an aching afternoon of practising her swordsmanship.

In the rum light she could make out Alina clearly, and as she approached, Samantha also made out the darker shapes of Sundance, Autumn, and even Siabhor. The unicorns greeted her kindly, they had all sensed the apprehension of the human camp that day and unease was growing amongst them.

"I'm getting scared now. I don't think I'll be able to kill another person." Samantha confessed.

Alina lowered her velvety muzzle to the human. "Your friends will be beside you, there is nothing to fear."

Siabhor grunted. "I am going from one battle to another. I will fight against the bad humans, also."

Samantha smiled, glad of this small comfort with what loomed ahead.

Nineteen

Dawn broke over the Great Forest of Enchena to find two enemies in silent readiness for battle. Lord Mgair rode ahead of his meagre troops, leading them from the Valley to face Hrafn, King of Enchena, and his invincible soldiers.

In the distance, the sharp glinting of many a sword and shield could be seen through the trees. The Gardyn halted, Mgair rode up and down the ranks in last minute preparation, straps were tightened, swords drawn and prayers said. Samantha tightened her grip on Legan's reins, feeling extremely unprotected with the rough Gardyn shield and leathers.

Jillis and the other bowmen were sent to follow Siabhor into the trees ahead. Everything was set. Finally the last moment of peace passed and cries rose from both sides.

At Lord Mgair's command the Gardyn charged through the trees, weapons raised high. Hrafn's own men began their attack and were met with a shower of arrows from Jillis and the others.

Samantha spurred her steed, racing nimbly between the great trunks with others at her side, human, horse and unicorn. Her first attack was well aimed and all worry left her as her sword swung down and everything became automated as she suppressed the nausea that swept through her. Her first stroke fatally wounding a soldier of the enemy, but as fighting ensued all around her she found that she could not concentrate on every angle.

This proved her undoing as an Enchenian soldier rushed at her from an unexpected angle, but luckily tripped, falling heavily against her pale steed. Legan shied violently, throwing his rider. Samantha landed heavily on the blood-splattered ground, she struggled to get up, staggering in the churned mud. She looked wildly about, Legan had disappeared and her attacker had not risen from his fall, two Gardyn arrows protruding from his back. Samantha started to move through the throng of fighting, when another soldier confronted her. Both hesitated, he from shock of meeting a mere girl on the battleground, and Samantha with aversion to killing another. Her sword reluctantly clashed against her foe's, the metallic sound lost in the ongoing battle scene.

The enemy soldier swung his sword down hard at her and Samantha wavered in her block, stumbling back. She hit the ground hard and cold fear swept through her as the soldier raised his sword for the deadly strike.

Something dark swept quickly between them, and Samantha watched with a mix of horror and relief as the soldier fell back, throat and face slashed, becoming unrecognisable in death.

Siabhor returned and stood by Samantha, panting slightly, claws stained and fur matted with blood. He turned his head and let out a sharp bark, and through the packed trees and fighters a grey unicorn struggled through. With all her strength Samantha dragged herself up and onto Alina's back, lying low she let the kindly beast carry her from the fray.

They stopped a good distance from the fighting, but still there was the terrible clamour of battle. Samantha let herself drop from Alina's back and sat quietly until her head had stopped spinning, barely aware that she was crying. Then she stood up uneasily, gripping her sword.

"Where are you going?" Alina demanded, blocking the girl's path.

"I've got to go back, to fight." Samantha replied, forcing away the queasy feeling.

"No, you can help no more, you are already hurt. We must keep you safe, you are the Lost Soul." Alina argued, harsher than Samantha had ever known her, not realising how battle can affect even the mildest of beings.

Samantha leant against a tree, catching her breath. She shook her head. "No, I'm fine. Just winded, that's all. But this war is my fault and I'm not going to be the old, scared Sammy." She replied, thinking back on David's words.

Samantha glanced across at the mallus that had accompanied them. Siabhor was acting strangely, darting about, sniffing the air and listening keenly.

"And what's up with you?" Samantha asked him.

Siabhor didn't turn to face her, but replied quickly. "You stay quiet, listen and hide."

Alina and Samantha shared confused looks, all they could hear was the horrendous noise of the continued fight. But Siabhor looked up to the trees, obviously able to sense something else. A low growling emitted from the mallus. His actions were shortly explained. Just audible against the battle sounds the girl and unicorn could hear the familiar rapping of claw against the bark - the nightmare prowlers. Mallus were coming.

Suddenly from the treetops a light brown shape dropped down onto Siabhor. Samantha drew her sword and Alina prepared to charge the single mallus down, but Siabhor gave a bark to ward them off. He fell to the ground with the weight of the light brown mallus, but quickly, and expertly kicked back, flinging the creature away. Siabhor instantly pounced with teeth and claws to leave nothing but a bloodied and ragged body of the attacker.

Samantha crept slowly forward with disgust. The torn body of the mallus was small, with longer limbs than any she had seen, Samantha looked across to the panting Siabhor.

"Ikhneumòn." He spat. "There should be another. The rest of the pack will not be far. We leave, now."

"What? I don't understand." Samantha stuttered.

Siabhor's growling continued. "That is an ikhneumòn, a tracker, from my old pack. They travel in pairs so the other will have gone to tell Sahr that I am here." He scanned the forest surroundings. "They will have sensed the battle and come to scavenge; now if they meet me, they kill me."

"We'll go to the Treefort and wait until the battle is over." Alina strongly suggested and waited for Samantha to mount again.

But the girl shook her head. "No." Her mind raced with plans and ideas, thinking quickly she added. "Siabhor, I know how we can upset the battle *and* get Sahr and her lot gone for good."

The two creatures gazed at Samantha, they knew that any trickery was risky, but they had already learnt to trust her.

*****

The timing of Samantha's plan was crucial if they were to succeed and make it seem as though the power of 'Lady Samantha' was not to be contested. Siabhor had gone, acting as bait for his old pack. Samantha rode astride Alina back to the battle area.

Above the terrible battle din, Siabhor's signal came as an eerie mallus' call. Samantha drew her sword and Alina cantered slowly through the fighting masses to where all could see them.

Alina shone magnificently and there was a sudden hush. Samantha spied some mass rushing towards them from the depths of the forest that was yet to be seen by either army, and then raised her sword high.

"Bewares to my foes, I call nightmare and myth to strike you down!"

Suddenly there were shouts and cries from where Hrafn's army was at its densest, there was chaos in the ranks as hideous creatures sprang down onto the enemy, causing many to drop their guard with fear. A deep and throbbing horn was winded and the retreat was commanded. All of Hrafn's men backed warily away.

At first the Gardyn moved after them in a glorious and foolhardy charge, but Mgair's horn called them back with its valiant note. The place of the First Battle emptied, leaving only those who had fallen, disfigured beyond even the help of Hrafn.

What had happened, and was told over and over again by Gardyn to regale their great Lady Samantha, had been a risky gamble. Siabhor had purposefully stayed away from the fighting and let the mallus find him. Such was his old pack's anger and hatred, that when he ran into the fray, they followed heedlessly.

No human war had ever happened in their forest, so the mallus were at first confused, but quickly their instinct had kicked in and teeth and claws tore at whatever person was before them.

Siabhor got away unharmed as soon as he led the other mallus into the clash, but the majority of the pack weren't so lucky. Sahr, who was first in the chase, finally lay as an unmoving carcass on the forest floor along with seven of her pack. Those that lived scattered, some with wounds that would not heal and cause death within days.

By the time Hrafn's army returned to force battle, the wood-wise Gardyn were nowhere to be found.

*****

The Gardyn army had retreated back to their hidden Valley, where they were greeted by Sundance, the only individual from the Valley not to have gone to battle, by order of Alina.

The mood was both sombre and exhilarant. One of Autumn's unicorns was wounded, but not seriously; Siabhor had come away completely unscathed; but they had lost a fifth of their men and had many more injured in that one attack. For many it had been their first experience of battle and everyone was deeply affected.

Samantha's trickery had come just in time, the King's army was well-trained and well-armed and even in the forest they held an advantage in full-on combat. Their only real hope now was in ambush until more Gardyn had arrived from other towns. The fastest riders were immediately sent out to help direct them.

The rest of the Gardyn spent the remaining day quietly tending injuries. Samantha was sitting alone with Tobias outside their small tent, as Jillis was still with the other archers. The friends were trying to put the horrors of the day behind them when there was an unexpected flutter of wings as a small bird descended to the ground before them.

Samantha looked at it and smiled slightly. "Aw, pretty." And indeed it was, with bright red underneath and streaked breast contrasting with blue-grey wings.

"Shoo!" Tobias waved at the bird and startled it, but it did not fly far, only to the edge of the trees. Tobias looked at Samantha. "You've already got mallus and unicorns, you're not having a bird of prey too." He said, only half in jest.

Samantha sighed and leant stiffly back, bruises had begun to come up where she had fallen and her shoulder had to be bandaged. The day wore on and the camp fell to sleep early after the day's fatiguing events, with only a minimum of guards and scouts about the Valley.

Samantha dreamt of another long journey, of a brightly coloured guide who led her over the hills to the mountains near the sea. As her sleep became deeper it seemed she was looking into another person's memory with unknown, yet familiar cliffs and lands stretching before her.

She awoke from the deepest sleep imaginable and the visions took a while to fade. At first Samantha wondered where she was: home; the Valley; the palace; or elsewhere?

She struggled up and walked slowly out of the hut. Now she was outside beneath the cloudless, night time sky she felt wide-awake. There was a flutter of wings as the small falcon returned, its bright colours dulled to grey with the night, its presence unnatural at this hour. It passed in front of Samantha, then glided towards the Valley edge, stopping as though to check she was following. Samantha took a step towards the small bird, but a noise behind her made her stop.

Tobias was emerging from the shelter, eyes bleary with sleep, but clearing when he saw Samantha preparing to leave once more.

"I woke up and you weren't there." He explained. His gaze scanned the dark Valley, a silver shape was moving from the distant end towards them, a shadow by its side.

"You have to go, don't you?" Tobias asked, guessing further than Samantha had planned.

"I just feel there's something I've gotta find out, I'll be back soon." Samantha reasoned.

He half smiled. "Well, I suppose there's no stopping you. There never is. May Minaeri watch over you."

Tobias lingered, while Alina and Siabhor loped up to them. Samantha mounted the unicorn and the trio of friends moved to leave the Valley. As they reached the borders, Samantha turned to see Tobias return dejectedly to their shelter.

Twenty

As soon as they had set out, the small bird emerged again. It darted swiftly before them and would pass to and fro, steadily leading the trio east. They passed quite close to the enemy camp, but neither person, nor horse stirred. Their winged guide led them hurriedly out of the forest 'til the great wall of the city of Enchena loomed in the darkness, which then receded into shadow behind them.

Samantha was unsure what time they had begun this journey, but by dawn the capital was left far behind and the mighty hills and mountain peaks that had seemed so distant were now standing out clearly before them. None of the travellers had ever been so far east, their faith was completely in their feathered guide.

If Alina or Siabhor were tired, they did not show it, walking and trotting mile after mile. Although the two had become friends, each wanted to prove to the other their stamina, as if they were still natural enemies.

*****

While the most famous trio in the Gardyn army were travelling steadily eastward, the rest of the rebels were waking in the hidden Valley to find their Lost Soul gone. Tobias had of course said goodbye to Samantha during the night, though he had awoken to the hope it was all just some bizarre dream, because he was dreading having to tell Lord Mgair.

He left the shelter and walked dejectedly over to the main council area, wondering what to say. Tobias didn't have long to dawdle, because Mgair had already found out that Samantha was missing and sent a runner to fetch Tobias. The lad came hurriedly towards Tobias, with a worried look.

"Tobias Deorwine, sir. Lord Mgair wishes to see you immediately."

"And I him. Is he in his tent?" Tobias asked.

"Yes sir." The messenger turned on heel and strode through the meeker dwellings, leading Tobias to the main camp. At the opening, he stood aside and let Tobias pass.

Inside, a lamp was still lit, because the sun had yet to shine over the trees into the Valley.

"Did you know, young Deorwine, that the Lady Samantha has gone? She fled during the night." Mgair was sitting in the furthermost corner of the shelter, his voice husky with sleep and disappointment.

"You know already?" Tobias glanced away.

"Aye, that unicorn Autumn came trotting up before dawn asking if Alina was in the encampment. The mare hasn't been seen all night either." Mgair raised himself up and moved threateningly towards the younger man. "Now, if your Lady has run back to Hrafn-"

211

"She hasn't." Tobias cut in. "Be assured, sir, that her absence is innocent, and helpful only to the Gardyn."

Mgair peered suspiciously at Tobias. "You seem well versed in her activities, perhaps you two are traitors together."

"What do you think you are saying?" A furious female voice came from the entrance. Both men turned to see Jillis standing with arms crossed, glaring in at them. "Lord Mgair, I will thank you to not accuse my brother of treason every time you are at a loss."

Mgair was momentarily caught out by the fiery young girl. "I am sorry, but the Lady Samantha is missing again, and your brother seems to be the only one informed."

Jillis glanced at Tobias before facing Lord Mgair again. "Lady Samantha has a will of her own; not my friendship, Tobias, or any wall of soldiers could keep her from whatever duty she has. Surely you would not wish our saviour to be stopped so easily."

Without waiting for a reply, Jillis caught Tobias' sleeve and led him out into the open. She walked, stony faced, until they were away from camp, then she turned to confront her brother.

"What is going on, really?" She asked quietly, dark eyes pleading.

"She's not gone to Hrafn, you can be sure of that. I woke last night to see her leaving with Alina and Siabhor. Something was calling her, I could tell, so I did not stop her."

"I believe you, and in her. Right now, we need to bunker down. There's no way we can defeat Hrafn until more Gardyn come." Jillis shrugged and walked away, the air of a powerful lady fading back to the plain serving girl.

*****

The three travellers continued on their journey, the miles dropping away and the countryside a blur. Their feathered guide led them steadily to the looming hills, avoiding all settlements that were scattered across the land. Rests were brief and few, as urgency drew them on through the day and on into the following night.

At nightfall, Samantha was almost falling from Alina with fatigue of a hard day's riding. Since dawn they had covered many miles eastward and the terrain was becoming uneven with larger hills and valleys rising about them as the introduction to the greater mountains.

The small falcon must have decided it was too dark to continue and perched on a branch of a short, deformed tree in a sheltered lee.

After an undisturbed sleep, they woke again and were led off with the rising of the sun. This day's journey proved to be much shorter than the last, and before midday they had reached their mystery destination.

On the top of a large hill a small house stood, stone walls worn by years of storms and all the weather that the mountain range could bring. The bird flew ahead to the dwelling, leaving the trio of friends to climb cautiously up the slope. As they reached the building, the door flew open and an old man peeked out expectantly. At the sight of the travellers he grinned, his wrinkles deepening; and he signed enthusiastically for them to come closer.

Samantha slipped off Alina's back and stood by Siabhor at the entrance. Now they were on level footing, the old man was distinctly short, nearly a foot shorter than Samantha. He had a crop of wild white hair that fell scraggily past his shoulders and the overall effect of his appearance would have been comical if it hadn't been for his steely grey eyes.

"You've come, you've come! You are late, but at least you are here." The old man said jovially with a clap of his hands. "Come in." He invited Samantha and Siabhor, then looked up to the grey unicorn. "Cousin, I will have to ask you to stay outside, you will not fit!"

He turned and rushed inside, Samantha and Siabhor could do nothing other than follow him. The entrance room would have been considered large, if it had not been cluttered with all manners of equipment, some recognisable for navigation and stargazing but others that Samantha could only guess at. She stood gazing at the contents of the room, then remembered the old man.

"Excuse me." She began, but then had to rush to follow the peculiar white-haired man to the back of the building. "Excuse me, but who are you?"

The old man stopped and turned to face her, bushy white eyebrows frowned at her question, had he forgotten introductions?

"I am called Danu, Erudite and Priest of Minaeri, at your service." He gave a quick little bow, then looked up to her again. "You have met my counterpart in your world surely, you know Elisabeth." His attention was suddenly diverted to Siabhor who was sniffing cautiously at some contraption, and Danu shouted a warning to the mallus, making Siabhor jump back, knocking into other items.

214

Samantha stood, dazed. "Who - who's Elisabeth?"

"She's the gatekeeper." He answered shortly, rearranging his possessions.

"Gran?" Samantha asked, realising that the old woman must have a real name. "Then she meant for me to come here?"

"Yes, yes." The old man replied with frustration. "But you are late and we must get on."

"But what…" Samantha began, but again Danu had wandered off further into the building.

A heavy door stood ajar where Danu had entered another room and Samantha gave it a rough heave open. The sight was very different to the rest of the house, the stone wall was bare and the floor uncluttered. In fact, the only thing that furnished the room was a great stone slab set up like an altar in the middle of the room. The only light available came from candles in this solid room.

"What is this place?" Samantha whispered, afraid to break the silence.

"Come, sit." Danu instructed, his previously cheery face now matching his grave eyes. The old man sat stiffly down before the altar and waited for Samantha to join him. Siabhor lingered uneasily by the door before following like an obedient dog to sit protectively close to the girl.

"I know more than anyone about Minaeri." Danu started quietly, closing his eyes. Before them, Danu seemed to suddenly age and Samantha wondered how old he truly was.

"I have long studied the First War, where the very first beings fought against a great darkness and the

215

victorious heroes were blessed. Our Lady Minaeri, among them.

"I know of her tale in detail. She was the Goddess of Prosperity in another land and allowed her people entrance into Enchena." Danu opened his eyes again and looked sternly at Samantha. "And now you are here to finish her work, for she meant this land to be a happy place." The old man seemed terribly saddened by some knowledge that he did not share.

"But I don't understand. Why me of all people, and how are you so sure?"

The old man shook his head slowly. "The first I cannot answer now, but the fact that you are whom we seek, that is undeniable. You came through the gateway unforced and unaccompanied, true?"

Samantha nodded slightly.

"Only one with... well, with certain attributes can pass in such a way. The only other that can do this is the King of Enchena. You see, you must be our Lost Soul because you were able to pass through alone and unharmed."

Samantha sat, still confused.

"But now, we are wasting time that we do not have if the Gardyn will survive." He said gruffly, "Samantha, Lady of Gardyn, I summoned you here to enlighten you. The danger of the Gardyn; they will be destroyed without your help, and the help of Minaeri. It is my duty to see you receive the knowledge you need."

"You know how we can defeat Hrafn?" Samantha asked eagerly.

Danu's following silence unnerved her, and he slowly shook his head.

"But then, how do I find out?" She asked cautiously.

The old man sighed, "You must pass into another state of consciousness, past life and death. There you will discover what part of you already knows."

"Is it dangerous?"

"I will not deny that there might be implications, but do not worry, you will be guided by - by someone important." Danu struggled up to his feet and Samantha followed suit. "Trust me and everything will be fine." He said, indicating for her to clamber up onto the altar.

Samantha did so and lay her head down on the rough stone surface, feeling terribly nervous yet also excited. At this point Siabhor interrupted, thrusting his hairy face up at Danu in a terrible growl.

"What are you doing?" The mallus demanded.

Danu, who seemed quite unperturbed by this, replied calmly. "Samantha will just fall to sleep for a while, that's all."

Samantha listened to the voices, but already felt herself falling from consciousness. A sudden chill raced through her body as she passed through the states of life and death to awake to another time.

Twenty-one

In the conscious world, Siabhor was left staring uneasily at his friend who lay on the altar, looking as though death had taken her.

"Why don't you go outside? No offence meant sir mallus, but you smell like the pits of death and you make the room stuffy." Danu's sharp voice came.

Siabhor growled unhappily at the old eccentric, but grudgingly moved to leave the stone room. At the door he turned his hairy face back. "How long before she wakes?"

Danu shrugged. "How should I know, it could be a minute, a day, or never." The mallus hissed again, then turned to make his way outside.

Outside, the sun shone down on the unicorn who grazed nervously, often lifting her head and whinnying gently with worry. As the mallus left the house, Alina walked swiftly towards him to hear all he had to tell.

"What you say hardly brings hope to whatever quest we are on." Alina's audible thoughts quivered in the summer air. "Why is she putting herself through this?"

"I do not know, do not know." Siabhor answered, sadly shaking his head. "The mad old man say she must discover something. Something to do with Minaeri."

The unicorn lifted her horned head to the west, her superior sight making out the dark blur on the horizon of the mighty forest of Enchena. "I would stay with Samantha until the land crumbles with age, but I hope we return home much sooner, I miss the others."

The two unlikely friends stood side by side, gazing silently out over the many miles between them and the forest. Alina suddenly gave a whinny of fear.

"What? What is it?" Siabhor wheezed hastily, crouching down protectively to the ground.

"Can you not see?" Alina replied quite distressed, horned head held high with a steady gaze. "To the west there is a shadow on the land, it flies steadily eastward. Something ill comes, we are not safe."

Siabhor moved quickly out of the way of Alina's skittering hooves, then looked across the land with confusion. "You have better sight than I, but perhaps it is just a cloud across the sun."

"No, it moves against the wind, it is a foul omen." The unicorn started backwards, then neighed out with all her strength. "Danu! Oh Praede help us!"

Moments later the old man came rushing out. "What has befallen you, noble cousin, that you would draw me away from the shrine of Minaeri?"

"There is a darkness approaching." She replied quickly, and with a nervous rear she turned to look again to the distance.

"I have not the sight of your kind." The old man murmured, then tottered back into his house, shortly returning with a shiny telescope. He peered through it for quite a while before looking back at his guests, bushy white brows raised in question. "I see nothing, dear Alina, but even my skill cannot compete with the unicorns' when it comes to reading omens. Yet I wonder if you are just a little tense and are reading what is not there."

Alina snorted with frustration. "Danu, O wisest of humans, perhaps it is that my senses are heightened and not deceived. Something foul comes towards us with great speed."

"Oh well, there is nothing we can do but wait and see." Danu replied, exceptionally calm. "Now be still and do not bother me until the enemy is at my gates! I would watch over the Lady Samantha in peace."

*****

Minutes and then hours slowly passed, Danu rarely left Samantha's side, and often Siabhor would enter the stone room to watch over his dormant friend. Alina was resigned to wait outside, and with the summer heat beating down her fears were quieted, almost forgotten.

These three members of the Gardyn were unlucky, and perhaps Alina's warning should have been heeded more readily; or maybe Danu knew how things were to progress and would not want it any different. The afternoon was passing into early evening when in the distance shadowed riders moved with great haste eastward. The light was poor and it was only Alina that could see the dull gleam of royal armour, that was lightweight, made for the messengers of Enchena.

The unicorn's distraught cry brought Danu once more from his vigilance. "Is it come, Praede's daughter?"

220

"Yes, they come, armed men of the King. We must wake Samantha and flee before they reach the hills."

"We cannot wake her, such a thing would kill her." Danu said with a shake of his aged head.

Siabhor came up, growling his displeasure. "These hills offer no hiding, we must leave now or we be cornered in your nest."

Danu did not reply immediately, but looked out thoughtfully to the west. "Alina, dear, how long until they reach us?"

"I would say but an hour." She replied, intrigued.

"Well, hopefully your friend Samantha shall be awake by then, if time is short I know of a secret way through the mountains. It will take you far from the capital, the forest and your friends, but you will not be caught." Danu stood, scratching his coarse chin in thought. "But you, O Star-bright One, get yourself about the back so you do not shine like a beacon! I believe these are only messengers to summon the scattered armies of the King, and they may pass us completely."

Alina obediently trotted to the other side of the house where she continued to fret and worry, even though she could see the danger no more. Siabhor lingered uncomfortably out front, as a shadow himself he would not show up, but he had no wish to remain alone and soon entered Danu's house and curled up outside the stone room like a faithful dog.

*****

At first everything was dark and blurred and Samantha felt as though she were going through some terrible sickness, her senses causing confusion as her mind and body parted.

221

Then everything became clear. She was standing on a cliff, taller than any of comparison, and there was a gentle breeze pulling at her hair and clothes. On the breeze there was a hint of a voice, and as Samantha strained to listen the voice grew louder. It seemed familiar, a woman's voice, but not her mother's as she had first guessed.

As happens in dreams, the words made little sense to the ear, but told a story to the mind. *"Enchena, as it was."*

Around the cliff all was dark, a distant sun started to rise up on the infinitely distant horizon, its rays barely strong enough to light the land below the cliff. But as she gazed down to where the rock receded to darkness, Samantha could see further and further down until eventually she saw a desolate, grey land far below. As dawn came to the grey land, Samantha could make out the bare landscape of the land and what would be large creatures that roamed the rocks and grasslands.

"Inhabited by the great Lords until Minaeri was blessed."

At that point two things happened for Samantha: she was suddenly aware of the entire, terrible tale of the First War where, in another land, the victors were blessed with immortality and their weapons made sacred to become the first Gods; and the land below seemed to rush upwards towards Samantha as though her sight extended and magnified so that the barren land appeared close enough to interact. The strange, roaming creatures were swiftly identified-

"Dragon lords, who fought to extinction."

To Samantha's horror one of the huge reptilian monsters turned and cried a challenge. Now Samantha knew that she was truly at a great distance because the sound delayed in travel, but was not lessened in volume

222

nor lost its terrifying cry, more terrible than anything found in Enchena today. Samantha could not move from it, fear failed to register with her limbs and she was subjected to watch the grappling dragons whose claws were at least as big as the watching girl.

"Minaeri came to an empty land and made it fit for those that worshipped her and wished for space to live."

Then, with time in fast forward the dragons disappeared until only the old bones were left, and even these vanished to form the mighty hills that rose to the east, beyond where the modern capital stood, close to the sea.

Then a figure moved across the land, following a path of sunlight. Samantha's gaze focussed on them, a tall lady riding a unicorn so white everything else became dull as the sun glinted on his coat. Wherever his feet fell plants and trees shot up to cover many empty miles with lush forests and meadows.

The rider had the look of a great lady, but also the appearance of a seasoned and proven warrior with a shining sword by her side. Try as she might, Samantha could not make out this strange lady's face, but as was possible in dreams she instinctively knew that she now beheld the goddess Minaeri on her faithful steed Praede, and that it was Minaeri who lent her voice to guide Samantha.

The goddess now dismounted and the unicorn moved from view. Minaeri drew her sword, a beautifully crafted weapon with a large pale blue jewel inset in the hilt, which she removed from its metal clasp, before sheathing the blade.

The blue stone was lifted in salute to the full moon that hung faintly in the daytime sky. Light flashed through and what Samantha recognised as a portal, forming via the light of the day-moon and blue stone.

"Path to Caelum, people of Minaeri. Come citizens and prosper in the given land."

And although it was impossible to see through the portal, Samantha could clearly see the other land Caelum. On the other side of the portal, people crowded to leave their overpopulated land.

As their pathway opened, people poured in, most spreading far to claim the best land, but one individual had lingered.

"Ragoul, bane of Minaeri - the goddess he adored."

Samantha saw the young man, who would be handsome if his expression were not so dark and hateful. Again, in the way of dreams and visions, Samantha knew that he was a young priest from the Temple of Minaeri who had worshipped the goddess unquestioningly, until a beloved friend and father-figure fell sick and died with prayers unanswered. From then on, Ragoul had studied Minaeri with obsession. In all the worlds and lands, only he knew how to end immortal life and he had the blackened heart to do the deed.

Creeping behind the goddess with silent footfalls, Minaeri wasn't aware of him until it was too late. Ragoul leant forward, tightly gripped her sword hilt and withdrew it quickly. Finally alert to her danger Minaeri spun around to confront him, but Ragoul moved swiftly to thrust Minaeri's own sword into her in a violent attack.

Samantha tried to scream, but her horror did not register and the wind whipped away her breath. A pain was felt in her own heart and she looked down to see her hands clamped to a bleeding chest.

Confusion clouded her thoughts, but her gaze was directed again to the goddess who lay dying in a growing pool of her own blood. The pale blue jewel had been dropped and the portal broken,

"Broken untimely, it now becomes an uncontrolled power loosed to open at random."

Above the fallen Minaeri, Ragoul stood tall and proud, sword still in his grasp, his fervent gaze on his victim. The goddess took one last shuddering breath and lay still. With her death a bright light seemed to descend over her body, two fragments broke away and, shining brightly like two stars, they danced towards the murderous Ragoul and were absorbed.

"Power of the goddess given to her slayer, but fate allows him only to receive the power to give life and control life-giving water. Control of fire, death, destruction and ultimate power remained to the soul."

As with the dragon lords, time sped by. At first slowly, showing the rise of Enchena, then faster and faster. In a blur a temple was set up about the old portal-ground, then aged 'til only two statues remained against the force of time. Ages passed in seconds, then it suddenly stopped. Samantha found herself looking out upon the present-day land. She could see the two armies, currently apart and preparing.

Then she finally found her voice, as words came unbidden. "But where is Minaeri, how does her soul exist?"

In the distance, like a cloud of mist, a pale mass appeared. It rushed forward with amazing speed and became more like a spectre rushing up to Samantha on the cliff, a ghostly face staring out.

"She will come again." The voice said as the misted figure grew increasingly closer and faster. It then grew to an almighty shriek. Samantha awoke with a start, knowing who she was meant to be.

Twenty-two

Cold sweat dampened her forehead and her pulse raced as she thought over the vision. Samantha struggled to sit up and found old Danu supporting her with surprising strength. Siabhor's hairy face peered out from a dark corner of the room and he rushed forward, truly glad to see his friend conscious again.

"Steady now, you've been through a lot and it'll take a moment for you to get your balance, too bad we haven't got a moment to wait." Danu was mumbling, hurrying to help Samantha get up from the altar. "Siabhor, dear monster. Go out; see where the riders do travel, and tell Alina your friend is awake."

Samantha watched with blurred vision as the mallus left, his hard claws scraping wildly on the stone surfaces. Samantha looked down at Danu, who stood barely shoulder height to her.

"What's going on?" She asked groggily.

"Messengers of the King are travelling east." Danu began, helping Samantha to walk slowly out of the room and outside. "They are not hunting for you, but I fear

227

they will come here as the only shelter, demanding beds for the night."

The old man continued talking as he led the still sleepy Samantha to the fenced off area behind the house where the ground met the first real tor of the mountains. "And I'm afraid there is no time for you to escape to the west, so your journey is to be much longer, and darker."

They made their way to a tumbled pile of rocks where Alina and Siabhor waited nervously. Already the heavy beat of fast horses could be heard by the small party.

"I have packed you as much as I can spare, now you must go." With difficulty, Danu slung a bag over Alina's high back and Samantha waited with confusion at how they would pass and escape with the rocky tor in the way.

Her bewilderment was greater as Siabhor moved forward on all fours and seemed to disappear into the rocks and debris, even moving round Samantha could see no way through. Then Alina followed Siabhor's path and a concealed, twisting entrance became apparent. Samantha followed on, as she slid through the crevice all light was blocked and she had to move slowly, hands outstretched in the darkness. Further on the walls moved out and she could no longer touch them and fear started to well up inside her.

Ahead of Samantha a glimmer appeared. Even in the pitch black the unicorn held the quality of shimmering as a dim star. Alina let out a friendly whinny, but the sound was distorted and echoed through the stony area to give a terrible, unearthly sound.

Siabhor started and his claws scattered across the stone, and his low hissing of displeasure could be heard.

"Where are we, and where are we going?" Samantha murmured, afraid of setting off echoes.

"There are Hrafn's messengers abroad so we cannot return immediately eastward. Danu has told that this tunnel, though long, will lead us to safety way from the greatest danger." Alina's passing thoughts seemed to shout out in the silence of the rocky tunnel yet remained clear and without echo, which made Samantha marvel again at the unicorn's form of communication, as she had at their first meeting.

"First a stinking city, then tunnels, bare land, more dark tunnels…" Siabhor grumbled unhappily to himself. "And now we go to danger, so the old madman says!"

As a shadow he could not be seen, but the girl and unicorn could hear him starting away through the darkness, obviously mallus had the quality of seeing through any darkness. Samantha clambered onto Alina's back and the unicorn slowly following the mallus into the black tunnel ahead.

*****

The dark trek took what seemed a long time, away from sunlight the travellers could only guess at time and distance though they covered many miles. At first the tunnel had gone straight and made easy travelling, but then it began to slope and twist about yet continued east. The trio kept doggedly on, short walks with brief stops when they were tired, or found the path particularly difficult.

How many hours had passed in slow, stumbling darkness, how many miles passed by the tired feet, hooves and claws. Samantha did not know whether she was conscious or still asleep as she trudged along in

229

monotonous blackness, no sound other than the repetitive tapping of hoof and claw, no sight other than the ghostly glimmer of Alina who continued to shine in the lightless tunnels.

As they moved on, constantly eastward, it got warmer and warmer within the cavern, and with no movement of wind it became quite stuffy. Maybe it was just their desperate desire to see light once more that tricked their eyes, but there seemed to be the faintest light. Samantha was just able to make out Siabhor's outline against the lighter rock.

"Maybe we're coming to the end." Samantha ventured in a timid voice that seemed to shout through the silence in which they had been travelling in for so long.

With lighter hearts and more hopeful spirits that they were nearing the end of their terrible dark journey, they laboured on. Then they stopped. The ground had started to shake and from far ahead came a terrifying, roaring noise.

Alina whinnied with fear and Siabhor leapt and tried to scramble up the rock wall.

"The earth will crumble!" He barked. And true, the tremors were shaking loose rubble from the top of the tunnel onto the frightened trio. Then as suddenly as it had started, it stopped.

They all stood still for quite a while, terrified that they may upset the balance of the tunnel. Finally Siabhor spoke in his hissing whisper. "We must go back, there be nothing but danger ahead."

Samantha, who was wondering where she had heard such a noise before took a while to reply, and murmured. "No, we must definitely go forward."

The light grew stronger and the heat more intense as they moved on. Samantha had dismounted from Alina's back, trusting her sight now to keep her feet from stumbling. Siabhor no longer ran ahead of them, but crept slowly, unsurely, often trying to find purchase on the walls that gleamed strangely black and crumbled from beneath his claws like charcoal.

No more roars echoed down the tunnel, but small tremors often occurred. The light was yellowy-red, and it was strong enough now to see perfectly well along their rocky path.

Alina had trotted ahead to look at something that had caught her eye and she whinnied back to the others. Samantha approached curiously to see Alina gazing at a large slab of marbled rock that stood out clean and clear against the scorched rock surrounding it.

"Do those marks have meaning?" Alina asked with great interest, her pearly horn tracing the deep grooves.

Samantha inched round until she could easily see the words engraved into the marble. "Yes, it's writing, but I don't know what language, I've never seen this type before -" She paused, tilting her head and frowning in concentration - the style seemed strangely familiar - as she looked it was as though the lines moved to appear legible. "Wait!" Samantha cried out. "It - it says,

We who reigned for many years,
Tyrants o'er a desert land.
Though come to light our greatest fears;
As the reptilian realm was man'd

"Though given o'er to human tale,
Yet Our kind shall ne'er fail.
Beware …"

231

Samantha stopped and gazed at the tablet, "The - the rest seems to be worn away." She muttered, but fell silent as the words before her lost meaning.

Siabhor grunted unhappily. "It is clear though, it is telling that we should beware what is ahead and return to the west where we are wanted."

Samantha ignored him and looked to Alina, who seemed to read her thoughts.

"There are no stories told of these eastern lands, except that somewhere there is a large stretch of water they call the Sea. I did not even know these tunnels existed."

Samantha nodded and continued down the strangely lit path, she did not tell the others, but she felt a sense of foreboding, as though she knew what was ahead…

Confidence was very low in the small party; Siabhor, the most obviously afraid, skittered and hissed at the slightest sound or tremor of the ground. Alina seemed to be walking along very calmly, but her thoughts seeped out.

"In their wake a forest rose up…"

Samantha realised that she was repeating stories to herself, to take her mind off of the situation. Only the thought that she had to be strong for the others was stopping Samantha from sprinting back down the tunnel as she had wanted to do since reading from the tablet. On they trudged, the tunnel that had seemed to be so close about them before, now widened and grew tall enough to create shadows in the juts of rock. The ground was strangely warm underfoot, all the signs came together to make Samantha steadily less easy, for surely she already knew what they were to soon come across.

Finally, they came to the source of all the noise, heat and light. It was more terrible and horrifying than anything Alina or Siabhor could have conceived. The tunnel in which they had been travelling for so long led to a cavernous void, large enough to fit a small city within, and it was bathed in a reddish light that emanated from one of the occupants...

The three travellers stared up, feeling themselves shrink into insignificance. Samantha was left speechless as she stood in the strange warmth that suddenly swept over her, mixed with an icy breeze that made her feel as though she were running a fever. Surely not, these creatures had died out thousands of years ago. Yet, here, in the middle of the monstrous cavern, circling a large underground valley of grass were two great lords of ancient times...

Twenty-three

Dragons.

Huge beasts beyond the comprehension of mortals, they towered to titanic heights, their huge reptilian bodies shrank all surroundings out of proportion. The two dragons were more amazing and more horrific than imagination allowed, the heads were armed with deadly horns and folds in scaly armour, the elongated necks swayed above massive, lizard-like bodies that were carried about the underground plain by strong, sturdy legs and incredible claws and talons. To finish the mythical picture, above their shoulders sprouted huge leathery wings that folded tightly about the spine unless they used them for balance.

One great beast was the colour of sunset, blood red and tinged with darkness. From him came the reddish glow as the furnace within him shone out through hide and scale. The other beast was of winter hue, pale grey, white and blue. Curiously, from him came frost and icy-cold that conflicted his companion's heat.

The dragons at first seemed oblivious to the three strangers and instead appeared to be in the middle of a battle, mighty streams of flame would erupt from the red dragon, some scorching his opponent, but many missing for the white dragon was well practised in dodging and would throw out a blast of ice in an attempt to put out that eternal furnace of his foe. Both were equally matched in all movement, cunning and force. Sometimes flame and ice would meet and form a temporary globe that remained only as long as the dragons provided its source.

Eventually the prehistoric lords were aware of the presence of the strangers and they stopped amidst their thunderous battle, staring down with wonder at the trio. Fearsome heads the size of large vans were lowered almost to the ground so that the glassy eyes could scrutinise the intruders.

"You have come." The first words came like rumbling thunder, from the open beak of the white dragon.

"Then again, the truth-"

"Was so clear that the future-"

"Could not be misread."

Samantha stood speechless, her head spinning. The two Dragon Lords had spent so long in their cavern, words and thoughts were predicted and shared precisely and each finished the other's sentences.

"Greetings to the Great Lords of both past and present." Samantha shouted up, thinking back on terms of her dreams and an inner courtesy that began to emerge. "I am Samantha, Lady to Gardyn, Lost Soul to Enchena."

"Your salutations and titling-"

"Are most correct, but we-"

"Do not care for mortal names,"

"We know who and what you are."

The dragons peered down, their fierce, scaly faces closer to the peculiar trio than they would have liked.

"She is one of Minaeri's." The pale dragon said abruptly, staring with glassy eyes towards Alina.

"But he is one of Her Foe's." The red dragon added, glaring at Siabhor with narrowed eyes.

"Yet they are both dear to Minaeri reborn." Samantha spoke up adamantly.

The dragons moved back, apparently satisfied.

"Then they may stay. I am Leukos, and-"

"I am Caminus." The red dragon finished.

"Yes…" Samantha replied hesitantly. "Well, this is Alina, descendant of Praede, and Siabhor, who has become equally noble. We came this way be-"

"Because you did not wish to meet your foes."

"Yes, even though encased under stone and mountain, we see all."

Samantha was baffled, Alina and Siabhor even more so. "I don't understand. All the dragons died."

"No, we survived, we-"

"Were the strongest of our kind,"

"None could defeat-"

"Us. We survived when all-"

"Others fought to extinction. When the goddess Minaeri-"

"Came, we agreed to live in peace with the humans who would-"

"Occupy our land. We sought sanctuary within the mountains."

The dragons fell silent after the brief tale, allowing their information to sink in.

"Our age is great." The red dragon finally said. "And so is our wisdom,"

"Add to that our insight." Leukos continued with a nod of his scaly head. "This is why you have come to us."

"I don't understand, we only came this way-"

"You came because fate directed you here." Caminus interrupted Samantha.

"You have questions, and there are things-"

"That you must know to survive your war."

Samantha stared, open-mouthed at the two beasts, her neck aching from looking up for so long. "I do have questions, but there are so many and I'm afraid to know the answers."

"Only three of the questions you have in your mind are worthy, ask wisely and we will answer as only we can." Leukos informed.

"Only three? How can I choose three from the hundreds I have?" Samantha muttered to herself. Her mind reeled, taking her back home, reminding her of her journeys that brought her here. Foremost in her mind was David, the boy she had had a crush on, the first person she had ever seen die.

"David." Samantha murmured, she blinked away the unshed tears and looked up pleadingly to the dragons. "Is there any hope for him?" She shouted out.

"No." Caminus answered simply.

"What, no explanation?" Samantha gasped. "Wait, that wasn't a question. But I do want to know why David can't be saved."

Caminus and Leukos growled and looked to each other, then nodded unwillingly. Leukos lowered his ice-blue head to answer her, uninterrupted by his companion. "The answer you seek is almost as important as the meaning of life, for this involves the meaning of Birth and Death. When an individual is born, he or she is completely pure. By this I do not mean they are entirely good, or entirely evil. Instead, they are untainted by ideas of right and wrong, the way the great Creator intended all life to be. It is through life, and choices that a person becomes good or bad, and it is in Death that these measures are important.

"When a person dies, their soul retains all the good that they have amassed over their life and all evil remains in the body which rots away. Then the soul is free to ascend to what you call Heaven. The better the person, the better the afterlife for that individual."

Samantha stood speechless, taking in what information she could, there were so many things she wanted to ask at this point, but she held her tongue for fear of wasting her granted questions.

"It is within the power of all gods and goddesses to create life." Leukos continued. "But there is a reason that life should not be restored to those already passed on. When your friend David died, all the good within him was released with his soul. The human King merely brought his body and spirit back to life, which means all that was good about the boy is forever gone and he has been left as a shell, full of all the evil and hatred he has incurred within his life. The David you knew will never return." The dragon finished, lifting his head back up to the dizzy heights of the cavern.

Samantha wavered slightly in her stance. She controlled her expression, careful to keep looking composed; the opposite of what she felt inside. Perhaps she had asked the wrong question, perhaps she had wasted one precious answer, but she had needed to know before she could move on. Now she turned her thoughts to the serious task of phrasing the question that now burned in her mind. "What will happen to the Gardyn if we remain in Enchena and fight Hrafn?"

This time there was no conference on whether or not to answer this question, and both dragons reacted immediately. Samantha jumped back with fright as the two great beasts backed away from one another, the grumbling, growling noise within them increased, as though they were calling up on all their energies. Caminus shot out a huge burst of flame and Leukos caught it with an icy blast. A globe of molten liquid and shimmering ice formed, but unlike the smaller ones the trio of friends had seen, this one lingered and blurry images could be seen. Samantha concentrated on it and the images sharpened, she could see the forests, and Autumn's Valley. The viewpoint shifted and she could now see the Gardyn forming, preparing for battle. There were hundreds of them, many more than when Samantha had left, and all were now well armed.

Her gaze shifted to the front of the lines, where the horsemen were mounting, Samantha searched and saw a single girl within the group. It was herself, but not as she remembered; neither as the scared schoolgirl back home, nor as the aloof lady that she had become in Hrafn's palace. Instead she saw the image of a tested warrior, her pale face showing courage and defiance. There was no sound to the image, but noise would have been unnecessary, Samantha knew enough of war now to see that the Gardyn were mounting a desperate and final attack on Hrafn while he was relatively vulnerable.

The image blurred and time shifted forward, Samantha could again make out herself, sword elevated as she helped rally the troops as they were hopelessly overcome by the King's men. A hail of arrows came from overhead, and many uniformed soldiers fell to the bloody battleground; Jillis and the archers were shooting furiously into areas of packed uniforms from their positions in the trees. They were so engaged in their task that they were unaware of the approach from behind them. Many were killed in the boughs that they rested on, but Jillis, whose attacker was so surprised to find a young girl here, was knocked backwards and fell twenty feet or more to the rugged ground. Though the images were noiseless, Samantha knew that Jillis had landed with a heavy thud, and that noise would have been lost in the din of battle.

The Samantha in the vision threw herself from Legan and pushed through to get to her fallen friend. Three soldiers fell by her sword by the time she had reached Jillis. The young girl was on the ground, her shallow breathing irregular. The vision moved higher, as though from a bird's eye, and though the distance had increased, Samantha could still make out every detail of what was shown:

Hrafn had been prepared and brought in more archers, the ground was covered with blood and the bodies of Gardyn;

Men with long spears made their final deadly strike on a once beautiful silver unicorn who was already splashed with her own bright blood;

240

An opportunist mallus attempted to flee the fray, and almost succeeded, when three arrows in his back brought him down.

All these visions of horror, Samantha watched. The battle had been pitifully short and now all surviving Gardyn were on their knees in lines before Enchenian soldiers. A girl, who had just watched her best friends die, was brought forward to Hrafn, then led away towards the capital city. Hrafn was giving a speech, but Samantha could not hear his words, the King then turned, an order was given and all the Enchenian soldiers stepped forward with swords raised. The real Samantha closed her eyes as a hundred blades met a hundred rebel necks...

"They will fall." Caminus began.

"So far only luck and blessings have delayed their destruction,"

"But even with reinforcements, the King's army-"

"Will defeat them, then claim the powers of your Soul. Their only chance is to reform-"

"Out of the reach of even Hrafn." Caminus finished abruptly, and both dragons stared at Samantha with those huge, glassy, unblinking eyes.

Samantha's breathing became shallow, she was not surprised to find her cheeks wet with tears. She worried for her friends, she wished they were safe. She wished, not for the first time, that she was back home in Yorkshire. One question was left for her, her mind raced again, this time her memory took her back, not so long ago, to the vision she had had of Minaeri and the portal to Caelum. Perhaps there was hope there. She looked up, and was surprised to see truth in the large crystalline eyes of Caminus and Leukos.

241

"Where is the blue stone of the day-moon?" She asked, almost without realising she did so.

If a dragon could smile, Caminus and Leukos would have done so, instead their scaly mouths opened stiffly to reply. "The stone was reset into the sword, belonging to Minaeri, that had been dubbed Black Hart and taken by he who would become the human King of Enchena. He did not know what power could lay in it now the goddess was dead, otherwise he would have dealt with it differently."

"As it was." Leukos continued Caminus's tale. "The man kept it 'til his death and it remained by his tomb in the Temple of Gates-"

"Until the temple wore down with age and the sword was placed with honour in the treasury of the King."

"It lays there still, rusted, its purpose and meaning forgotten, awaiting Minaeri to claim it once more."

Samantha listened, no longer needing the ball of flame and ice, but receiving her own images of the young Ragoul taking the sword of Minaeri's, she saw him age and finally die at the hand of his own son so that he could pass on the powers he had gained. She saw the sword, which was once a shining beacon covered in rust and dust and left to be forgotten in the palace treasury.

She blinked, knowing what she had to do. If the Gardyn were no longer safe within the King's domain, perhaps it was time to take them out of Enchena. Samantha innately knew that the gate to Caelum could be resurrected if only she had that stone. She glanced behind, Alina and Siabhor had backed away to the rocky wall, leaving Samantha isolated.

"We need to get back to Hrafn's palace." She called back to them. Looking up to the dragon lords she shouted out. "Caminus, Leukos. You are truly great lords of the eternal ages, but now we must hurry home. If there is anything we can ever do for you…" Her voice trailed off.

The two dragons nodded their appreciation to her kind words. "All we ask is that our existence is kept secret." Caminus replied.

Samantha bowed down, then returned to her friends, she looked into the tunnel before her with regret. One more long, lightless journey. Her hand reached out and rested on Alina's wither, the mare's grey coat felt rough with the dried sweat of fear for Samantha and what she had seen.

"Let's go back home." Samantha said quietly. Siabhor immediately responded and bounded happily away from the great beasts that inhabited the underground cavern.

"Wait." Leukos demanded with a small roar. "Your path is no longer dark."

"To return to your friends in time you must go over land, not under it."

"Cross to the other side of our confines and you shall find a narrow passage-"

"That will lead you out into the light. That path, though unknown to you will be swifter."

Samantha stood silently, then looked across the area, the other side was cloaked in shadow, even with the dragon's strong light. "We thank you again." She said distractedly, then began to walk straight past the dragons.

Alina and Siabhor looked at each other hopelessly, then followed on. The ground beneath them cracked with their steps, threatening to collapse into dust with their weight. They worried unnecessarily though, for the scorched ground supported the dragons so easily, the weight of the three friends was quite insignificant. The area was almost a mile long and they were continuously walking into shadow as they moved away from the dragons with Caminus' red light and Leukos' paler light.

Eventually, they reached the solid wall of the cavern again, their eyes scanned the dimness for the passage the dragons had mentioned. It was Siabhor who spotted it first, a gaping opening that was large enough for all three to move comfortably through; although it would be a very tiny crack for a dragon. A slight breeze came from the tunnel, the fresh air bringing hope to the trio, and a greater longing to see the sky and feel the wind once more. They set off into the tunnel with the happy knowledge that they were going home. This short journey was monotonous, every step just as the last, yet the enticing breeze leading them tirelessly on.

Twenty-four

One last turn of the tunnel and the trio were blinded by the light, there was no hesitation as all three rushed to leave the tunnels that had confined them for so long. At this point, one last, horrific bellow came from below and loose dirt began to shake from the walls. The rush of joy became a rush of fear and the trio scrambled to leave the crumbling tunnel. Stumbling, they made it into the sun, covered with dust. Behind them, the walls seemed to stabilise for a moment, then caved in, closing all access to the mythical dragons deep within.

All stepped blinking into the early morning sun, a cold wind whipping at their hair, fur and clothes. As Samantha's eyes adapted to the light she looked about her in amazement, it seemed that all the world lay before her, they were high on a mountain that was set on an island with hills that ran steeply to dark blue waters. As she looked to her left, across the sea, Samantha could make out the coast of what she guessed was mainland Enchena. She struggled to remember all that she had heard back in Autumn's Valley, Rian had told her once of the lay of the lands: *'And off the coast of our country, a Drake Island, used only as a port, as Mount Draco takes up most of it…'*

"Drake Island." Samantha murmured with wonder. She stepped forward and was surprised to find her foot crunching through freshly fallen snow. "Surely it's not winter already!" She exclaimed.

Alina had dropped her head, snuffling at the snow which lay no deeper than an inch. "It is a warning that winter will come early this year, and the snow will be heavy." Alina replied in her own fashion, "But do not worry, this snow will melt as morning moves on. Winter will not truly be here for a couple of moons."

Samantha nodded, but shivered in the cold morning breeze. She looked out again, narrowing her eyes against the bright light that bounced off the snow and near the shore, where the land flattened, Samantha could see a town and port.

"Alina, be careful not to be seen." She said hurriedly.

Alina shook her head. "We are too far, and the snow hides my form."

Samantha realised she was right and continued looking down at the port-town, wondering and hoping. "We'll have to go by sea to get back home. That means going down to the town." She looked about. "Siabhor!"

At her call the hairy monster of a mallus bounded back into sight, his elongated limbs splaying in the thin covering of white snow, Siabhor was obviously elated to be above ground once more. He looked up to Samantha and Alina with his ugly face and grinned, baring his sharp, yellowing teeth.

"We will be back home soon, yes?"

Samantha grimaced. "I'm not sure. But there's a town down there where we can find out how soon we can get back to Enchena."

Siabhor's face fell and he stood up on his hind legs, looking down the slope of the mountain to the town that lay by the port. He hissed and crouched down again. "I is not going into human places again." He spat adamantly.

"For Minaeri's sake, Siabhor! I'm not asking you to. Imagine the reaction if I walked into the town accompanied by a unicorn and a mallus!" Samantha retorted. "Anyway, we don't even know if there are any Gardyn there. I'm guessing the best way would be to try some passwords in the taverns, Rian says that's usually where you can find help." She continued talking, as though to herself, then her eyes flicked up to look at her friends. "If we go down the mountain, I'll head to the town alone, you two will have to hide in the trees again."

*****

The town was only a few miles from where they had come out of the mountain and the downhill journey made the walk a lot less arduous for the tired travellers. Samantha often glanced behind her and was surprised how concealed the tunnel entrance had been, now all that showed to a keen eye was the sign of fresh rubble seeping out of heavy foliage. They had been making their own tracks through the forest, but were unworried about getting lost with such an obvious descent. Soon, though, they came upon old trails and paths that must have been made by the island inhabitants, but little used. They followed one of the most worn paths as it threaded through the forested

247

slopes of the mountain down towards the village. Soon it was time for Samantha to leave her friends in the safety of the trees and carry on alone, wishing that she had not left her sword back home in the Valley.

The town was still in the cold, early morning and the ships strained against their ropes in the dock. Samantha looked around as she walked along the cobbled streets; the few people out and about ignored her as they got on with daily life. Samantha looked at every sign above every door, hoping that Gardyn rules applied to the island also.

Finally, she found what she was looking for. With a final glance at the murky sign, she pushed open the heavy tavern door and stepped in, the fishy stench of the harbour was overtaken by the smell of ale, food and tobacco. She looked about, due to the early hour the place was almost empty. Samantha set her face to appear unemotional and unafraid, a handy trick picked up from city life back home. She walked over to the bar and leant on the smooth wooden surface, waiting for the worker's attention. The man behind the bar was short and stocky, looking both fat and strong, his hair was receding to leave a bald area on top of his head and his eyes had the sharp, wary look so common in Enchena.

"Can I help you love?" He grunted, his straying eyes making Samantha uncomfortable. "You look like you need feeding up."

"No, that's okay. I don't have any money. I'm looking f-"

"Between you and me love, you don't have to pay by money." He said slowly, his chubby, worn face with leering eyes leaning forward.

Samantha was disgusted. "Ew! No. Will you just tell me where I can find Bern's uncle." She replied angrily.

The barman shrugged. "Don't know of no uncle, but his aunt's in the back. I'll go fetch her while you think some more."

Samantha was extremely glad to see the barman turn and go and she sat facing the wall until she heard him return.

"This is the lass, I just hope your nephew don't come in, Minaeri knows we've had enough vagabonds wanting you lately because of him."

"That's enough." A deep, female voice commanded. Samantha turned to see quite a hefty woman with thick muscles under her men's clothing and sharp eyes that bore into Samantha's. "I guess you'll be wanting a back parlour to talk." She said, and without waiting for a reply led off through a far door.

Samantha followed her into a room furnished with a large wooden table and chairs. The woman held open the door for her, then glanced outside before pushing it shut and sliding the latch across securely.

"You'd think we'd have a better passphrase. All it takes is for one curious person to find out that Bern was an old Gardyn conman and we're all exposed." The woman complained, then stared at Samantha who had seated herself at the table. "My name's Rosa. And you are?"

"Um... Lucy." Samantha lied. "Lucy Smith." Perhaps it was better to leave the name of Samantha behind, even with other Gardyn.

"Well Lucy, you look famished. It's a bit early for it, but I'll be back with stew, and then we'll talk." Rosa left, locking the door behind her, leaving Samantha all alone. She wasn't long in returning with a large bowl of steaming hot stew and what seemed like a whole loaf of bread. Samantha hadn't realised how hungry she was and quickly tore into the meal.

Rosa sat down and looked at Samantha strangely. "You know, I've been thinking. There aren't many Smiths on this island and I can't place you with any of them."

"No, I'm actually from the mainland. From Enchena."

Rosa looked at the girl with interest. "Really? Then you must tell me all of what's happening there."

Samantha hesitated, then slowly told all that had happened as though she had merely heard of it. Rosa listened patiently as the girl paused every now and then to eat and think ahead in her story. By the time Samantha had finished she had wiped her bowl clean, Rosa leant back in her seat looking plainly amazed.

"Well I never! I had heard rumours of a Gardyn uprising, but I never would have guessed…"

Samantha fidgeted uncomfortably, there were parts of her fabricated story that would still reveal her.

"... the Lost Soul, eh? The Lady Samantha. I bet she's a grand one." Rosa blinked and seemed to come out of her reverie. "Forgive me. I'm sure you didn't come here just to update me on mainland happenings."

"Oh yes... I mean no." Samantha stumbled. "I was hoping you could help me. I desperately need to get back to Enchena and by sea would be quickest, but I don't know who to trust."

Rosa sat with her arms crossed, looking thoughtful. "Well, any boat would take you, they don't exactly oppose the King, but the fact that you're Gardyn won't worry them." The woman peered at Samantha. "But I wouldn't trust some of the captains with a lass like you. I know! Captain Muggahan, on the Gilded Rose. That's the closest thing we've got to Gardyn, and they're all respectable on that ship."

Rosa smiled at Samantha, but the lass appeared rather uncomfortable. "What's wrong, Lucy?"

"Oh, it's just that there's some special... um, cargo. I want it to be safe and... and no questions asked."

The girl looked so afraid at this point that Rosa was unsure what to say. "It's nothing... illegal, is it?"

"By Minaeri, no!" Exclaimed Samantha. She paused, wondering how to phrase it. "It's just that some people wouldn't understand, might even be afraid."

Rosa shrugged. "Well, as long as you're not packing one of our mythical dragons or something to take home with you, I don't see the problem." The older woman laughed at Samantha's worried face. "Come now, surely whoever you're working for wouldn't give you cargo impossible to ship."

"That's the thing, I didn't know we'd come overseas - I mean, I'd come..." Samantha kept her eyes on the older woman, hoping her hurried sentence had not revealed too much.

"But Lucy, my dear, we are on an island. The only way on or off is by boat." She stared back at the girl. "How *did* you get here then?"

"I walked. There was a tunnel that ran from the mainland range to this mountain, but it's caved in now." Samantha replied, trying to sound as though it was nothing.

"Draco mountain?" Rosa sounded amazed. "But that's a volcano! How, by Minaeri, was it safe?"

"A-a volcano?" Samantha mumbled weakly.

"Aye. Not that it's erupted for as long as we can remember, but it's always rumbling and threatening."

"Oh." Samantha suddenly realised that the dragons had been mistaken for lava activity. She paused, wondering whether or not to correct Rosa, but remembered her promise to Caminus and Leukos. She looked back at Rosa and shrugged. "The lava pool must be very deep. I was in no danger. But it is still impossible for me to take that route home."

"What with it being caved in? I guess it would be quicker by sea anyway. Very well, when do you want to leave?"

"As soon as possible."

Rosa paused, thinking. "Captain Muggahan is usually in here 'bout midday. You can speak to him yourself."

"Is it possible for me to stay here 'til then?" Samantha asked half-heartedly.

"Of course." Rosa stood up, collected Samantha's bowl and spoon and left, locking the door behind her.

*****

Samantha had spent so much time around Gardyn in the past months that she had picked up their fear of betrayal. As soon as Rosa left, Samantha ran over and checked the door. Locked. She paced the room, perhaps Rosa had locked her in to keep her safe from others, perhaps the older woman had guessed who she really

252

was and had gone to fetch soldiers, or others faithful to the King.

Samantha rushed over to the tiny single window of the room, it was unlocked. She pushed it open, but it jarred and would open no more. The fishy stench of the port flooded in, making Samantha nauseous, so she yanked the window until it was closed again, then huddled into a corner to await her fate.

Time passed slowly, and eventually, by the light filtering through the window, Samantha could tell that it was midday. Yet still Rosa did not return. Another hour dragged by and Samantha was growing hungry again, she went and tried the door again with despair. As she turned the latch there was a click and the door was wrenched from her grasp.

Samantha jumped back, eyes wide with fear and surprise. She reached instinctively for her sword, forgetting that she had left it behind.

A stranger entered, a short stocky man with dark, yet greying hair. Rosa followed in afterwards, pausing to lock the door behind her.

"Captain Muggahan, this is Lucy Smith. Lucy, this is the captain of the Gilded Rose."

Samantha didn't reply, but looked to Captain Muggahan, whose dark beady eyes glared out from a weathered face.

"You'll be the lass that wants to Enchena, eh?" The captain asked gruffly. "What's this cargo then? I don't like secrets on my boat."

Samantha dropped her gaze. "If you promise that you will take it, I will tell you, even show you if you want."

The captain moved over to a chair and sat down. He looked up to Samantha and shook his head sadly. "I make no such promise. Now it is up to you to reveal your secret, you have nothing to lose."

Samantha glanced about, she didn't want to say too much in front of unnecessary persons, and Rosa was still in the room, lapping up all information. "It's live cargo, waiting beyond the town to be collected. They're perfectly safe and follow my wishes."

Captain Muggahan also looked towards Rosa and knew instantly that Samantha would not say anything in front of the barmaid. He sighed and stood up. "Well, let us see this 'live cargo' and I will judge for myself the danger."

Rosa hurried to unlock the door and stood aside to let them out. When passing her, Samantha smiled hopefully. "No chance of some dinner?"

*****

Samantha left the inn, stomach full and hopes high. As she marched quickly towards the edge of town, Captain Muggahan matched her stride and asked no questions. Walking uphill, it took longer to cross the fields and reach the trees. As they approached, Samantha caught sight of a familiar silver flash and smiled, beside her Captain Muggahan was looking expectantly about him.

"Hey, Alina, Siabhor. I'm back." Samantha shouted out. As she stepped within the trees' shadows.

The beautiful grey unicorn came towards them. "Samantha, I was growing worried. Who is this?" Alina turned her horned head to the captain.

Captain Muggahan stood wide-eyed, his breathing quickened. He shook his head, the unfamiliar sensation of unicorn telepathy disturbing him.

"You should know not to worry about me." Samantha replied with a smile. "And this is Captain Muggahan, he owns the ship that'll take us back to the mainland." She glanced to the captain hopefully.

Captain Muggahan cleared his throat and regained his composure. "Of course, unicorns are most welcome aboard the Gilded Rose." His eyes narrowed as he stared at the girl. "Samantha, eh? I was told your name was Lucy."

"Oh shit." Samantha muttered. "Long story. Um, Alina, where's Siabhor?"

Alina snorted. "Out hunting." She replied with disgust.

"I thought that unicorns were herbivorous. Why would one want to hunt?" Questioned Captain Muggahan.

"Ah, well, Siabhor isn't exactly a unicorn." Samantha phrased delicately.

Alina snorted again. "He is nothing like a unicorn." She added with a backward flick of her ears.

"What is he then?" Captain Muggahan asked suspiciously.

"Um, have you heard of…" Samantha paused and took a deep breath. "Have you heard of mallus? The thing is, they're not a fairytale and one of them is our friend."

A clicking noise originated from the deeper forest and all other noise was stilled, all birds and creatures were quieted to an eerie silence as the rapping of wood drew nearer. Samantha and Alina were unperturbed, but the captain tensed and stared with horror. The source of the noise and atmosphere swung down from the high branches and landed in front of the captain.

Captain Muggahan gasped in horror and drew his sword. The large, spindly creature crouched before him, murky hair bristling as it growled through a blood-stained mouth.

"No!" Samantha shouted, running forward. "Siabhor stop it. Captain Muggahan, sir, this is Siabhor, he is a mallus and my friend. I trust him completely."

Captain Muggahan paused, the young girl who had seemed so nervous and afraid, now stood up to him without hesitation. He nodded and released his grip on his hilt.

"And I thought that mallus existed only in children's nightmares. Very well, you seem to have control of the creature. But with these on board, I can only trust a skeleton crew." Muggahan looked thoughtfully down to the town. "It would be near impossible to get them through the town, even at night. There is a cove, deep enough for my ship to anchor, a couple of miles south in the shadow of Mount Draco. Meet us there at sunset."

Twenty-five

The sun, low in the sky, turned the rippling waves of the sea to an orange-red gleam, the few clouds in the inky sky reflected the colour until everything faded to dusk. In the hour that is between day and night, a small ship pulled into a cove of Drake Island and moored, two sturdy boats then made for the shore. As they crunched onto the gravel, a man stepped out of the lead boat and left the others to secure them, he stroked his dark beard and looked about, questioning this rendezvous.

Almost immediately a young lass stepped out from her shelter to greet him. Behind her, walking with nervous fire was the most beautiful creature in existence, a silvery unicorn upon whom all the stars trained their gaze. Hardly visible, there was also a large shadow, moving irregularly across the ground.

The men by the boats stared, they had been warned by their captain, but nothing could have prepared them for this sight. They tried to hide their apprehension though, and said nothing as they loaded their peculiar guests; the unicorn in one boat, the girl and the monster in the other.

Eventually, with a little manual effort, they were all aboard the main ship.

All three passengers found the motion of the ship unnerving, and as the crew cast off, poor Siabhor panicked and clambered up the mast - the most tree-like structure the monster could see. This of course made the look-out very unhappy, but the lad feared Captain Muggahan's anger much more than a tamed monster.

Alina had sensibly lain down out of the way of everyone, so as to minimise the rocking she experienced.

Samantha stood at the edge of the deck, gripping the rails with both hands and staring ahead as the Gilded Rose sailed into oncoming darkness, trying to forget the queasy feeling in her stomach.

"Here you go lass." Captain Muggahan made Samantha jump as he held out a mug of murky liquid. "It'll help with the seasickness."

Muggahan frowned as the pale-faced girl took the drink gratefully; in his point of view, lasses were best left ashore.

Samantha took a sip, the liquid was warm and bitter, making her pull a face of dislike, but it lay heavy inside her and calmed her stomach.

"So." Muggahan began gruffly, his arms crossed and his balance perfect against the waves. "Here we are, out at sea. The Lady Samantha and no one to aid her."

Samantha started as she realised what he had just said. She looked worriedly towards the captain and began stumbling over her words. "S... Samantha? You must be mistaken, my name is -"

"I know what you said your name was. But even if the unicorn hadn't let it slip, I could have guessed. I have more brains than that over-nosey inn-worker, Rosa, as well-meaning as she is."

Samantha looked down suspiciously at her drink, fearing it to be drugged or poisoned.

"Don't worry, the drink is fine." Captain Muggahan grunted. "You're worth more to me alive and well than otherwise." He glanced to the mystical creatures. "The unicorn would fetch a pretty penny too, but that mallus would have to be killed if such a thing is possible. I do not side with or against the Gardyn. My priority is my ship, she doesn't come cheap and there is much to be lost in going against a king like Hrafn. But don't worry, Lady Samantha, I have made no definite decisions, yet."

With that, Captain Muggahan turned and walked easily away to his cabin.

It was dark now, the last glow of the sun had since died and the heavens were lit with infinite stars. On the deck of the Gilded Rose, lamps had been lit in the fore, mid and aft. It was by this lamplight that Samantha staggered uneasily across the tilting deck to the silver unicorn which still lay out of the way of the crew.

"Something troubles you Samantha." Alina watched her friend with familiar worry.

Samantha nodded and repeated Captain Muggahan's words.

"By Praede. Why do humans have to be so complicated and devious?" Alina said, with more pity than fear. "I should not worry too much Samantha, I have sensed that the captain is good at heart. And though it is morally wrong for me to interfere thus, when he dozes I shall try to persuade his thoughts."

*****

In the distance, a yellow pinprick of light remained steady, drawing them on. It was still many hours 'til dawn when the single light accumulated and spread across the dark horizon to show the lights of a port-town. There was a rush on deck as Captain Muggahan's crew prepared to dock. Orders were shouted to and fro. Samantha huddled down with Alina, the girl was tired, forgetting when she had last slept properly, but anxiety and fear kept her tired eyes straining to see in the darkness. Alina too was anxious, though she tried to hide it, for she knew that the human captain had yet to make up his mind.

Suddenly there was a hush, all that could be heard was the creaking of the wood and the breaking of the waves on the hull. A whisper went round the crew, the men's murmurings sounding like a soft breeze. They were pulling into the silent docks and stealth was fundamental. The crew moved about quietly, signalling to each other. The lights on the Gilded Rose were extinguished as she was securely moored. When all of their tasks were completed, the crew went below deck as pre-ordered, leaving Captain Muggahan alone with the trio of friends.

"Captain Muggahan, have you made your decision?" Samantha asked as defiantly as she could manage.

The captain didn't reply, but stared out to the midnight sea, still deliberating.

Samantha continued. "If you let us go, you will be remembered for it by the Gardyn if we win this war, Hrafn would be none the wiser. If you don't, it will be worse for you."

Muggahan grunted as though unimpressed, but he was wary and his thoughts were clouded by those projected by the unicorn. "I have several grown men at my call. What can one unarmed little girl do?"

Samantha boldly held his gaze. "I am not alone, I doubt very much that Alina and Siabhor could be subdued with your 'skeleton crew'. I am also not unarmed, I may not carry a physical weapon, but surely you have heard the stories. Perhaps I should turn a curse of fire on this ship to set an example."

"Do not threaten my ship." Muggahan growled with a hint of panic.

"Then do not think you can threaten my freedom." Samantha's eyes narrowed, then she hissed behind her. "Alina, Siabhor. Let's go."

Siabhor leapt without hesitation from the ship to the dock, then turned his hairy face to watch Alina jump nimbly down.

"One day, everything will be clear." Samantha said to the captain as she straddled the side of the ship. Then the girl dropped down from view.

Captain Muggahan seemed to come out of a reverie. The girl had defied him! A shout went out and soon guardsmen were rushing through their town to find the girl and her mystical beasts, but a unicorn is one of the fastest things alive and the trio were already on their way west.

*****

They moved on through the night, steadily westward until all three were dropping with exhaustion. It was an early dawn that found the trio hidden from sight, finally able to sleep and not worry for a few hours. It was with the midday heat that they were ready to go again, they used the main river of Enchena to guide them back towards the Great Forest. They travelled with caution, as they were relatively unarmed and even though Samantha had used her power of fire to intimidate Captain Muggahan, she still felt unable to control it at will if they were spotted and confronted.

There was an urgency as they travelled, what Samantha had seen in the Dragon's Orb plagued her while she was awake and had haunted her mind while she slept. She feared that they would be too late, that even with the Sword of Minaeri the Gardyn would still fall.

When the forest and city of Enchena came into view after a solid twenty-four hours of travelling the trio were so overjoyed to see home again that their anxiety was temporarily allayed. They made for the north of the city wall, aiming for the tumbled rocks that marked the tunnel through which Samantha had escaped from the palace. They stopped beside the dark entrance, Samantha leant against the sturdy boulders, she felt as though she would drop from tiredness and felt sorry for Alina who had carried her many miles over the past days. But whereas the old Sammy from England would have given up long before now, Samantha glared determinedly at the city; the feeling of duty, responsibility and justice pushing her on beyond exhaustion.

"When you get back to the Valley, fill them in on everything and get everyone prepared to leave." Samantha instructed Alina and Siabhor. "Tell them I'll return shortly."

"You will not be going alone." Barked Siabhor.

"We have been through so much together. We will not leave you now." Alina added, looking down dearly at the girl. "After all, how will you return in time without me?"

"And how will you be getting through tunnel and into palace without Siabhor?" The mallus asked.

Samantha watched her friends, reflecting how a few months ago she had felt no real connection to the people in her life, yet now she had two dear, albeit odd, companions that would sacrifice everything to help her.

"Well? We go now and be back sooner." Siabhor finished and moved away into the tunnel, glad to be continuing with his strange friends, yet still muttering about another dark journey.

As they got closer and closer to the palace, memories and nightmares flooded back to Samantha. Hrafn had kept her a prisoner, not only within high walls, but within her mind also, for too long. The old feeling of guilt returned as Samantha recalled how she had been willing to betray the Gardyn.

All too soon, the pitch black of the tunnel was broken by the faintest gleam of light above them. Siabhor's claws were black silhouettes as he reached up to the hefty wooden planks.

"Wait!" Samantha hissed, making the mallus pause. "Maybe we shouldn't be doing this now. It's dangerous, and it's gonna be impossible during broad daylight."

"We have come too far. Put your fear away." Siabhor hissed back.

"I have to agree with Siabhor." Alina added. "Any delay is dangerous for the Gardyn. Your friends are with you."

Samantha sighed, staring into the darkness. "This is going to be difficult." She mumbled.

"But you know where the sword is?" Siabhor questioned.

Samantha nodded without realising that neither could see the gesture. "It's in the palace treasury, third floor up in the North Wing." She replied, thankful of the King's pompous tour when she had resided in the palace.

"Then Siabhor shall take you by the quickest route to the treasury." Alina instructed. "And I shall wait here."

Siabhor grunted and raised one of the planks slowly. The dim light of the barn flooded into the tunnel to temporarily blind the trio. The mallus silently shifted a second plank and moved aside to allow Samantha out. Samantha scrambled up, out of the tunnel, careful to stay behind several bales in case anyone should enter the barn, she then turned to help lift more of the wooden floor to allow Siabhor's wider torso through, and eventually Alina.

But as soon as the unicorn sprang nimbly up, the stables went mad with the sound of whinnying horses and stamping hooves as the mystical creature drove the lesser ones mad with want.

"What's going on?"

"The horses - what's wrong?" Male voices called out as confusion hit the yard.

"Alina. Get back quick." Samantha hissed urgently. Alina obediently slid back down into the darkness of the tunnel and immediately the horses began to calm down. "You can't come out if the horses are going to act like that. Perhaps... perhaps you had better wait for us in the forest."

Alina's grey face peered out from the darkness, her pale horn protruding above floor level. "I will do no such thing. When you have retrieved the Sword of Minaeri, I shall listen for your call and carry you swiftly away."

Samantha grinned. "You are spending too much time with humans, Alina. You have become very stubborn."

"We go quickly, before we are found." Siabhor hissed impatiently.

"Okay Alina, you win. Keep out of sight." Samantha murmured to her dear friend, then stepped back. She helped Siabhor to loosely replace the floorboards, closing Alina back in the tunnel.

Siabhor moved along on all fours to stand beside the door of the barn. Samantha crept up beside him, but reached out her arm to hold him back for a moment,

"Siabhor, we need to get away undetected. So no confronting anyone, but if..." She paused and took a deep breath, aware of what she was about to allow. "But if someone does see us, make sure they don't have a chance to shout out."

The mallus looked up at Samantha, looking her straight in the eye. With a low hiss of acceptance, he left through the door, keeping low to the ground. Samantha followed him, her heart thudding with fear as she moved quietly out onto the yard.

265

Now that the horses had calmed down, the stable workers appeared lax in their jobs. They were making the most of the absence of higher ranking lieutenants and captains, who would ordinarily be barking orders whenever things got too quiet, but were currently all congregated in the Great Forest for a final clash with the Gardyn army. The workers chatted idly about the King who, in his eagerness to destroy the final band of rebels had somewhat neglected the protection of his city, leaving it in the care of lower-ranked soldiers and elderly lords of the court.

This flaw in the King's plan allowed Samantha and Siabhor an easy approach to the palace wall. Samantha glanced up to the dizzy height of the North Wing, while Siabhor flexed his claws and, standing up on his hind limbs felt for a secure hold on the brick.

Samantha lowered her gaze and clambered onto the mallus' hairy, bony back. Siabhor's sudden vertical leap made Samantha gasp, but she managed to prevent a scream as she clung on tightly, her eyes closed against the height. They flitted up the side of the palace like a strange shadow, the climb was over in seconds. Siabhor balanced easily on the narrow ledge outside the window, unworried by the drop behind him.

"Please hold tight." Samantha managed to mutter in a petrified voice, then, with difficulty she raised her leg and kicked out suddenly, the heel of her boot smashing through the glass of the window.

Samantha and Siabhor worked quickly to smash away the rest of the pane and dropped through, landing on the fragments of glass. Samantha paused, there was a cut on her leg from the forced entry, so while Siabhor darted about the room, she quickly ripped off her sleeve to tie around the injury.

Samantha looked up, sweeping her hair out of her eyes, the treasury was as she remembered, full of glittering jewels and ornamented weapons all arranged in cabinets and on stands.

Siabhor suddenly gave a bark as he found a huge cabinet with glass doors, inside which several swords and scimitars were presented. Samantha rushed over, trying to hide her limp, her eyes lit with the sight of all the blades, each one worth more than all the contents of the Gardyn armoury.

As Samantha opened the cabinet carefully, Siabhor started to slink away, he could smell the fresh blood of the girl and, friend or not, it was stirring his hunter instinct. He shook his head and tried to think otherwise; he would not try to kill her again.

It was then that Siabhor heard it. His senses had been heightened by the smell of blood and were tingling, and now there was a new sound. Distant running. It sounded like several individuals, all heavy, or weighed down.

"They come." He hissed, darting back to Samantha.

Samantha was glancing over each sword, all were beautifully and intricately made. Then something caught her eye, half hidden with a velvet cover, instead of gleaming and delicate, it was dull and looked roughly-made, it seemed so out of place next to all the fine weapons. She heard Siabhor's warning hiss and span round.

"What?"

There was no need for an answer, for now even the girl's less developed hearing picked out the sound of quickly approaching men. Without knowing what she was doing, she reached into the bottom of the cabinet and drew out the odd sword. It was then apparent that it was not roughly made at all, it was just rusted beyond use, yet still the details of a long blade, peculiar hilt and a large dull stone could be seen.

Siabhor glanced up in confusion, he thought humans were extremely strange creatures. But he had no time to wonder any more. There was a pause, the only sound was a slow clicking as the door of the treasury was unlocked, and three armed guards burst in, swords raised.

Siabhor didn't hesitate. He leapt on the man nearest to him, who looked at the monster with surprise and fear, but his shout was quickly silenced. Siabhor looked up from the corpse, his fur splashed with blood, the desire to kill that Samantha's blood had induced now satisfied.

Across the room, Siabhor saw one guard already dead on the floor, the second approaching to attack nervously, his sword rose, but before it could fall Samantha had already cut the life from him. A shocked expression was on the man's face as he fell beside his comrade.

Samantha stood tall, an aura of strength and glory emanating from her. In her hand she grasped the sword, but no longer was it rusted. The blade gleamed a silver so dark it was almost black. The hilt was of a strong black metal, the sides branching up to surround the hand with antler-like prongs. The stone that was fixed to the top gleamed with its own pale blue light.

Samantha turned to face the mallus, but Siabhor had never seen her look like this. He peered incomprehensively into her eyes which looked darker, unfocused.

"Mallus... my counterpart has a peculiar taste in friends." The voice that came from Samantha's mouth was much deeper and richer. "We must hurry."

Siabhor ignored the suspicion he felt and loped obediently towards the window, it would not be long until more guards came. Samantha followed, then paused at the window, she closed her eyes and silently mouthed words that Siabhor could not make out. When she reopened her eyes she looked with mistrust at the mallus, as if meeting him for the first time.

"Must be quick." Siabhor hissed, perching on the ledge.

Samantha nodded and clung onto the back of the mallus once more. The climb down was even more daunting than the climb up, as Siabhor expertly dropped several feet to cling onto the wall again lower down. They had almost reached the ground when Siabhor felt Samantha's grip weaken, the girl gasped and suddenly dropped.

She didn't have far to fall, and she landed with a dull thud in the flowerbeds at the base of the tower. Samantha was left blinking in the bright sunlight, trying to catch her breath. Hovering above her head was the muzzle of Alina. Samantha sat up, Minaeri's sword still in her tight grasp, she looked at it with wonder, what was a rusted blade now made a glorious weapon.

"Move." Siabhor hissed. "Too many humans."

Samantha understood him and clambered up onto Alina's back. The unicorn took off immediately for the stables.

269

"Wait." Samantha said as a sudden daring took her, she glanced over to the forests that rose beyond the city. "Let's show the Enchenians what they're missing."

Alina and Siabhor didn't need to ask, and Samantha's daring was contagious and they raced with boundless energy, into the centre of the city, sending guards fleeing with fear. Such a sight had never been seen in Enchena, the crowd parted with many shrieks and screams as the mallus loped along the main streets followed closely by a unicorn of such beauty that she silenced all fear and upon her back a young woman whose pale face showed a warrior's determination.

Even guards and soldiers hesitated, so amazed by what they were witnessing. The mighty golden gates wavered slightly as they began to close, but a spurt of speed and the slow wits of the Enchenian Guard allowed the trio to exit before they crashed closed.

In their wake the crowded streets of Enchena burst into excited mutterings so that by nightfall, even with the guards' attempts to quieten it, the story of a monster, unicorn and girl riding through the city was known by all. Rumours began to spring up also, as the city's inhabitants, who had been kept in the dark by their King, searched for answers.

Meanwhile, the trio of friends were moving steadily through the forest towards Autumn's Valley.

"Alina, stop." Samantha managed to say, then slid off the unicorn's back, stumbling as she hit the ground, her energy sapped.

Alina yawned, glad to rest for a brief moment, but as she looked at Samantha, fresh worry awoke. The girl's face was almost grey in colour and she could hardly stand.

"Let's - let's rest a while." Samantha struggled to get her words out. "We can... move again after - after sleep."

"Yes." Siabhor said simply, settling down on the ground, his tired limbs outstretched.

Alina stamped a sore forefoot. "No. There is no time. Samantha, you are ill, you need to be with humans."

"I'm fine. Just tired." Samantha argued meekly. "So tired..."

"Samantha! I demand that we continue." Alina's thoughts were full of righteous anger. "I can get us home very quickly. Siabhor is not so fast, he can meet us at the Valley."

Samantha shook her head, every small movement making her uneasy. "I can't - I just can't." She insisted.

Siabhor looked between the girl and unicorn. "You get on, Samantha, or I be biting your legs!"

Samantha smiled timidly. Alina lay down and Samantha stepped astride her. Soon they were off. Samantha had only ever ridden as fast when Alina had rescued her and David from The Dark Being. Again their surroundings blurred as Alina really started to race, moving nimbly and confidently between trees and forest growth, spurred on in desperation as she felt Samantha's body collapse over her back.

Alina only slowed down when she drew near to the Valley's borders, where she trotted through the dense bush, now reinforced with Gardyn fencing. The unicorn threw up her horned head to give a screaming neigh.

271

The Valley came   alive. Mgair,   Rian   and
the Deorwines were rushing over from the encampment,
and Autumn came cantering over with Sundance at his
heels.

Samantha felt Alina smoothly stop and she knew she
was home. There was no energy left in her limbs and she
began to slip off the side.

"Beware." She muttered, then hit the ground.

Twenty-six

Samantha gasped as cold water trickled over her forehead. Her eyes flickered open and she could see Jillis leaning over her with a damp cloth. The tent was dimly lit with lamps and Samantha guessed that it was reaching dusk.

"You're awake." Jillis acknowledged softly.

Samantha tried to sit up, but Jillis restrained her.

"No, you're still weak. You need to save your strength for tomorrow."

"What... what happens tomorrow?"

"Our final strike." Jillis answered without meeting Samantha's gaze. "We have grown in number since you left; we will take Hrafn by surprise and finally finish this."

Samantha struggled against the younger girl's hold, managing to sit up, though her head spun violently. "No, you don't..."

"Alina told us all she could. But Lord Mgair has decided that the Gardyn will march out one last time to create glory that will be remembered for a thousand years." The girl still refused to look up, and Samantha

273

heard the shame in her voice. "And now you are back with us, we might have more of a chance to at least survive."

"We can't, I refuse to let it come true." Samantha gushed, making no sense to the maid. "Bring Mgair to me at once."

Jillis stood up and rushed out, hope returning again; perhaps Samantha *could* stop dawn's terrible slaughter.

Soon, the bulk of Lord Mgair entered the tent in which Samantha had again lain down.

"Jillis Deorwine has told me that you wished to see me urgently." Mgair said, his tone patronising as he humoured the Lost Soul that had caused him nothing but strife. The lord pulled a seat close to the bed.

"Yes, there is no need to fight tomorrow, instead we're going to head north to the ruins of the Temple of Gates. The Gardyn will finally be free of Hrafn forever." Samantha watched Mgair carefully, she could see his mistrust and desire to command working against her.

Lord Mgair's face coloured and his voice now held a warning edge. "It has been decided, by those more educated than you, Lady Samantha, that this final battle is our best option."

Samantha sat up again, anger flooding her veins at the lord's ignorance. "No. This is your selfish attempt at glory. I have passed beyond death, danger and exhaustion. I have seen things beyond comprehension in the past few days and you dare to suggest I know nothing?"

As her fury flooded out, sparks of flame flickered momentarily in mid-air before disappearing into the evening air. Lord Mgair leant back, staring at the girl with a mixture of fear and anger, but still she continued.

274

"I have seen what will happen if we go to battle tomorrow. Every person and creature in this Valley will be killed! There will be no glorious stories, other than how the King of Enchena can crush all who oppose him." Samantha's eyes strayed into the shadows, where she could see the pale face of Jillis, and the painful sight of her death arose in her mind.

"You have no proof." Lord Mgair shouted back. "You have been misled. A few hallucinations brought on by madmen. Your sadistic predictions are nothing more than the imaginations of cowards!"

"There is nothing cowardly about Caminus and Leukos. The visions were real." Samantha retorted, frustrated by his blindness and insinuations.

"Caminus and Leukos? Who are they?"

Samantha faltered, she had not meant to reveal the source of her insight of the future and would not break her promise to the dragons. "I… I cannot tell you." She replied weakly.

"Ah ha!" Mgair shouted, leaping out of his seat, pacing the tent. "So this is the true reliability of your information. Miscellaneous sources."

"This coming from the man." Samantha's voice dropped to an icy muttering. "Who has acted on the orders of a cloaked stranger that nobody knows?"

Lord Mgair stopped, his face purple with fury, leaning close to the girl. Samantha thought he would lash out, but instead his words came in a chilling whisper.

"Tomorrow morning the Gardyn will go to war. Their grand Lady Samantha will be there, fronting the charge, or you will be tried for treason." The lord turned and stalked out of the tent.

Samantha felt a cool breeze touch her face and the fire of her anger faded, leaving her crying late into the night.

*****

It was a clear day with a beautiful dawn that brought no cheer to the hundreds of Gardyn that assembled at the western end of the Valley. Whispers had spread about The Lost Soul's vision and subsequent argument with their Lord Mgair. The soldiers were quietened with the terrible knowledge that they were marching to their deaths.

Lady Samantha sat numbly on her horse Legan, slightly apart from the other mounted soldiers, whose numbers had swelled from just twenty to nearly a hundred.

"Samantha? I've come to say good bye."

Samantha looked blankly down. Jillis was kitted, all ready to leave with the archers who would go ahead of the main army. Samantha just nodded her acknowledgement of Jillis' words.

Jillis seemed to be fighting with herself, she sighed and put a hand up to gently stroke Legan's neck. "I don't really want to die. Because I believe that you can still save us."

"No." Samantha replied in a dead voice. "No more tricks. I can do nothing, except watch the Gardyn become pointless martyrs."

"I don't believe that. You have done so much already." A male voice joined the conversation. Samantha raised her gaze to see Tobias approach.

Tobias put a protective arm around his sister. "Well Samantha, it's time for you to become our saviour. This army would follow you."

As Samantha looked at him, she felt her heart swell, she could not bear the thought of him and his sister lying dead on a bloody battleground. But what could she possibly do? She shook her head with bitter resignation.

"It's not just that. Mgair was right, the Gardyn will perish, whether it is here, or on the journey north. To get to the temple it would take three days of slow travelling with many unarmed families. Nothing could stop the King's Army catching us."

"You could stop them." Tobias said simply. At Samantha's blank look his calm snapped. "Oh come on! Who escaped the King, his guards and the mallus? Who... who tamed a mallus and enlisted the unicorns to our aid? Who gave the Gardyn safe places to live? And who has, on several occasions, pulled dangerous stunts to disrupt Hrafn's army?"

"I had help." Samantha replied with a slight smile at the memories. She caught Tobias' eye again and his fire was contagious.

A single shout went across the quiet Valley. The archers were being summoned.

Samantha felt herself coming to life again. She looked at Jillis' petrified face and knew they were following the wrong path. After all, hadn't the dragons been pleased with her idea of taking the Gardyn to Caelum?

"Okay. Jillis, don't let the archers leave. Tobias, keep Mgair out the way - I don't care how you do it."

"Well, he already sees me as a traitor. I'll just have to prove him right!" Tobias said with attempted cheeriness.

The three hesitated, looking between each other, all fearing what the day may bring.

277

Then Samantha spurred Legan into action, racing towards where the unicorns lingered. Jillis ran towards the archers, while her brother darted off to find Lord Mgair.

"Where is Lord Mgair?" He asked a random soldier urgently.

"Still in his tent." The soldier replied briefly, then turned back to his comrades.

Tobias nodded and jogged towards the Lord's canvas shelter. Mgair's horse was tied up outside, and by the post were coils of spare rope. Tobias cursed what he was about to do as he stooped to collect it.

He paused. "May Minaeri forgive me." He muttered, then stepped inside.

Lord Mgair was sitting by his grand writing desk which looked out of place in the rough outdoors, he was busy pulling on his boots and armour. Aware that someone had entered, Mgair turned and scowled when he saw it was Tobias.

"What do you want?" He snapped.

Tobias slowly moved forward. When he spoke it was in whisper. "When did you start caring about what others wanted, my lord." Behind his back, Tobias was letting out a small noose.

Lord Mgair's grew angrier. "Ah, of course. A traitor like you, listening with your heart to the false Lady Samantha." Mgair took a stride towards Tobias, trying to intimidate the boy.

Tobias moved quickly with reflexes trained and tuned by army training. The noose of the rope twisted about his hand and Mgair found himself flung to the floor, Tobias kneeling on his back, quickly tightening the rope around his arms.

The wind had been knocked out of him, but the Lord quickly got over the surprise and found his voice. "Traitor! Help!"

His pleas shrieked out, and almost immediately a loyal Gardyn stood in the entrance. Rian looked down with fury and confusion, he dragged Tobias from Lord Mgair, his other hand grasping at the hilt of his sword.

"What, in the name of Minaeri, do you think you are doing Deorwine?" He demanded.

Tobias tried to keep eye contact with Rian, but found he could not.

"It's him." He explained weakly, pointing to the fallen Mgair who now struggled to turn over. "He expects to lead us to our deaths when Lady Samantha plans to lead us to safety. He would not listen."

"You mean Samantha has had another of her mad ideas?" Rian spat.

Tobias just nodded glumly, but he hardly cared about what punishment he was about to receive, in a few hours they would all be dead anyway.

Rian let go of the dejected Tobias, a grimace on his face. "I am so sorry about all of this, Lord Mgair." The warrior said, kneeling down by the lord and helping him sit up.

"Ah, Rian." Mgair murmured in simpering tones. "You are a true Gardyn."

Rian smiled and nodded, his hand feeling across the floor for something. "My lord, my life is devoted to the success of the Gardyn." A cloth grasped in his hand was suddenly stuffed into the lord's mouth and Rian secured the gag before standing up, dusting off his hands. "Lady Samantha has not done us wrong so far."

He looked over at Tobias as he left the tent, he gave a wry smile. "I never saw, or did anything here. Make sure Samantha does not fail us."

*****

A flurry of angry thoughts passed between the unicorns as Samantha approached to see Alina facing Autumn; Sundance hiding behind his aunt, and Autumn's remaining herd behind their leader.

"You have seen the end. I forbid you to go to this war." Autumn was telling Alina.

"And I saw that I died with honour beside my friends."

"Your human friends." Autumn corrected angrily. "You would reject your herd, and me, to be with the humans?"

Alina lowered her head ashamed, it was true that she had become too involved in human affairs. Autumn, feeling these thoughts, stepped forward and nuzzled her affectionately.

"Your heart is too big, Alina. And your only fault is that you care too much. That is why I love you, and I would never wish you any other way."

"E... excuse me." Samantha interjected quietly. "I've just come to say that the battle isn't going ahead."

"The humans have come to their senses?"

Samantha frowned and matched the form of thought to the brown stallion, Billan.

"Not yet, but they will do." She answered truthfully. "The Gardyn will head north to safety while I distract the King and his army. But I need your help."

"What now?" Autumn asked warily.

"It's just that, to give the Gardyn enough time to get to their destination, I'll have to keep the King occupied for at least a full day." Samantha began to explain. "That'll mean that the army can't catch up with the Gardyn no matter how hard the soldiers ride. But that'd also mean that I'll be left behind if I ride Legan. So… so if one of you were to take me north…. you are so fast…" Samantha's voice trailed off and she stared at the ground.

Autumn snorted as Alina's ears pricked and the mare took a step forward.

"Alina will not do this for you." He replied, his thoughts forming slowly as though undecided. The stallion ignored Alina's crestfallen thoughts.

"I would gladly carry you." Sundance spoke up.

"You?" Autumn seemed confused by the younger stallion's offer. "No, Samantha needs speed. In fact, I shall take you."

Samantha looked up, a wide smile spread across her face. "Oh thank you, Autumn. I… I really appreciate it!"

"Well, we will be rid of you and your problematic race."

Samantha thanked him again, then turned Legan to ride back to the Gardyn troops. She rode to the very front, where the archers were gathered, both angry and nervous. Samantha felt her confidence slide, but smiled when she saw Jillis, hoping to set her friend at ease.

Samantha was perched nervously on Legan in front of the Gardyn army, trying to look as brave and incredible as they all thought her. She almost squirmed as all focus was trained on her. By Minaeri, she hated making speeches, she remembered giving an English presentation back in school where she had turned bright red and the rest of her class had just laughed at her.

281

"I, er…" Samantha started feebly, only too aware of the eager, admiring stares of the average soldiers; the doubtful yet curious stares of their captains. She cleared her throat and started again.

"I'm sure you all know by now, that while I was gone, I found an alternative for the Gardyn. I can get us all away from Hrafn forever." Samantha paused, looking around to see the effect of her words. To her surprise, the majority looked sceptical instead of exultant.

Muttering was arising in the silence Samantha had left.

"…Lord Mgair said…"

"…cowardice…"

Samantha held up her sweaty hand to get their attention again. "Lord Mgair is a pompous git!" She said loudly. There was a ripple of shocked silence through her audience. "Look, you all know it, it just happens that I'm saying it!

"Your wonderful Lord Mgair has a need to end this gloriously, even if it means sacrificing all of you. He thinks anything other than one last brave, reckless front would be cowardice. I say this is ridiculous. Do you think Hrafn will regale how inspiring our battle was? More likely we will be scorned in history as a sloppy peasant revolt." Samantha paused to take a deep breath, pleased to see soldiers starting to nod with agreement.

"And what of your families? After you are mercilessly slaughtered, who will take care of them? Who will protect them?

"The option I offer is to go north to the Temple of Gates. For in the beginning of your history of Enchena, your ancestors were brought here by Minaeri from the land of Caelum so that you could populate this land. I

282

can take you through, take you out of reach of Hrafn and all evil rooted in Enchena.

"I must impress that it is *not* the cowardly way. I think it is just as brave and noble to save your loved ones and ensure the survival of the Gardyn and their hope as it is to be a martyr. And we… we will find a way back one day, and bring freedom to the whole of Enchena." Samantha's breathing was quickened with excitement, but the crowd around her stood, quiet and uncertain. Samantha sighed, suddenly frustrated that these people could not see she was trying to save them.

"If you wish to stay and fight a pointless battle, you will find your Lord Mgair sitting in his tent, muttering, paranoid of traitors and dishonour." She stopped again and no one moved. "You have half an hour to prepare and regroup."

There was hesitation once she had finished. But as each soldier came out of their reverie, they rushed away to follow their Lady's orders.

Samantha watched them leave. In the dispersing cavalry, she recognised two of the men that she had gone to steal horses with.

"Rinar! Philip!" She called out, then pushed Legan on to meet them. "I need you two to ride ahead. Get to Treefort as quickly as possible and get the families ready to leave. I'll get the others to gather your possessions."

Philip agreed immediately, yet Rinar observed Samantha in the same steady, calculating stare as his cousin, but also nodded.

Samantha waited long enough to see them ride through the Valley wall, then turned and hurried away to the Deorwine tent.

Twenty-seven

There was an air of excitement as the Gardyn gathered once more by the Valley edge. But this time it was the feeling of adventure, unsure of where their paths would lead rather than before, where it had been the depressing knowledge of how the day would end.

Samantha walked about the army, having given Legan to the Deorwines to use as a pack horse. Her eyes were keen and her senses tingled. Everywhere she went, soldiers bowed their heads and mumbled their praise. Samantha began to feel invincible, that she could pull this off.

Samantha suddenly glimpsed a familiar figure, hairy and low to the ground, loping towards her. "Ah, Siabhor. I was hoping to find you. You'll have to go with the main army, you wouldn't be able to keep up with the speed that I need from Autumn."

The mallus growled, his yellow, narrowed eyes refusing to meet Samantha's, his whole body seemed taut, nervous even, and his claws raked at the earth. "The end is here." He growled, his tone fiercer than Samantha had ever heard.

"What? No, it's not. We aren't going to fight Hrafn anymore." Samantha replied.

Siabhor finally looked up, glaring at her. It seemed as though a red mist covered his eyes as the hunter in him arose. "No. It is the end of Siabhor having strange friends. You think I will leave the forests for you?" The mallus hissed and spat. "No more running with unicorns, befriending humans. Siabhor go back to mallus, have new pack. I am glad it is over, I can be mallus again, hunt again."

Siabhor turned and, saying no more, he ran as fast as he could, leaping into the trees at the first chance and disappearing.

"But…" Samantha's voice faded. The familiar click of claw against wood ended. Samantha realised she had been foolish to assume that Siabhor would come with her, he was a wild creature of these forests, nothing could change that. But… she had hoped… she had valued her odd friendships. What about Alina, would she too choose Autumn and the herd over her friend?

"Samantha?" A strong voice called her.

Samantha hastily wiped a tear from her face and spun round to see Rian leading his horse, all ready to leave. "Rian, I want you to lead the Gardyn to Treefort. Then head to the Temple." She tried to keep her voice steady, and let her eyes stay out of focus so they did not tear up.

Rian stared at her, how absurd it was that the future was in the hands of a young girl. "Of course, Lady Samantha. How much time should we allow for the diversion?"

Samantha shrugged, although it was hardly the time for such a careless gesture, "With Autumn's speed, I'd say set off ten minutes after we have. No more though,

I want the Gardyn through look-out range while I have the King's Army's full attention."

The famous Gardyn warrior nodded, then actually stood back and bowed. "Minaeri's blessings, Lady Samantha. Good luck."

"You too." Was all she managed. It was time.

*****

"Why are you nervous, Samantha? You did something similar with Alina." Autumn's thoughts came steady as he raced through the forests.

"I hadn't really planned anything that time, it just happened." She gasped, then paused as Autumn swung left to keep on course. Samantha felt odd riding this chestnut stallion who was wider then Alina - and faster. "And we went when the army was asleep, *and* we weren't getting the King's army to chase us."

Autumn said no more until he came to a stop near to Hrafn's camp.

"Good luck, Samantha. Is there anything else I can do to help?" The stallion asked as the girl slid from his back.

Samantha ran a hand through her knotted hair and took a deep breath, "Thanks. Um, I need lots of dry wood, dry grass. Um, pretty much anything dry."

As Autumn trotted off, Samantha turned to face the direction of the enemy camp. First she'd draw their attention, then she'd attack from the south to clear the north road for the Gardyn to escape. She closed her eyes and concentrated, she pushed beyond hope, and an image began to form in her mind.

The trees had been cleared, there was row upon row of small tents. The horses were grouped on the city-side. Morning was growing old, yet there was a quietness in

286

the camp, it seemed as though all the soldiers were waiting for an imminent call of war, and were prepared thus. In the centre, stores were piled high under a rough canvas.

Samantha muttered to herself, not since the time she had lost control in front of David had she thought of her powers. She begged the gods and pure luck for this to work. She knew from the single training session with Rian when they had attempted to tune her power of combustion, that it was triggered by fear, anger and woe.

Well there was plenty of fear already coursing within her, and Samantha forced herself to think of all the hurt Hrafn caused to spark anger in her soul. Finally, she thought of Siabhor, Alina, even home, Yorkshire. She would never see any of them again.

Samantha's legs suddenly gave way and she collapsed onto the ground. She opened her eyes and her breathing was laboured. There was a sudden shout, faded by distance, that indicated that she had accomplished her task. That first burst of flame had really taken it out of her, but Samantha knew that the fire would start to spread from the stores across the camp and would be difficult to extinguish.

Autumn had been trotting in, twigs and dry bracken between his teeth, he would drop them near Samantha then trot away to collect more, coughing as the dust and dirt tickled his throat. The sharp sound woke Samantha from her reverie.

Samantha knew she had their attention; now to draw them south. She knelt down and scrambled together a rough sphere of dry material, she projected all her emotions into it 'til the fuel burst into flames.

Samantha was so surprised that it had actually worked that she almost dropped the burning sphere. Although the fire crackled fiercely against the wood, the flames licked coolly over her hands and arms.

'Hot air expands and rises...' All of Samantha's science lessons came unexpectedly to the front of her thoughts. Samantha couldn't believe that school was having use in real life and turned her mind to altering and heating the air around the sphere, then slowly loosening her fingers and lowering her hands. The ball of flame hovered in mid-air, a shimmer of heat about it.

Samantha grinned. There was a snort from behind her as Autumn came to drop off more fuel and Samantha realised that she was wasting time.

She concentrated on the sphere and it jerked up, then hovered again. Samantha closed her eyes and saw ranks of soldiers. Into the picture a flaming ball flew from the south and exploded into a line of confused soldiers, its flames spreading among the men with unimaginable ferocity, scorching the ground, yet the trees appeared untouched.

When Samantha opened her eyes, she saw that the sphere had gone. But this was no time for pride. Samantha knelt down again, gathering together another ball of dry fuel.

She worked hard, combusting each sphere and making them fly into her enemy, but she could only control one at a time and the exertion was draining her.

Autumn came rushing towards her, his worried thoughts preceding him. "Samantha, there is the glint of armour coming through the trees, they are close."

Samantha looked up and peered into the forest. At first she could see nothing. Then there was the unmistakeable glint that could only be the King's army.

"Well, at least we know my plan has worked so far." Samantha said, a quiver in her voice. "Okay, we'll wait 'til the last moment, then disappear."

*****

As the enemy ranks approached, the number of archers and spearmen increased, all were apprehensive, they knew that the Gardyn Lady controlled the forests. But to speak of it was cowardice and punishable by death.

The captains steadied their troops, their leader, Captain Losan trotting along the frontline, then to the rear where the King and his heir rode amidst heavy guard.

"My lord, do you order the charge?" Captain Losan asked in a lowered voice.

The King did not reply immediately, his attention taken by an explosion of flame in the left flank. The lieutenants shouted orders and threats and the soldiers continued marching in silence, disregarding those that shrieked in pain or lay blackened on the ground, yet their eyes filled with a fear that they dare not reveal.

Hrafn scowled, it had taken him much longer to master his powers than it had for Samantha. Today was not the first time he had feared the girl was stronger than he, for she did possess the more destructive powers. This doubt, and the pressures and distractions about him caused Hrafn to falter in his spells. He still managed to resurrect the fallen, but he had not healed them and soon there were several charred bodies screaming and cursing as they fled through the ranks causing more unease than

289

flying firebombs and the prospect of marching to battle did. The scorched corpses were slain with a single command and Hrafn was resigned to fight the Gardyn with a mortal army.

The King looked to Captain Losan, ignoring the questioning looks David kept shooting him. "Give the order. Orion, old friend, bring me glory."

Captain Orion Losan saluted, then spurred on his bay charger, sword held aloft to signal engagement. Shouts rang out across the front and the soldiers on foot drew their swords and began to run, the slowest persuaded to go faster with the lick of the whips. Once they were engaged, the mounted lieutenants would charge into the fray.

At least that was the plan. As the soldiers ran forward to the light, where the forest was less dense and the Gardyn were obviously making their last stand, they heard a female voice shout out.

"Fall back and reform!"

The soldiers came to the place of battle and halted in surprise, causing their captains to shout and curse. The area was empty, with no clue as to where they went.

Captain Losan came trotting up, wondering why battle had not commenced and glared about the woods, a fury welled up in him, but he felt almost split with a kind of respect for his foes.

*****

Autumn had galloped as fast as he could, while still leaving no prints to show whither he had fled. He had gone south until he thought they were far enough away from the human King to veer west and skirt round them to take the troublesome Samantha back north and finally be rid of the Gardyn.

Samantha shouted out to stop when she noticed the change in direction. Autumn grudgingly slowed and halted, watching the girl dismount and come to face him. Exasperation settled like a heavy cloud about him and Samantha knew to be careful.

"I'm not done yet, sir." She barely managed to whisper.

"You have caused a diversion and allowed your kind unseen passage to the north. That is what you promised to do."

"I promised to keep the army distracted so that they could not catch up." Samantha said defiantly, but not daring to meet the unicorn's gaze.

Autumn remained still, he did not share his thoughts with the girl, but the rush of thought within his mind almost gave off heat. After all, the great Nmirr had not been the only stallion to hold wisdom, Autumn had his own store, enough to let him lead a herd at such a relatively young age.

"You wish to stay, chance capture, to save your kind." The unicorn's shared thoughts came slowly. "While I wish for this to end. I admire your willingness to help others with no want of personal glory... I have a few ideas…"

******

Captain Losan's face was set to a permanent scowl as he marched back from the makeshift horse pen - unlike several lieutenants and captains, he cared that his warhorse was treated right. In the night time forest, everything was seen by the flicker of small fires dotted about the area.

That afternoon there had been another volley of flame attacking the ranks and drawing them further south, further from their main camp, so with dusk creeping upon them, the King's army had retreated back to where they had initially expected battle. The area was open enough and clear of scrub to set up a temporary camp, the little fires built to provide light, rather than warmth on this hot summer night.

Losan continued past the small tents that were eerily quiet and towards the royal canvas. Two soldiers sat at the entrance that they were meant to guard, but as the captain approached they leapt to their feet, standing tall. Losan ignored them and pushed open the canvas door to step in, letting it swish shut behind him.

Two faces looked up at him, both lit by the candles that they had been forced to light so as not to conduct their council in darkness. With the tent flap down it was stuffy inside and there was a sheen of perspiration on Losan's forehead as he sat on the King's right side.

"Well..." Hrafn started, his quiet voice quivering with anger. "We have lost over a score of men to this ridiculous attack and flee technique. I want this dealt with, captain."

Losan nodded. "It is too dark to do anything now, my lord. But with your permission, before first light I'll take the cavalry south-"

"South?" David grunted. "You're blind if-"

"David, keep your voice low." Hrafn hissed, canvas walls were not sound-proof.

David frowned, but continued in a quieter tone. "Look, I know Samantha." He lied, then took note of the captain's skeptical sneer. "Okay, maybe not well, but I understand how people of my world think. Sammy knows a lot of wars and tactics, more than any History exam has given her credit for. What I'm getting to is that

292

she's probably drawing us south so the Gardyn army can attack our main camp, the capital, or anything to the north."

Silence followed David's speculation. Hrafn looked at him hopelessly and Captain Losan shook his head gently and was next to speak.

"You may have wisdom of your old home and what is in the minds of the young, but you know little of actual armies, David. The Gardyn, begging your pardon my lords, are wiser and braver than our curses tell. They will not be run by a young girl, even if she is part of a prophecy. It is even less likely that they would allow the individual who holds the balance of this war to take on the might of our army alone."

David looked up, his eyes meeting Captain Losan's. His eyes shone with defiance and David suddenly wondered why the head of the King's army and a faithful friend of Hrafn's for many a year was so eager to ignore the heir's idea. Was it just that Captain Orion Losan hated David, or was there some other reason behind that fixed glare.

"Hrafn." David was one of the few to get away with calling the King by his name alone. "You appointed me your heir after the murder of Tagor. Trust me. Send soldiers north for your own protection."

The King waved his hand to signal an end to David's asking. "I will not waste soldiers on a wild goose chase and an unsupported idea. I'll spare a scout to travel north at dawn tomorrow. Now, captain, continue with your plan."

*****

The sun had been in the sky for barely an hour when Captain Losan halted the contingent of cavalry. Ahead

293

of them the trees fitted their trunks together so tightly that the way was impassable.

Losan ordered two of his men to ride swiftly along to see how far the natural barrier went. A smile crept over his scarred face when they returned to report that it encircled an area, like a wall or fortress.

Twenty-eight

The chop of axe and blade against wood and the groan of trees could be heard half a mile away, but Samantha and Autumn were already much further north.

After a second attack on the army, Samantha and Autumn had hidden deep in the forest, waiting for the King to make camp. Then, following Autumn's instructions, Samantha had created another ring of trees that mimicked the Treefort created for the families. Then, as much as she wanted to wait and see if the enemy would be fooled, she agreed that it was time to leave. By midnight they had set off to the north.

Autumn galloped tirelessly through the dark hours, spurred on by the thought of being rid of the humans' problems. His strong legs carried himself and Samantha on through the dawn and day, pausing only to drink and take in the forest signs.

Although the Gardyn army had set off over a day before, they were in sight by midday.

Everyone turned and cheered as their lady approached. Samantha grinned as she slid off Autumn's slick chestnut back. She was surprised and overwhelmed with happiness when two familiar figures caught her eye.

"Alina! Sundance! What are you doing here?"

"I could ask the same thing." Autumn added, an air of dissent settling about him.

The silver mare with her golden nephew focussed on Samantha. "We both wanted to say a final farewell to you, and to see this thing to the end."

Samantha laughed and wrapped her arms around Alina's silky neck. "Thank you, my friend." She mumbled.

"Well..." Autumn's thoughts came hesitantly as he watched the loving embrace. "I suppose that can be forgiven. But now I'll escort you back to the herd, it is all over."

Samantha stepped back. She did not need shared thoughts to know how uneasy Alina and Sundance were and her eyes darted between the trio of unicorns.

"Sir, we are not deserting the humans until the last has passed through their gate." Sundance was the first to unlock his thoughts and feelings. His brave, young head held high. "You cannot force us to return now, you have no hold over me, and my father's sister has given no word of commitment to you, yet."

The atmosphere bristled about the chestnut stallion, a quiver of fear about the others. It was as though he would strike out and Samantha almost quailed when Autumn directed his horn at her, but the stallion just snorted and turned away in a fury of hooves to become a flame streaking southwards.

Samantha joined the northward trek, falling into line beside Tobias and Jillis. Alina chided Sundance, but both continued on happily enough, moving about the humans, often giving children brief rides.

That night at camp, the Gardyn celebrated. Tired feet found energy for dancing and voices were raised in song. Everyone knew that salvation was closer than ever before.

As the sun reached its peak the next day, people broke free of the mass they had travelled in and raced each other uphill to the worn stone that was the focus of a thousand weary travellers.

All that was left of the Temple of Gates were the main pillars and fallen arches. Mosses and grass crept over the crumbled stone and it was easy to believe that it was well over a thousand years old. Only two statues had stood the test of time and as Samantha walked up to them she felt the flicker of recognition from her vision. Two young warriors that were exactly the same, stone arms raising stone swords to create an archway. Samantha did not know why two warriors had statues erected in the Temple of Gates, and if she had not had more pressing matters she would have liked to have found out.

Samantha drew out her own sword, the Sword of Minaeri, and wandered the temple alone, Rian had ordered none to enter until the Lady Samantha commanded it so.

Samantha gazed about the hilltop, in her mind's eye she could see the temple as it once was, standing strong and proud, to remind the people of Enchena of their roots and to be humble and thankful. She felt almost a connection with the place and her heart was crushed with tears that she could not explain.

Eventually she turned back to the statues, glancing up at them. Looking more carefully she saw the handsome faces expressing some sort of pain. Samantha sighed and looked again, her brow furrowed with what she saw. The sun had fallen slightly in the sky and had settled as a halo behind the left figure. Behind the right was the faint glow of an early risen moon with full face.

Samantha felt a warmth surge from the sword into her and understood. It was time.

*****

Samantha sat on Legan, keeping above the heads of the Gardyn, the hilt of her sword held aloft. The light of the sun and the day-moon played in the blue stone, sparks of dazzling lights were given off, then united beneath the crossed swords of the statues to give a shimmery, pale blue and silver haze.

The Gardyn, who lined up three abreast murmured in wonder, but wonder turned to apprehension as the people were unwilling to step into the unknown. Samantha frowned and wondered what to do, her eyes searched the crowd and locked with Jillis', the maid smiled as she understood what to do and started to push to the front, she would lead them through.

Suddenly the crowd parted as a golden flash barged through, propelling itself through the portal with a wild leap. It was all that Samantha could do to hold Legan steady as Alina trotted through, neighing aloud to her brash nephew as she followed him through into a world not meant for them.

There was a shocked silence and nobody moved, nobody knew what to do and stared up at Lady Samantha who sat, as amazed as any of them. Jillis took the initiative and hovered in front of the portal, took a deep breath, and stepped.

It was all the incentive the masses needed and soon everyone was passing through, disappearing through the bluish haze in ones and twos, mothers grasping the hands of their children, some hesitating, but none refusing.

Those that passed Samantha were mostly women and children, Rian had kept nearly a hundred men behind, the Gardyn's best warriors, as cautious and prepared as ever.

And they all lived happily ever after. How many times had Samantha, and all the Gardyn, wished for their brave story to end thus, yet how many times had the happiness been tainted as it seemed fated to always be.

The cry they had all been dreading came.

"Look to the south!"

There was a pause in the flow through the portal as all turned to look away down the hill.

There was a sudden gust as the wind changed direction from westerly to coming from the south. Dark clouds were accumulating and being blown north with an ill omen that could not be misread. There was the gleam of armour and the phantom sound of galloping hooves. Hrafn had wised up to the Gardyn's actions.

The remaining Gardyn panicked and pushed towards the portal; Rian ordered half his men to aid and control the main section, the other half prepared for the rapidly approaching army.

Nearly nine tenths of the Gardyn had already disappeared through the portal when the first wave of attack came. Rian and his men ran down to meet them, arrows flying at the pure cavalry of the enemy, who retaliated with sword and spear.

Rian, his mind racing, shouted for his men to stay put. He turned and rode his horse cantering up the hill to where Samantha could be seen over the last fifty or so Gardyn. He glanced over his shoulder and could see the slower section of the King's cavalry coming to join in what would become the slaughter of his people. But there was something else that Rian could see that no one else had yet noticed, a splash of colour to the south west.

"Samantha, you must be safe. None of your arguments." Rian shouted, pushing towards where she sat on her own horse. Their eyes met and Rian felt his heart go out to the young girl. "This is where your story ends." He said quietly, then gave a sharp smack on Legan's pale rump, making the horse dart forward. Rian watched dejectedly, long enough to see the portal fade away.

*****

Legan bolted through the gateway, Samantha held on desperately, but felt her grip slipping. She landed unceremoniously in long meadow grass and quickly looked back. The portal, which had been maintained by her alone, shimmered and faded. She fancied that she heard the voices of the Gardyn on the other side crying out. This made little sense to her and Samantha gasped, tears started to roll down her cheeks and she struggled to stand up, slipping on grassy tussocks.

"No." She pleaded. "No!"

A strong arm reached out and held her steady. "There are some things you have to let be." The voice of Tobias muttered in her ear.

"I have failed them." Samantha whispered, leaning against his sturdy frame.

"No, you have given a future to many Hrafn would have killed, and a hope to those in Enchena that the King can be overcome."

"Samantha?" Jillis took her hand, the maid was crying but her face was beaming. "Look - look at your people."

Samantha turned slowly, fearing to see broken families and friendships.

The sun suddenly came out from the clouds with blinding light. A soft breeze moved through the large meadow in which over a thousand people stood, crying, laughing, dancing. Beyond them were fair cities and no longer would they live in a shadow of fear and ill-will. If heaven existed, this was it, the dreams of the Gardyn were coming true for this small group.

In the very centre of the crowd, a beautiful young girl leant over to a sad, yet noble lady.

"Freedom. We are free." She murmured.

Other books by K.S. Marsden:

Witch-Hunter ~ *Now available in audiobook*
The Shadow Rises (Witch-Hunter #1)
The Shadow Reigns (Witch-Hunter #2)
The Shadow Falls (Witch-Hunter #3)

Witch-Hunter trilogy box-set

Witch-Hunter Prequels
James: Witch-Hunter (#0.5)
Sophie: Witch-Hunter (#0.5)
Kristen: Witch-Hunter (#2.5) ~ *coming soon*

Enchena
The Lost Soul: Book 1 of Enchena
The Oracle: Book 2 of Enchena

Northern Witch
Winter Trials (Northern Witch #1)
Awaken (Northern Witch #2)
The Breaking (Northern Witch #3)
Summer Sin (Northern Witch #4)

Printed in Great Britain
by Amazon

69671841R00173